Valdoro's Mistress

Evelyn Stewart Armstrong

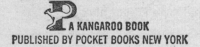

A KANGAROO BOOK
PUBLISHED BY POCKET BOOKS NEW YORK

POCKET BOOKS, a Simon & Schuster division of
GULF & WESTERN CORPORATION
1230 Avenue of the Americas, New York, N.Y. 10020

Copyright © 1976 by Evelyn Stewart Armstrong

Published by arrangement with Macdonald and Jane's Publishers Ltd.

All rights reserved, including the right to reproduce
this book or portions thereof in any form whatsoever.
For information address Macdonald and Jane's Publishers
Ltd., Paulton House, 8 Shepherdess Walk, London N1, England.

ISBN: 0-671-81303-X

First Pocket Books printing February, 1978

Trademarks registered in the United States and other countries.

Printed in the U.S.A.

Only intrigue, violence, and passion were law in her new homeland.

INDIA: Given to Don Miguel as servant and lover by her father, she lived without shame on the handsome hidalgo's magnificent estate. Soon she would bear his child—and then her power over him would be greater than ever.

DON MIGUEL MOURAL: Mysterious, aristocratic, both kind and coldly indifferent, the wealthy hidalgo had many enemies who opposed his plans for the future of Argentina. Not the least of them was Alfonso Sánchez, whose reasons for hating Don Miguel were not entirely political.

DON ALFONSO SÁNCHEZ: The unscrupulous owner of silver mines that bordered on Valdoro, he schemed to see Don Miguel destroyed. Even as he plotted the downfall of his rival, he relentlessly pursued Marta, his rival's wife.

And MARTA GONZALES MOURAL:

Although she shared both her home and her husband with India, she alone deserved to be mistress of Valdoro—and no savagery of man or nature could separate her from her burning dream!

Books by Evelyn Stewart Armstrong

Daughter of Valdoro
Valdoro's Mistress

Published by POCKET BOOKS

 *Are there paperbound books you want
but cannot find in your retail stores?*

You can get any title in print in **POCKET BOOK** editions. Simply
send retail price, local sales tax, if any, plus 35¢ per book to
cover mailing and handling costs, to:

MAIL SERVICE DEPARTMENT
   POCKET BOOKS • A Division of Simon & Schuster, Inc.
   1230 Avenue of the Americas • New York, New York 10020

Please send check or money order. We cannot be responsible
for cash.   *Catalogue sent free on request.*

Titles in this series are also available at discounts in quantity
lots for industrial or sales-promotional use. For details write our
Special Products Department: Department AR, POCKET BOOKS,
1230 Avenue of the Americas, New York, New York 10020.

1

"Come and look, Marta!" my aunt called to me from the other side of the cabin. "I can't see anyone who might be Don Miguel—though at this distance it's difficult to tell—and what are they doing with those bullock-carts?"

She was standing at the open porthole; the bright sunlight reflecting off the water made shifting patterns on her thin animated face. I did not want to come and look, to take my first sight of Buenos Aires, with or without Don Miguel. I was feeling sick—I who throughout the long voyage from Spain had experienced hardly a qualm. At that moment I wished the journey to be twice as long, or the precarious peace between Spain and England—it was the year 1803—to be broken so that our ship might have been captured by an English vessel. Anything that would delay me; that would stop me being united with my husband. I was suffering from nerves.

I told myself that he *was* my husband. The marriage contract had been signed months ago in Spain, and soon would come the religious ceremony. True, until that had been performed the marriage was not irrevocable, but I knew I could not withdraw now, matters had gone too far for that. It had been my decision, and I must stick to it.

"Do come and look!" my aunt repeated. ". . . I suppose he wouldn't hang about on the shore when there's no boat ready to bring him out to us. Oh, would you believe it, they're driving the bullocks out into the water! The poor beasts will drown!"

I crossed the gently swaying floor and joined her at the porthole. Through it drifted a multitude of sounds: the slapping of waves, the creak of rigging, voices, the thud of feet and all the noises of a ship preparing for port. I gritted my teeth and looked.

Our mail-ship from La Coruña was lying at anchor in the roads. Before us stretched a great tract of rippling sea, not clear and blue as I had expected, but dull and muddy-brown. Far ahead lay land. From this distance I could see no proper wharf, just a flattened shoreline with buildings rising behind it, an assortment of buildings large and small, clustering around and in front of a huge squat mass over which a flag fluttered lazily. Too far off to be recognized it must be the Spanish flag, and that broad expanse of stone would be the citadel.

Across the fawn-grey sea little boats were making their way to the shore. Our ship did not ride off-shore alone. Earlier that morning when I had been on deck one of the officers had pointed out its companions to me, identifying the craft and their respective nationalities. Two quite nearby, at least as big as our own, were English.

"Since our friend Napoleon made peace last year they come here openly," he had said with a laugh. "And if the peace doesn't last, they'll find the same old excuses to come here nevertheless."

"What—to fight?" I had asked, wide-eyed.

"*Dios*, no! To smuggle—as they have done for centuries! The English are great traders," he added with a touch of sarcasm.

"But why is it allowed?"

"It is not *allowed*." He smiled. "But it happens—it suits both sides, you see. In the Viceroyalty goods were needed—and still are. Not enough comes from Spain to satisfy the colonists."

Tía Amalia was quite right. Beyond the boats which speckled the sea like a swarm of water-beetles there were, at the water's edge, a number of bullock carts. Two of them were moving forward, straight out into the sea.

"The drivers must be mad!" my aunt continued.

"Perhaps the men are just letting them cool down in the water," I suggested. "They certainly won't risk drowning their beasts—they are too valuable to them."

This practical explanation seemed to satisfy my aunt, and having agreed that there was no one on shore finely enough dressed to be Don Miguel—though to me it was impossible to tell at that distance—I left her to watch, and sat down again beside my bunk.

I was now facing the reality that I was about to be deposited in a foreign country, a Spanish-speaking country certainly, but in all other respects totally unlike the land and the life I had left behind. Perhaps I had made a dreadful mistake, perhaps Serafina had been right, perhaps at seventeen I had gambled my life away. What had possessed me to marry in haste a total stranger?

I shut my eyes, I could not even recollect his face. Separate features I could remember; the straight nose, the well-shaped mouth, and above all the dark and brilliant eyes; but when I tried to put them together they refused to make a face, they became a hotch-potch, a nothing. My heart quickened as a seed of panic grew within me.

I didn't know him at all. I could count on the fingers of one hand the number of times I had met him. Yet I had married him. The civil contract had been signed at my home, and then off he had ridden to the coast as if nothing mattered but sailing to South America, leaving me to gather together my trousseau and to follow him some months later. I had written to him, care of a bank in Buenos Aires, to tell him the date of my departure; from him I had heard not a single word. Of his arrangements in South America I knew nothing.

"Marta! Are you feeling ill?"

I opened my eyes. Tía Amalia was standing in front of me, looking at me anxiously. I smiled and made myself answer brightly. "No, not a bit. I was just wondering how it will feel to be on land again."

"Very welcome, I'm sure!"

There was a knock on the cabin door; it was a seaman asking for the last of our luggage. Then the Captain's cabin boy appeared.

"Señoras, the Captain says could you be on deck in a few minutes?"

"We will come now."

No, there was no going back.

We were in the boat, sitting amidships with the Captain. He was going ashore to deliver personally certain important mails, and escorting me as the passenger of the greatest consequence. As Señorita Marta Gonzales I would have been totally insignificant, but as the Señora Doña Marta Gonzales Moural I was a lady of rank, to be treated with deference.

Tía Amalia did not look at all comfortable, the result, no doubt, of being lowered over the side of the ship in a kind of canvas chair to the bobbing boat below. If I had had the option of using a wood and rope ladder, as the men did, I would have taken it, but decorum and long petticoats ruled out the possibility. Once safely aboard I cast a quick eye over the piled luggage; it seemed to be all there, the personal trunks and portmanteaux, and my precious dower-chests.

"Captain, how much farther are those men going to drive their bullock carts?" My aunt had found her voice. "It really does look a ridiculous proceeding."

She was quite right; other carts had also left the shore; the first ones were a long way out yet the water had barely reached the animals' bellies, and they were still advancing. The Captain chuckled, his eyes narrowing in a net of wrinkles, his black beard twitching.

"They're coming out to meet us, señora!"

"To *meet* us?"

"Don't you know? The water is so shallow for such a distance that the boats can't get in. We go as far as we can and then we transfer into the carts. It works very well."

Tía Amalia crossed herself. "*Dios,* who would have believed it. . . ."

"It's a very practical solution that we've imported from home, and will no doubt serve until the Porteños find a better way."

Being a country girl I had never heard of it, but serve it did. The boat grounded when we were a long way from the shore, and the patient beasts, now nearby, and up to their chins in the muddy water, turned and positioned the great cart against the shallow cutter. The Captain climbed in, and he and one of the sailors helped me and my aunt to join him. The luggage followed, and I held my breath as the large chests were manhandled across into the cart. It would be too dreadful if one of them slipped; sea-water would be ruination to the contents and would spoil the chests into the bargain. I sighed with relief when they were all inside, then peered anxiously at the floor for signs of water seeping through the wooden slats.

"It's all quite safe, señora," the Captain assured me. "We take good care."

"Of course."

I was being silly; I wasn't the first bride to be transported in this way.

Slowly, laboriously the bullocks responded to the cracking whip and hoarse shouts of the driver, and we moved in towards the shore. The cart was uncovered and the sun shone hotly on our heads. I arranged my shawl and regretted that I was not wearing a better gown. This mulberry one was not new, and I had worn it a good deal on the voyage, but it was not shabby, and it was silk. It had seemed foolish to risk splashing one from my trousseau. But as Don Miguel's wife perhaps it was not fine enough—what would he think? My stomach gave a lurch at the thought that a man who considered himself my husband was waiting for me somewhere ashore. What would happen when we reached the wharf? Surely the Captain would help me —he couldn't leave me stranded—I had no address for Don Miguel . . . panic rose again, half choking me.

The cart creaked, the water rippled, and the smell of land grew stronger in my nostrils. Already the strangeness began to impress itself. The scents were foreign; there were strong odors, spicy fragrances; then my nose twitched at a waft of something rank, unpleasant.

"You can smell the tannery," the Captain remarked. "There it is—over there—and the big building nearby is the *saladero*."

"What is that?" I asked, not really interested, but glad of any conversation as a relief from my thoughts.

"A place where meat is salted down, so that it will keep. It's a new thing commercially. The cattle are brought here for slaughter, the hides are tanned for sale and the beef salted for shipping up and down the coast."

"What a good idea!"

Madre de Dios, the cart was beginning to rise in the water! Soon we would be on land. No longer muffled by the sea, the axles began to creak louder and louder; looking out to one side I could see the churning, muddy sand. The sounds on the wharf were buffeting me, voices calling, men shouting to each other as they moved sacks and cases. All at once there seemed to be a tumult of excitement and bustle. The cart lurched to a stop. Half numb with nerves I found myself being helped from the cart. I was on solid land at last, and my bags and chests were lying like flotsam at my feet.

At my first meeting with Don Miguel I had not shown to best advantage, since I had a live hen clutched under my arm at the time. Besides which I—but no, I must first set out my situation clearly and in full.

My father was of a good family; his father had left him a respected name, a little land, and less money. So much less, in fact, that he could not live as an absentee landlord in comfort. Therefore, rather than run into debt maintaining social position he resided on his own property. He did away with the expense of a town house and society life, and was his own bailiff. So I was born at the Quinta Gonzales and had known no other home.

It must have been a great grief and trouble to my father that he did not have a son, but he bore it well. I never heard from him a word of reproach nor from my mother a single expression of regret. There were three of us daughters, Serafina, myself, and Luisa the youngest. Three daughters—and hardly a dowry among us.

Most girls of our birth would have had an easy, indolent life; we were brought up to work. Serafina did the lighter work in the house, and helped in the kitchen with the cooking and preserves. I looked after the chickens and helped with feeding the other animals and tasks that kept me mainly out of doors; this was my choice for I hated to be confined too much within four walls. Luisa did a variety of things according to necessity and her own inclination, which was not much towards work and against routine and monotony.

My mother saw to it that my sisters and I were well brought up, properly trained and educated, but our visits to town and our opportunities for social life were infrequent, to say the least. In some ways it was a free and easy country life, but in the evenings, when the work has done and we all sat together in the *sala,* we had to read and sew and behave as well-brought-up young ladies should.

The *quinta* was a group of very old buildings roofed with large pink tiles and set around a courtyard, not a formal patio with tidy ranks of flowers in pots, but a true courtyard which was the hub of our comings and goings. On two sides were store-rooms, stables and barns; the chickens and some of the other livestock came and went as they pleased, the more curious ones invading the kitchen when they felt so inclined. On this particular morning there were no hens to be seen when Mama told me she wanted one for the pot, so I had to go into the fields and find them. It was I who knew all the hens individually, and mentally marked down any that had gone off lay and would be next for eating. Today it was the turn of a particularly silly creature, but she was not so silly that she did not sense that I wanted to catch her, and she led me a fine dance until, with a mixture of cunning and speed, I laid hands on her and tucked the flapping squawking bird under my arm.

It was only as her protests subsided that I heard the sound of hoofbeats on the road which ran nearby, and looking over the low stone wall I saw two riders nearly abreast of me. It was plain from their clothes that they were gentleman and servant. The former was somberly but richly dressed: I saw an excellent boot, finely cut breeches and coat, and the glimpse of an ivory-handled pistol at his belt. The broad-brimmed Cordoban hat half-shadowed a patrician face. The servant, wearing good livery, looked a capable fellow; he led a pack-horse which bore a fair amount of baggage.

And there I stood gazing at them, my feet bare, my petticoats still tucked up from my recent pursuit and showing an indecorous stretch of ankle, and my hair beginning to break loose from its pins. In such a situation Serafina would have remembered her station, would have dropped her eyes modestly and fled without more ado. I, flushed with triumph over my feathered captive, stood there like any peasant girl and gave look for look. A pair of brilliant dark eyes treated me to a long stare as the three horses drummed down the dirt road beside me. Then they had passed me; they were cantering on, on past the archway which led to our courtyard, on along the road to Torillo, our nearest town.

Travelling strangers were always interesting and rated a few minutes' gossip as we worked, though I did not expect to see them again. But the day which had started so quietly and normally gathered momentum and excitement as it wore on.

The next event was the arrival of the *alcalde* to see my father. This was most extraordinary, for the *alcalde* rarely left town except on official business and with an escort, and this was obviously a social call. After the required courtesies had been exchanged Papa and he closeted themselves in the *sala* with a bottle of Papa's best wine, and talked and talked, while we outside could only speculate. We could think of no reason why he should come. If he had wanted to buy stock or produce he would have waited till Papa came to town— and what other incentive could he have to ride the long miles between us? So we sat in the big hall, working and waiting until Papa called Mama to join them. Now we heard three voices, but the doors were too thick and heavy for us to catch any words.

When the doors opened, Papa, without a word, went out and across to the stables, while the *alcalde,* hat in hand, gave us all his formal goodbyes. His horse and Papa's came up to the door, and quickly the two of them left without more ado, accompanied by the grooms and riding more swiftly than I would have thought comfortable for so corpulent a man as the *alcalde.*

I had never seen Mama in such a state. She was quite distracted, yet there was pleasure and excitement in her confusion. To our utter frustration she refused to tell us anything, saying we must wait until Papa returned. All our pleadings made no difference. So we spent the rest of the day in speculation, never coming anywhere near the truth. Papa had said he might not return for dinner; and when the time came we dined without him, and then tried to settle to our sewing. I would have discounted the mystery as a male fuss over their own affairs; but Mama was plainly holding such an anticipation in check that it must concern her, and therefore us. To our disgust she sent us off to bed early, but Luisa was pert enough to say that we were too excited to sleep and if Mama had anything to tell us when

Papa returned would she please do so. Mama almost agreed.

We went to bed, chattering among ourselves in the big room the three of us shared, and waited. Before long we heard the sound of horses entering the courtyard. Papa said good night to the groom, who led the horses to the stables, and proceeded towards the house and into the hall where Mama must have been waiting to greet him. Luisa crept out of our room and said she could hear them talking downstairs. Serafina called her back to bed; and some minutes later there was a gentle tap on our door and Mama's voice said, "Are you still awake, *chiquitas*?"

We sat up in bed like three jacks-in-the-box as Mama came in and set down her candle on the dressing table. We were goggle-eyed with expectancy as she looked at us each in turn.

"Well?" said Luisa.

"I don't know how to tell you. I don't know where to start!" she said, sitting down on the end of Serafina's bed.

"Go on, Mama!" I urged.

"We shall have a distinguished guest at dinner tomorrow," she announced.

This was very surprising, for relatives and friends were entertained at home very rarely, and strangers never, but surely it could not be as portentous as her manner indicated.

"Who is he, and why is he coming?" asked Serafina, the practical one.

"His name is Don Miguel Moural, and he—and he . . ." she stammered, and the words came out then in a rush—"and he wants a wife."

We were not told everything that night, but Mama's blunt announcement was enough to make us aware of the importance of the situation. Now we were all grown up we were almost resigned to spinsterhood, for Serafina was twenty, with no *novio* in sight. Everyone guessed we were virtually dowerless, and she had had only one offer, from the son of a man who owned a tiny parcel of land adjoining ours. From his viewpoint marriage to Serafina, a well-born girl who would bring him at least a third of Papa's land, would be very desirable; but the family were peasants and the son such a boor, so utterly unprepossessing in looks and manner that Serafina said that she would rather take vows than marry him. Papa would not entertain the match.

Serafina would make a splendid wife, but a man has to be madly in love to defy his family and take a dowerless girl, and such a man had not appeared. And Serafina, though good-looking, had neither the startling beauty to ensnare a man against his common sense nor the vivacity and allure to attract him equally strongly; she was a dear, sweet person, quiet, capable, unselfish; but time was running out for her. She was the eldest and must marry first. If she did not find a husband soon, the chances for Luisa and me would become nonexistent. On the face of it, Don Miguel's possible offer was a wonderful opportunity.

"But—the dowry?" Serafina had asked.

Mama told her that Don Miguel was prepared to take a dowerless wife. This was almost incredible.

"Why?" asked Luisa.

Late that night Luisa confided in me her worst fears for Serafina. For an *hidalgo* to consider a wife below him in station and penniless, with two younger sisters, there must be something seriously wrong. Either he was very old, and just wanted a drudge, a nurse, or a comfort for his last years, or he was a cruel rake who would beat her. Or perhaps he was a cripple, blind, a hunchback, or monstrously ugly . . . what could it be? I too had grave doubts, and could not wait to come to the truth of it.

Serafina herself must have had some suspicions, for as we started work in the kitchen she said to Mama, "Is Don Miguel old, Mama?"

My mother gave Serafina a quick look, but the morning sun showed only grave interest on her calm face.

"Old? Whatever gave you that idea? Your father judged him to be in his early thirties, certainly not more. A very good age for you, *chica*."

"Then what is it?" pressed Luisa. "We're not in his class—he doesn't even know us—and with no dowry —*why*?"

Mama looked embarrassed and my heart sank. There was something. Something terrible for Serafina.

"There is nothing wrong at all, if that is what you are thinking," Mama answered. "Your father would not consider a match which would be distasteful." She was choosing her words, and we waited. 'There is just one condition to the marriage. Don Miguel has lands in South America. He is going to live there. So, of course, must his wife."

"Live . . . in South America . . ." Serafina gasped.

"But it's the other side of the world!" cried Luisa. "We'd never see—"

"No, no!" Mama said quickly. "You would not be cut off from us. There would be letters, and he has promised you would visit Spain periodically. He has a great deal of money . . ."

Her voice tailed off. Serafina had gone very pale, but I hardly noticed because I was thinking: South America—how exciting to go to that great continent! She would be seeing new things, making a new life. It would be frightening, but fascinating. . . .

"If he's so rich why pick on us?" Luisa was saying. "Doesn't he know any women? And surely there are plenty in South America—they're not all Indians."

Mama began to be impatient with Luisa.

"Of course he knows *hidalgas*! But it seems they do not want to leave their families. And he wants a Spanish wife, not a South American. And don't ask me why, for who knows what goes on in a man's mind? As for picking on us, he was introduced to your papa by the *alcalde*—"

Serafina dropped her peeling knife. "You mean he went to the *alcalde* and found out who needed a husband! Oh, how humiliating! I shall feel I'm on a market stall waiting to be bought!"

Mama put her arm round Serafina's shoulders and spoke briskly, with a warning glance at Luisa as if to say, Don't you dare make any more trouble!

"Come, child, don't be so silly! He is simply being practical, as we must be about marriage. If he needs to look further afield than his own circle who better to approach than an *alcalde*? Tonight he is coming to see you, but he is also coming for your approval. You will see him, hear about his lands and how he will live in South America, and if you do not like the idea he will go away and that will be the end of it. If you think you like him enough to consider the arrangement he will come again. All this had to be settled quickly because he has not time for a lengthy courtship. But tonight commits you to nothing, so there is no need for tears or hysterics."

"I'm not hysterical!" Serafina squeaked. "And I'm not crying—it's the onions! Very well, I'll meet him this evening."

And that was that. I could tell she was nerving herself to the marriage for all our sakes. But Serafina, so home-loving, so attached to the family, so fond of the orderliness of familiar things; for her it was going to be a difficult matter.

There was much to do that day, as we wanted to look our best. Mama's first consideration was for the meal and the house, ours for our appearance. There was no time to do much furbishing to our best dresses, and Mama, once the domestic matters were well in hand, gave Serafina all her attention. Luisa and I were expected to look our best, but simply in order to do Serafina justice; naturally we would keep in the background. But we both spent a lot of extra time on our hair.

By the time Don Miguel arrived we were all in a state of nerves. None of us had the faintest idea what to expect, and we were so strung up that when the *hidalgo* was shown into the *sala* three small gasps were distinctly audible before the introductions.

He was the complete antithesis of everything we had feared. Tall, well-built, and handsome. What was more, I at least could be forgiven for gasping, for he was the traveller I had seen on the road when I was subduing my captive hen. I remembered how I had looked, and thought: *Dios!* I have ruined Serafina's chances. Then in a split second I realized how different I was looking now. There was a very good chance he would not recognize me, dressed and behaving like a lady. The worst give-away was my wretched rusty-brown hair, which refused to turn ebony-black like everyone else's in the family; but even so a likeness would be unremarkable, for it was by no means unusual for a servant's child to bear a distinct resemblance to the patron's family, and nothing was thought of it, though I'm glad to say no such thing happened at our *quinta*.

I made my curtsey and saw a fine head of black hair, an olive-complexioned, lean-featured face and a pair of large dark eyes which gazed into mine with what in a lesser man would have been a disturbing boldness. But I knew this was an *hidalgo* with all the pride and assurance of his nobility. He had, I noticed, a scar on the left side of his face; it was about two inches long and must have been caused by a deep cut, but it in no way detracted from his appearance; I thought it gave him a dashing look. I had that one long stare from him, and then he bowed with no sign of recognition. I breathed more freely and found time to think how lucky Serafina was! At first sight there seemed everything to recommend him, and no drawback other than the intention to live in South America. That would indeed make the marriage unwelcome to her. I couldn't help putting myself in her place and wondering if it would be so difficult for me. A new life in a new world—there was a great attraction in the unknown.

During dinner we found Don Miguel altogether charming, without arrogance or undue formality, and an interesting conversationalist. His manner was at times as direct as his gaze, for he supplied information without much diplomatic circumlocution, plainly to give Serafina an idea of the kind of life she might expect. We already knew that his father was leaving his land in Spain with the title to his eldest son, and Don Miguel, the second, had been given all rights to his father's lands in South America. Now we were told that the land was in an Intendency of the Viceroyalty of Río de la Plata, and that the nearest town was called Varena.

"Does one see many Indians in the towns?" Mama asked. "I think I should be nervous of them."

"I assure you there is no reason to be," he told her. "They are quite pacified now, and accept us as their masters. Treated properly they are very loyal—more loyal and industrious than the *mestizos,* in my opinion. One's servants are mostly of Indian or mixed blood. Sometimes they need training—particularly house servants—I expect my wife to do that for the staff of my country house—but they are intelligent and speak Spanish quite well, so there are no difficulties."

During the evening a number of other pieces of information were placed before us. ". . . my wife will have this . . . my wife will do that. . . ." Serafina looked embarrassed, but it was honest: it told her where she stood. I, who should have kept quiet, could not resist a question or two, and found the clear look from those brilliant eyes as he answered a little disturbing. It would be easy for Serafina to fall in love with him, I thought. She must have thought so too, for when Don Miguel and his servant rode off into the dark, having assured Mama that they discounted the possibility of footpads and were in any case well armed, it was with the understanding that he would return within the next few days.

Two days later he appeared, and Papa allowed Serafina and myself to go riding with them. Luisa was furious at being left at home, but the arrangement made it easier for Papa to drop behind a little with me and leave Don Miguel to escort and talk to Serafina.

Then we discovered he wanted a firm decision in a week's time on his return from settling some business in Madrid.

As the days passed Serafina, who had accepted him as a possible *novio,* began to wear an air of desperate calm. Papa was happy that he had done his best for his eldest daughter in offering her such a suitor, but Mama was torn between sorrow at parting with Serafina and pleasure that she could make such a good marriage. One way and another it seemed settled, though I wished Serafina looked happier about it and less like someone condemned to the stake. Still, I supposed that marriage was a serious business for the bride.

Then Don Miguel was back, and coming to dinner to hear her decision. There was another day of excited preparation for our guest—and all at once, at the very last moment, everything was on the brink of disaster.

Serafina went up early to dress for dinner; when I entered the bedroom a little later it was to find her crouched over the dressing-table, her head buried in her arms, her body shaken with shuddering, uncontrollable sobs. I ran to kneel beside her and put my arms around her.

"Serafina, darling, what's wrong?"

Serafina raised her head, covered her face with her hands, and eventually broken phrases came between the gasping breaths.

"I can't do it! I can't do it! I'll go into a convent, but I won't go there. Never to see you, to live shut up in a house with those dreadful Indians—and everyone a stranger."

"Serafina, don't worry. You don't have to. Why didn't you say? I'll get Mama."

I rushed off to find her. All at once the house was in an uproar, our bedroom a battlefield, people dashing to and fro like soldiers in combat, question and counter-question whizzing past like grapeshot. In the middle of it all Don Miguel's horse was heard outside.

Papa went down to receive him, and Mama managed to expel everyone else but me from the bedroom.

We helped Serafina to her bed and Mama waved her smelling bottle under Serafina's nose, but it had little effect except to make her choke.

"Now, *chica*, no one's going to force you to marry him!"

"Don't worry about us—we don't want to marry!" I said firmly.

"If only it wasn't so far—and those Indians—it's like marrying a Turk—"

I completely failed to see the similarity, but was unable to consider the matter as Mama sent me to fetch a glass of brandy, drastic restorative measures being obviously necessary. I hurried downstairs; the house was now unnaturally calm, a lid of convention pressed tight on a seething emotional stew.

I was passing the *sala* door, it was slightly ajar. Papa was obviously breaking the news to Don Miguel, for I heard him say, ". . . I greatly regret it. But I do not think she will change her mind. It is nothing personal. Simply that she cannot bear the separation."

In the silence that followed I was about to tiptoe past, but Don Miguel's voice broke in abruptly with words so unexpected, so outrageous that I stood as if rooted.

"I see. Your second daughter, then?"

Just that. Not a word of regret, of sympathy, of understanding. What had Serafina said? "Like something on a market stall. . . ." We might as well be sacks of flour. Refused one sack he takes the next. Not an atom of feeling. Oh, Serafina was well rid of him!

Of course Papa would refuse. I pulled myself together and walked on, seething with rage. So handsome, so charming—but he didn't care a straw for a woman as a person: it didn't matter to him who was his wife as long as she could cope with his house and his wretched Indians. Anyone would do. I could still hear his cold voice saying, "Your second daughter, then?"

My inside suddenly turned over and my legs shook.

He had actually offered for *me,* this arrogant, insufferable man! Marry him? Under such conditions? It would be impossible. I would not marry a man who proposed to me as second-best, without even the pretense of a courtship, who so obviously considered me merely as a marketable commodity. No, I could not do it.

Yet four days later I found myself signing the marriage contract.

2

I stood on the wharf, not moving a muscle, as if by keeping perfectly still I could convince myself that I was calm. There was no sign of Don Miguel. Instead of being relieved I was now bordering on panic, for without him what should I do?

Beside me Tía Amalia was darting swift, bird-like glances on every side, but still Don Miguel did not appear. I noticed that a man had approached the Captain and was talking to him. He was a saturnine-looking person, discreetly well-dressed, not like a nobleman but some kind of middle-class professional; he had a swarthy skin, a long thin face and a hard mouth. The Captain left him and came to us.

"Doña Marta. Doña Amalia," the Captain said. "May I present to you Señor Ruíz, Don Miguel's steward."

The man bowed to us, a small stiff bow, as if he resented having to do it. The eyes that met mine were narrow and bright, with an unblinking gaze that reminded me of a snake, but his voice was respectful as he offered me a letter.

"Señora, this is from Don Miguel, explaining why it is impossible for him to meet you here. A carriage is waiting—perhaps you would care to read your letter there in comfort?"

It would certainly be better than reading my first message from my husband on the open wharf amid all the comings and goings. I looked at my pile of luggage.

"I will attend to your boxes, señora."

A servant had appeared and Ruíz was giving quick instructions, then he turned back and led the way to where a group of carriages and riding horses were standing. He handed us into one of the smartest carriages, then stood with his back to us while I broke the seals and unfolded the sheet.

My dear wife, I read. *It is most unfortunate that a matter concerning Valdoro has called me away for a short while. I shall greatly regret it if it prevents me from meeting you at Buenos Aires. I am leaving this letter with Baltasar Ruíz, my steward, a reliable man, with instructions that if I have not returned to Varena in time to catch the ship for Buenos Aires he shall take my place and await the mail ship there. He will make all arrangements for you and escort you to Varena as quickly as possible, where I shall by then be returned and anxious for your arrival.*

My respects to your good aunt Doña Amalia, and my apologies to you both.

He who kisses your hands.

Miguel Moural.

I read it through twice, and noticed that at the end he had first written *where I shall by then be awaiting you,* had reconsidered the phrase (repetitious or too cold, perhaps?) and had crossed out the last two words and added *returned and anxious for your arrival.* Yes, it sounded better. The opening *my dear wife* was delightfully informal, and the stylized closing phrase *he who kisses your hands* could be taken warmly and

personally if one wished. It was a good letter, nothing
flowery or false about it, and I was somehow com-
forted. I passed the letter to my aunt and leaned forward at the carriage door.

"Señor Ruíz, what arrangements have you made?"

The man turned and moved a pace towards me.

"Apartments have been engaged for you, señora,
and Señora Alvarez who keeps them will do anything
you require. A ship leaves in three days' time for
Varena; I have reserved a cabin for you. The carriage
is at your disposal while you are here, and when I am
not attending to Don Miguel's affairs I shall be happy
to serve you."

"Thank you. It sounds well arranged."

"Then with your permission I will take you to the
apartment."

He spoke to the coachman, mounted his own horse,
and in a few moments the carriage bowled off the
wharf into the streets of Buenos Aires.

We went rocking and swaying past warehouses, large
and small, interspersed with shacks and hovels of mud
brick, open-fronted booths, wine-shops and mean
dwellings. All the way I looked about me curiously.
The streets, I noticed, were badly paved—in places not
at all—and the roadway was littered with rubbish and
refuse, fly-beset and stinking in the hot sun. It was no
surprise to me that no one of any quality walked; the
pedestrians were all poor folk, mainly of Indian blood,
shoeless and shabby, with a few down-at-heel white or
near-white men, and a number of sailors and Spanish
private soldiers.

Until we reached the better quarters where soberly-
dressed servants could be observed, the only women I
saw were either old, broken down by poverty and hard
living, or strange creatures exotically dressed in silks
and satins of mixed and lurid colors, their arms and
necks jangling with bracelets and beads, their dark
faces lit by white teeth and large flashing eyes; they
looked like gay fantastic birds until one saw that the
bright plumage was often filthy and torn. They were

quite shameless, calling to the men, posturing so that
their bodies thrust against the gay stuffs of their dresses,
their hips setting the full skirts aswing while their tight
and scanty bodices suggested only too plainly as much
of their breasts as was not actually revealed.

I felt a sudden shock—they were *putas*! I had heard
of such women, but to me they had been unreal—
denizens of night-time and dark alleys, never to be
seen by respectable people. Here they were flaunting
themselves in broad daylight. Not all, I noticed, were
deliberately provoking the men. Some merely stood in
the doorways of shacks or drinking shops, gazing sullenly ahead at nothing, and somehow these were more
disturbing. I tried to tell myself that I was mistaken,
that they were just Indian girls who liked the white
woman's finery and wore it in their own haphazard
fashion.

Nevertheless I was glad there were no such women
in the better streets, where I could turn my attention to
fine buildings and exotic flowering trees. In the fashionable part of the town there were grand stone
buildings, great baroque churches, and tall houses with
Spanish wrought-iron balconies and *rejas* at the windows. When the carriage stopped in front of a neat
house with blue shutters it all looked reassuringly
Spanish, almost familiar.

We were introduced to Señora Alvarez; we had a
light meal, and we rested; then Señor Ruíz came again.
By now I was full of queries; whether it was correct
to betray my ignorance to a servant or not I decided I
must question him. And he was not really a servant,
more an agent, I thought. He must not even be ad-
dressed as a servant: I had taken that cue from the
Captain.

"Señor Ruíz, there are a number of things I must
ask you, for I know nothing about this country. How
far is it to Varena, and why must we go by boat?
And where is the *estancia?*"

"I will draw you a little map, señora." He brought
out a pocket book and pencil, and made a quick

sketch. "Here is Buenos Aires. Here is Varena—about three days' sailing along the coast—the ship is quite small, and not fast like the mail ships. We go by water because there is no good continuous coastal road and, besides, Don Miguel has a lot of bulky articles, furniture and so forth, which are much easier to transport by sea. They are going as cargo in the same ship."

"I understand now."

"Valdoro lies roughly here—inland, and upriver. This is the Río Oro, with Varena at its mouth. Varena is the chief city in this part of the Viceroyalty of Río de la Plata. The Intendency is called Tierra de Riqueza."

"What other towns are there?"

"In Riqueza? In this area, none. There are frontier posts and a few settlements, but for civilized living we must rely on Varena. It is a charming little city and was originally a garrisoned port. I am sure it will surprise you."

Was there a slightly malicious look in his eyes as he said that? No. How could there be? But now I did not want to question him any more, and when he explained that his time was limited as there was a cargo of Don Miguel's he needed to check before it was loaded on to the coastal ship, I was glad to let him go.

The three days in Bueno Aires were a delightful break after all the weeks cooped up on shipboard, but they were not quite as much fun as they might have been. For two women without a husband between them there were strict limits as to what we might do in the city. Most of the time we spent driving about in the carriage. We could not visit anyone, for we had no introductions. In addition, we were restricted by having so little money. It would not do to render ourselves penniless before we reached Varena, and Don Miguel had not thought of sending a letter of credit any more than one of introduction. The business which had called him away must have quite engaged his attention. Not that I had any idea of grumbling; my board and lodging and my comfort were assured; I expected nothing more and was grateful for as much.

On our drives we were frequently passed by other smart carriages holding well-dressed people of Buenos Aires society. I was uncomfortably conscious of being quizzed from beneath the high-piled mantillas and colored parasols. I would have been even less comfortable had I realized then that the efficient circulation of gossip made everyone well aware of the identities of the two women fresh from Spain.

Señora Alvarez struck me as being very much the woman of business, shrewd and cold; but she attended to us well, was pleasant and informative. She was no ordinary apartment housekeeper, she told us, and did her best to impress us with her superiority; the rooms were certainly well-kept and nicely furnished.

"Don Miguel himself has stayed here," she announced. "Forgive my asking," she went on, "but Señor Ruíz tells me that Don Miguel is building a great house on his *estancia* and intends to live there. Is it really so?"

"It is quite true, señora," I agreed, for he had mentioned the building, though as to the size of the house I was completely ignorant.

"Dios mío!" Señora Alvarez crossed herself. "What an extraordinary thing to do! Surely he does not intend to take you, his wife, to live in Indian country? It is not Christian to expose women to such danger!"

The heat of my anger overwhelmed my surprise. I collected myself and answered, "I think you must have misunderstood your information. I am quite sure Don Miguel would not take me anywhere which was not safe for living. The house cannot possibly be in Indian country."

I saw an approving gleam in Tía Amalia's eyes.

"I meant no offense, señora! It is a relief to me to hear that you know all about it, I'm sure. And of course you will not be going there yet. First you are to live in Varena, I believe? It's a pleasant town, though I dare say you will have a few surprises."

"Surprises? What do you mean?"

An uncomfortable feeling churned in my stomach —Ruíz had used almost the same words.

"Why, nothing, señora! Simply that you do not know the town, and things are never quite what one expects, are they?"

There was something like a challenge in the tight smile which made me retort, "I am going with an open mind, señora."

"I am sure that is the best way. And if you will take my advice, señora, you will not listen to gossip. Such towns are full of it, and it may be hurtful even if it should be unreliable. Now, if there is nothing more, perhaps you will excuse me."

When she had rustled out I turned to Tía Amalia. "What do you think she meant?"

"Nothing, I am sure, *querida*. What could she mean? She is just a jealous woman trying to unsettle you."

"Jealous? Why?"

"Such women don't need a reason. But you're young and pretty and married to a rich and handsome *hidalgo* —that would be enough for the dried-up widow of a horse-thief."

"A horse-thief!" I burst out laughing.

"On second thoughts he was probably a wine-merchant who watered his wares. I'll swear he gave her nothing but vinegar!"

Every hour I was grateful for Tía Amalia's presence. When the matter of my chaperonage on the voyage to South America had been raised, Don Miguel had said he would find out when some well-born Spanish lady who might agree to act as a dueña would be travelling. And Tía Amalia had simply said, "That will not be necessary. I am prepared to go with Marta."

It was the perfect solution. Tía Amalia was a widow with no ties in Spain; she would welcome the experience, she insisted. It was arranged that she should stay with me for an indefinite period; if at any time she wished to return to Spain Don Miguel would arrange her passage. She and I had always been close, almost like mother and daughter, for she had more in common with me than with serious-minded Serafina or frivolous little Luisa. Her practicality and her humor chimed in with my personality, and could be relied upon to lighten any difficult moments. Now my uncomfortable feelings of indefinite unease were swept away, if only temporarily, by my aunt's salty comments.

Only one incident stood out from our stay in Buenos Aires. One morning we ordered our coachman to drive us to the better-class market streets, which, luckily for us, were wide enough for the carriage to thread its way between the booths. It was a scene of great color, noise and movement, with the merchants and their assistants crying their wares, finely dressed ladies and gentlemen examining the goods while their servants stood by to collect purchases. It was plain that however the merchandise arrived in Buenos Aires, whether legally or by smuggling, the Porteños lacked nothing; never had I seen such a variety both of necessities and luxuries for sale. Before long we got out of the carriage, Tía Amalia having decided we could afford some ribbon which we needed to smarten up our traveling gowns, and we reached a booth where there was an excellent choice.

I soon found what I wanted, but Tía Amalia was torn between mulberry, claret, or dark lilac as a trimming on black. While she was coming to a decision I was tempted to look at the next booth which had a fine display of fans. They were of every variety; in the front were the cheapest, of printed paper with plain wooden sticks; beyond these were better ones, until one's eyes traveling back reached fanciful creations of feather and silk, of material embroidered and stitched with beads and sequins, or delicately painted with flowers or romantic scenes, with sticks of carved and gilded wood, polished ebony, ivory or tortoiseshell.

While I was looking at the fans I had the uncomfortable feeling of being watched; and although this was ridiculous in such a crowd I soon felt compelled to look around. I was right. A fashionable buck lounging only a few yards away was openly eyeing me, and was not in the least discomfited at being observed. He was a young man, and would have been called handsome, but I did not like the calculating look in his eyes nor the twist of his full-lipped mouth. Of course I looked away at once, and was almost relieved when the fan-seller spoke to me. I explained that I had no need of a fan, but was simply admiring his wares.

"Then I am flattered," he replied. "Perhaps the señorita would tell me which she considers the most beautiful? This one, perhaps?"

He pointed out one of colored feathers on gilt sticks, which I considered far too garish.

"Oh no," I said. "That one is far prettier." I pointed to one which had taken my eye, of pale gray satin sewn with silver and pearls.

"That is an excellent choice, señorita—or should I say señora?"

"Señora," I admitted automatically, preparing to turn away.

"Then I shall hope the señor will buy it for you," he said with an ingratiating smile.

I was glad to rejoin Tía Amalia who was now completing her purchase. As we walked away a few moments later I found the fan-seller beside me, offering me a package. I looked at him in complete surprise.

"The fan, señora. The señor has bought it for you."

I followed his gesture, and there was the young gallant, bowing and smiling at me. I was hot with anger and embarrassment. Did he think he could buy my acquaintance?

"He is not my husband!" I exclaimed, at which the man grinned knowingly.

"One can see he is an admirer, señora," he murmured, and still offered me the fan.

I thrust it away, and said angrily, "Tell the *gentleman* I do not accept gifts from strangers!"

With that I took Tía Amalia's arm and walked

swiftly away, hoping it looked like the dignified exit of an affronted married woman, and not the embarrassed scuttle of an inexperienced girl, which was how I secretly felt.

"What insolence!" Tía Amalia snorted as we stepped back into the carriage and drove off. Then: *"Caramba! Would you believe it! He is now on his horse, and I could swear he is following us! If this is a sample of Porteño effrontery it is as well our stay is to be short!"*

She was right. He was following us, and continued to do so until we reached Señora Alvarez's house.

As the door was shut behind us I sighed with relief and said, "Heaven be praised, that's the last I shall be likely to see of him!"

But the incident was not ended. Later in the day Señora Alvarez came tapping on the parlor door and handed me a small parcel. I unwrapped it—and there was the fan, its oyster-gray satin, silver and pearl more gleamingly lovely in the hand than at the booth. But I dropped it on the table as if it had stung me and looked at the wrapping. It bore no name, but inside was a sheet of paper on which was written in a flourishing hand the phrases: *Accept the gift; forgive the giver who only wishes to adore you.*

When I could control my voice I asked Señora Alvarez, "Where did this come from? And why did you think it was for me?"

"Did not the señora order it?" she asked in her turn, her eyes snapping with curiosity. "It came by hand, and I was told it was for the young lady staying here."

"No, I did not order it. And it is to go straight back." Hastily I folded the fan into its wrappings and thrust it at Señora Alvarez. "Please see that it is returned at once. The coachman will know where it was bought." My eyes lighted on the note; there was no fire in the room, so I crumpled the paper in my hand and pushed it into Señora Alvarez's fingers, adding: "And burn that on the kitchen fire."

Señora Alvarez raised her eyebrows, and looked as if she was about to make a comment, but instead she shrugged her shoulders and left us.

"If all Porteños are so insolent I shan't be sorry to leave!" I said emphatically.

"*Caramba, sí!*" my aunt agreed. "The sooner you reach Don Miguel's protection the better!"

We were in cramped quarters, for the coastal vessel had none of the space and luxury of the mail ship. But it was only for three days, and I intended to spend a lot of the time on deck. And so I did, in spite of a most irritating coincidence. Besides our party there was one other passenger on board, and after we had sailed I came face to face with him. It was the young man who had sent the fan. Determined not to let this disconcert me, I ignored him, and when the Captain asked permission to present him to us I refused. In any case I should have been doubtful of the propriety of being introduced to a strange man when I was on the way to join my husband.

I noticed that he and Ruíz exchanged bows, but their acquaintance seemed to be slight as I never saw them talking together. As Tía Amalia said, in Varena it was possible that everyone knew everyone else by sight.

The cumbrous trading ship beat heavily along in the coastal waters from La Plata to the Río Oro estuary, and as our cabin was so small and very stuffy in the daytime heat I was glad to spend most of the time under an awning on deck, in spite of our fellow passenger who frequently strolled nearby. I was relieved that Señor Ruíz did not feel obliged to give us much of his company. Then at last we were at anchor again.

We were just finishing our packing when we heard a boat tie up alongside, and all my qualms returned with extra strength at the thought that Don Miguel might be coming aboard. Sure enough, in a few minutes we were summoned to the Captain's cabin.

With Tía Amalia I went there, on legs that felt like green twigs, and entered with my eyes cast down, not from modesty but nerves. A tall figure turned towards us, and I forced my glance upwards, past the tasselled boots and light breeches, past the yellow waistcoat under the dark blue cutaway coat, on past the frilled shirt and white cravat, till I saw the face. With a surge of relief I found it recognizable. The features which had refused to combine in my memory now coalesced, and I saw it was my husband, as handsome as before—and probably just as coldly businesslike, I reminded myself. But now he was smiling and holding out his hand. Tía Amalia dropped him a little curtsey, but I could not do so: if I relaxed my knees I might well collapse at his feet. So I stood as straight as I could and put my hand in his, willing it and my lips not to tremble. He drew me towards him and kissed me on both cheeks.

"Welcome, dear wife."

Soon we were on land, driving in a splendid black carriage with yellow wheels, with Don Miguel riding beside us. We were going to the house of Doña Sara Guzmán, whose son, Don Gaspar, was the colonel in charge of the Varena garrison and Don Miguel's greatest friend. We were to stay there until my wedding ceremony; and a remark of Don Miguel's, intended to put me at my ease, did not entirely do so.

"Doña Sara has a heart of gold," he said, "and will do her best to help and advise you. You must not mind if you find her quite a formidable old lady."

As we drove I looked around at the town where I would live. At some distance from our landing point, jutting out on what looked like a little island in the waters of the bay, was a stone-built fort, oddly toy-like, with a battlemented top on which two sentries paced, and thick straight walls pierced by gunports which covered the harbor entrance. On the quay everything was on a smaller scale than at Buenos Aires, and the pace was slower, the atmosphere less mercantile, more homely. There were fishing boats at anchor, nets spread to dry, and a group of women with baskets on their heads carrying the silver and slate-blue loads which must be the last of the morning's catch. Beyond the wharf and its storebuildings lay Varena, the houses neatly aligned, a town hardly bigger than a village, I thought, all boxed compactly together.

The buildings on shore directly opposite the fort were barracks; there were soldiers drilling on an open space. I heard sharp orders and saw a flash of scarlet and the glint of steel. Further on were some handsome houses, and before one of these the carriage stopped.

We were shown through a massive door into the tunnel-like porchway; at the end of it I saw the corner of a patio, shaded, invitingly cool.

"Doña Sara is in the *gran sala,* señor," the servant said. "I am to take you to her."

The dark-skinned girl led us through the house and opening a door announced, "Don Miguel and his ladies, señora," which made him sound as if he kept a harem.

I had the impression of a large room, beautifully furnished, with a high ceiling, a tiled floor strewn with rugs, and large windows opening on to the patio. In a high-backed chair by a window sat an old lady in a black silk gown with a white lace fichu. Her silver hair was covered with a lace mantilla; beneath it was a thin and wrinkled face, with sunken cheeks and a complexion sallowed by time. But in this aging countenance was set a pair of eyes like polished agates, sending glances to and fro which snapped with liveliness and curiosity. A deep cracked voice exclaimed, "That girl will never learn to announce anyone in a proper fashion! Now, Miguel, perform your quite unnecessary introductions!"

The old lady nodded graciously to Tía Amalia, gave a thin and blue-veined hand to Don Miguel to kiss, and fixed her gaze on me as I made my curtsey.

"Come, child, sit next to me. You, señora, the other side. Miguel, pour us all some wine—it's not worth calling that silly girl to do it."

As I seated myself Doña Sara continued to scrutinize me. By now she will know how much the mulberry silk cost, and the quality of gold in my earrings, I decided. Folding her hands on the gold top of an ebony cane beside her chair Doña Sara leaned forward and asked sharply, "Did you have rough weather on your crossing, child?"

"For a short while, Doña Sara."

"And were you seasick?"

"A little queasy, no more."

"Good. That's one sign of a strong constitution. Well, Miguel, you did not choose her for her looks, but she appears healthy, and not unhandsome."

I felt myself blushing, and cringed inwardly to think that Doña Sara must know the full details of Don Miguel's search for a wife—which was more than I did. Now it was Tía Amalia's turn to be quizzed.

"And you, señora, what made you offer to come to the Americas with your niece?"

"Several things, Doña Sara," my aunt answered coolly. "First, my love for my niece. Then, too, a desire to do something useful with my life."

"A widow without children can be useful in Spain in many ways. You could have helped your priest."

"There are plenty of women to help the priests of Spain. There are not so many who will leave their homes to come here."

"True." Doña Sara sipped her wine and glanced momentarily at me. "Have you taught her well?"

Tía Amalia looked surprised. "Her parents have given her correct instruction. Marta is a good Catholic—" The old lady shook her head impatiently. "Not religious matters! Prayers won't cook meat for a hungry man! Does she know how to run a household—will she be a good wife? Don Miguel has had to take everything on trust."

"And so, you will realize, has Marta," answered Tía Amalia calmly. The old lady gave a snort—you could not call it anything else—but the corners of her mouth twitched. "Marta has been well trained in the duties of a housewife," my aunt continued. "I do not think Don Miguel will regret his choice."

"And Doña Marta, I hope, will be satisfied with hers."

Don Miguel had spoken on his own behalf. He was looking directly at me and smiling. In spite of Doña Sara I began to feel more comfortable. This lasted only a moment, for she turned to Don Miguel and asked, "Well, Miguel, have you arranged for the wedding?"

My heart gave a great bump.

"Yes, it is fixed for next Sunday."

I was amazed at Don Miguel's coolness. He might have been arranging a morning's ride. He turned to me as an afterthought and added, "That will be convenient for you, I trust?"

He doesn't know me, I thought, and I don't know him. . . .

"It is less than a week," I faltered.

"Did you wish for a delay?"

"No—I had thought it might be necessary—" The words came stumbling out.

"Then it is agreeable to you?"

"Yes."

What else could I say? How could I ask for more time?

"Then it is settled."

I soon realized I was not to see the house in which I was to live until after the wedding. It was not considered correct for me to go there before the nuptial mass. All I knew was that it was a house very similar to Doña Sara's, and that a capable housekeeper was in charge. It would have been in bad taste to ask questions about it; however, by dinner time I had found enough confidence to make a few more general inquiries.

"This territory is called 'La Tierra de Riqueza'—but why?" I asked. "In what way is it rich?"

Don Miguel gave the hint of a smile. "It is not rich in gold, which is what the *conquistadores* who named it expected. But in other ways it is." This was a subject on which he seemed pleased to talk. "The land is fertile. As for Valdoro—the name as you can tell is a corruption of 'El Valle de Oro,' Golden Valley— Golden River—no, there is no gold, and it is not even a valley."

"Then why call it that?"

"Well, there is a slight cleft formed by the river; from it the ground rises steadily until it opens out on to the great plains—the *pampa*. The *conquistadores* thought it was a valley which would lead them to an Indian city—full of gold, naturally. I have proved they were wrong."

"Did *you* ever think there was gold?"

"No. I didn't want gold. I wanted land. I've never had land. Everything else, but no land of my own." He paused, and then continued. "My father was a second son, as I am—and when his brother died unexpectedly he inherited not only land in Spain but certain rights in South America. My brother is not interested in South America; he is content to be heir to the Spanish estates. So, as you know, my father passed the South American deeds to me."

"And that is why you came out here?"

"Yes. Can you understand that I wanted to make a new life for myself, not to be second to anybody, to create an estate from nothing, to establish something that will last? It will be a new line, the Moural de Valdoro, in a new land."

His face was turned to me, his expression intent, his eyes gleaming. I had noticed that whenever he spoke of Valdoro his look altered, as if he were seeing his land in his mind's eye, and loving every inch.

"As soon as I could I proved the boundaries of Valdoro, I pushed them as far as it was possible for them to go. Now all that is mine—no one can challenge my right."

Now I knew what Serafina had meant. She had said to me, "There is something about him which almost frightens me—something strong and ruthless." Ruthless was too harsh a word, I thought. Intense would be better. I did not think it would frighten me, although

I now saw there was a side of him I had not suspected. So the desire to live in South America was not a wealthy whim; he had chosen a way of life from a fixed purpose, and I began to suspect that Valdoro was not simply a house he was building for occasional country visits. It was part of a plan about which I knew nothing. What was more, I too was part of that plan.

The night before the wedding Doña Sara announced her intention of retiring early.

"And so, Marta, should you. Now, my child, I wish you to come and say good night to me in my room. María will call you when she brings me my posset."

I guessed that this was an honor, and suspected that I was to receive some special good wishes on my wedding eve.

Doña Sara's room was large and dark. I crossed the smooth floor, past great cupboards and presses and chests which loomed in the shadows, over to the yellow patch of candlelight beside the huge fourposter bed. In it Doña Sara sat, propped up against a mountain of pillows, a lace-trimmed nightcap covering her hair and making a white blob over the sallow face patched with shadow. The maid put the posset cup on to the side table and was dismissed.

"Sit down, child." The candlelight was caught in the agate eyes. "No, bring that chair and put it here, so that you are sitting in front of me. How can I talk with my head twisted around? I am not an owl."

More like an old hawk, with that narrow nose and staring bright eyes, I thought, as I placed the chair and myself as directed. Doña Sara took the posset cup, stirred the contents and sipped a spoonful.

"Well, for the daughter of a penniless *caballero* you've made a splendid match," she said sharply. "Don Miguel is noble, and very rich."

I wanted to contradict the "penniless," but thought it wiser to stay silent.

"Very rich," the old lady repeated. "And very handsome. Handsome enough to make any young girl fall in love with him. And many have."

I met the old eyes squarely, and still said nothing.

"But you are marrying him, which makes you different. You have to be a wife, not a silly moonstruck girl. You have a job to do. Now, besides being rich and handsome he is also ambitious—I hope you know that."

I had not thought of it, but I agreed.

"You should be grateful for it. A man without ambition is a household cat, thinking of nothing but food by day and pleasure by night. But a man with ambition is a puma—a creature to be reckoned with. You are marrying a puma. Oh, you haven't seen it yet, but you will."

"Yes, Doña Sara."

"Is that all you can say? *Dios mío,* girl, I had you come here tonight to find out whether you're capable of keeping your side of the bargain! Miguel is like a second son to me, and I don't want to see him wasted on an empty-headed puppet who'll be no good to him!"

I controlled my anger and spoke firmly. "I hope Don Miguel will find I am no puppet. I am ready to help him in any way I can."

"Ready? That's something. But are you capable?" Doña Sara went on implacably. "Can you take second place to his ambition, can you help him and accept what you find, or will you go whining for assurance and comfort and safety and spend your hours fretting because he doesn't love you?"

The words were like a blow in the stomach. I realized that I had hoped for affection in my marriage, but Doña Sara was telling me that my husband would have no time for tenderness.

"I shall try to do what is best for Don Miguel— and our marriage will be my affair," I flashed out.

"Ah, you have some spirit! That's as well. I suppose, having warned you, I'll have to leave it to you to do your best. Remember that a man like Miguel has to be taken with his faults as well as his virtues. Well, you have my good wishes. Did you meet Miguel's parents? Did they come to see you, or ask you to visit them?"

"No, Doña Sara. Nor did they write to me," I admitted unwillingly.

"That's not surprising. You weren't their choice of a wife."

"That was obvious, even to me."

I did not mean to sound bitter, but it hurt.

"One cannot entirely blame them. They had been trying to marry him for long enough. Some hard words were said when he turned down their latest choice because she would not agree to live here, and he left home in anger saying he would marry the first woman who would go to South America with him."

I felt cold at heart. "I did not know that."

"So you see, you could hardly expect them to open their arms to you before your marriage. It doesn't matter; there's an ocean between you now; you've only Miguel to concern yourself with. I dare say his parents will soften to you when you've fulfilled your first duty, which you had best manage successfully and in good time."

"My first duty. . . ?"

Doña Sara clattered the spoon into her cup.

"*Madre de Dios!* You cannot be so innocent! When a man *marries* it is because he wants an heir! Miguel is founding an *estancia*—you must give him a son, and quickly!"

My heart was thumping, I was hot with embarrassment. "I hope I shall do so."

"There's no reason why you should not—though one can never tell. But you're young and healthy—better stock than the languid beauties here. I maintain people are like horses: too much inbreeding weakens the line. You're bringing fresh blood. So that's your first duty—give Miguel a son. A full nursery—that should be *your* ambition. And it will fit in with his. I know what I am talking about."

Until then I had not thought much about the physical side of marriage. It sounds naive to say that I had accepted the Church's teaching that marriage was for the procreation of children, and hoped to fulfill myself in that way, without having any clear idea how it was brought about. Animals I understood from my life at the *quinta,* and I had been allowed to infer that something similar happened with people—but it all seemed so strange, so impossible, and I feared it would be unpleasant, or worse, much worse. Now this cruel old lady was forcing me to face reality, to see only too clearly why Don Miguel was marrying me. I trembled inside to think of the lesson I should soon have to learn. I gritted my teeth. I must not show ignorance or fear in front of Doña Sara.

She was looking at me shrewdly. "Yes, you're quiet, but not without spirit. Maybe you'll manage. Miguel knows how to keep a woman happy and has the sense to do so as long as his ambition lets him. I have just two pieces of advice for you, so listen carefully. Accept what you can't alter; and don't judge a man from a woman's viewpoint. Now off to bed with you—you must be at your best tomorrow. Good night."

Disconcerted by the abrupt dismissal I could only murmur, "Good night, Doña Sara. And thank you."

Thank you for what? For frightening me, for crushing my hopes and giving me eccentric advice? Some of her remarks had been all too plain, the rest more than a little obscure. She was fond of Miguel, that was certain. Whether I should be able to live up to her standards of a good wife to him was much less certain. The interview had done little but increase my feelings of uneasiness and inadequacy.

3

I remember very little of the nuptial mass. I was too nervous, concentrating on keeping my self-control, on doing the right thing. First the drive, then stepping out of the carriage in front of the yellow stone cathedral, walking up the steps and through the great baroque door into the candlelit perfumed dark. It was all hazy. I recollect that I knelt so long in a state of nervous tension that I felt my leg muscles stiffening, my heart thumping, and my body was top-heavy. I took deep breaths and tried not to sway. Don Miguel had turned and given me a long unsmiling look as he took my hand in his, and when I felt the strength in the grasp of his lean fingers I gave a little prayer that I might live up to what he expected of me.

The wedding feast at Doña Sara's house was a whirl of color and sound, of people laughing and talking, people I did not know and whose names I could not remember. I recognized the priest who married us, a thin old man with a deeply lined face and somber eyes, and I heard him talking to Don Miguel.

He was saying, "I have found just the man for you

—a young man, Father Marcos. He will leave Varena any time you wish, and will be happy to live at Valdoro. He has a call to strengthen the faith and promote the welfare of the Indians."

"That is splendid, Father," Don Miguel answered. "I will meet him as soon as you can arrange it."

A few days ago such a conversation would have caused me unease, but now I knew that there were Indian workers on some newly established plantations; there was nothing to cause concern.

"Come, Marta, it is time for us to say goodbye to our guests."

There was a flurry of embraces, of remarks I did not register, for he had called me Marta.

I knew we had not been following all the old customs, the situation was not conventional; now the wedding meal was over at last we were going to Don Miguel's house—we were having no honeymoon. Tía Amalia had been there that day to see everything was ready; she was acting as maid to me until a suitable girl could be found and trained.

As Don Miguel's house was near Doña Sara's, we were soon there. We were met in the hallway by Tía Amalia and a middle-aged woman who curtsied to us and said, "Welcome, Doña Marta," with a tight-lipped smile.

"This is my housekeeper, Señora Ruíz," said Don Miguel.

I greeted her formally, then the coincidence of the name struck me.

"Ruíz? Are you related to . . ."

"*Sí.* My husband has the honor to be Don Miguel's steward."

"I did not know—"

"I trust, señora, you will find everything to your liking. I shall attend you tomorrow morning for my instructions."

Before such a young mistress she dropped her eyes rather too humbly, I thought. It did not match the persistence of that tight smile which was still on her lips as she curtsied again and withdrew.

Upstairs in the large bedchamber I looked about me, flurried by the unfamiliarity of everything, nervousness threatening to return. The furniture was elegantly Spanish, and grander than I was used to; the bedcurtains were of blue silk damask, drawn back against the posts; the floor was of polished wood, overlaid with fine rugs, and there to one side was my best dower chest of brass-bound Cordovan leather, while on the dressing-table, I could see my silver-backed brushes and my little trinket-box. Groups of candles were flaring in the branched candelabra on the dressing-table and beside the bed; I had never seen so many in a bedroom before. It was *hidalgo* extravagance.

I took off my mantilla and Tía Amalia began to unhook my gown.

"There, *chiquita mía,*" said Tía Amalia soothingly.

I stepped out of the gown and began to loosen my hair. It was like taking off a heavy crown, and the physical relief seemed to lighten my spirit. I went to the long window and pulled it ajar. The night was moonless. I had only the vague impression of a patio like a pit of darkness beneath, but I could hear the faint rustle of leaves and the splash of water—so there was a pool and a fountain. How pleasant that would be. The night was very warm, but a breath of air came wafting in, bringing a faint scent of flowers to mingle with the smell of burning candlewax. I was thankful that Tía Amalia did not chatter. I wanted quietness now after the hectic day. I could hear faint sounds from behind a second door which must lead into Don Miguel's dressing-room; so he—or perhaps a servant —was there.

Now I was in my nightgown, I climbed into the high bed. Tía Amalia bent and kissed me, we said good night and I was alone.

What should I do? Sit up, or lie down? Look wide awake, or pretend to be asleep? He was my husband, I was in the bridal bed. . . . How should I greet him?

Half lying, half sitting, uncomfortably aware of my heartbeats pounding, I leaned against the pillows and gripped the lace-edged sheets. Long minutes passed. I tried to relax; then suddenly the door opened and Don Miguel came in. He did not look at me at first. I saw his tall figure in a green brocade dressing-gown cross the room, heard his soft leather slippers flapping faintly on the wooden floor. He extinguished the candles on the dressing-table one by one. Then he turned and came over to me. He sat down on the edge of the bed and his look held mine.

"Well, Marta, all day I have waited for you to call me Miguel, and you have not done so once. I believe I am Don Miguel to you even in your thoughts. That will not do for me. I do not believe in such formality between husband and wife."

Was he teasing me? I could not tell.

"I will remember that—Miguel."

"Good." Now he looked at me gravely. "Marta, you agreed to marry a man you did not know. It was an arrangement for the benefit of both parties. I hope that when you know me better you will feel some regard for me."

"I am sure I shall—indeed, I do," I blurted out.

He smiled, that wonderful flashing smile which lit his face and made the somber dark eyes brilliant. "Then I am a fortunate man, and we are beginning well."

He stood up, took off his gown and slid his feet out of his slippers. He climbed in beside me. The bed creaked beneath his weight. Trying not to think ahead, not daring to look at his face, I noticed the ruffles of fine lace on the cambric of his shirt, the breadth of the shoulders beneath it.

"I hope we shall suit each other," I whispered. "I want very much to please you."

"That you should want to is enough. You do please me."

He turned to me, leaning on one elbow, and I knew

he was still looking at me. "How old are you now, Marta?"

"Nearly eighteen."

"Do you find thirteen years a great gap between us?"

"Indeed, no, Miguel."

"Good. With many couples the gap is much greater, but that, I think, is unwise. In our case I believe it is not too much. And I, being older, can teach you some of the things you do not know."

Of marriage he means I thought desperately. Is he going to be as cold and businesslike in the begetting of his children as he was in choosing his wife? I know nothing, nothing! I can only guess what must happen, and it frightens me. What should I do? What will I have to do?

I lifted my eyes in a quick nervous glance, and found him looking at me, not as he had done before, but with eyes that moved from my face to the curves of my body under the thin nightgown. I felt a sudden tightening in my throat, my breath came quicker as my heart pounded, and panic fluttered inside me. I gripped the sheet and tried to keep calm, but his face, lit by the remaining candles, swam over me out of the darkness, the eyes burning, and suddenly I felt naked —ah *Dios,* would I have to be naked?

His hand touched my shoulder, the fingers warm through the silk to my cold skin, sending a shock through me so that I started and recoiled. I had not meant to do so, I was ready to be dutiful, to submit —for one moment I shut my eyes. . . .

"Caramba!" His voice sounded loud and harsh. "Must you flinch away at the first touch! Such reluctance is not very flattering, however innocent you are!"

To my dismay tears began to prick in my eyelids. "It isn't that," I whispered. "I am ready to please you."

He gave a dry laugh. "Ready for martyrdom, it seems! That would give pleasure to neither of us, and in this matter it is best for both to find some enjoyment!"

I struggled not to weep.

"Don't look so stricken," he went on. "I know I am not much more than a stranger to you. I will not take my marriage rights without reasonable preliminaries. Set your mind at rest for a while."

He turned away from me, and extinguished the candles on the bedside table. I sat there stiffly in the darkness as I heard him settle down. Then gradually I slid lower in the bed and lay quite still until I heard him drift into sleep. After what seemed an age I slipped, exhausted, into unconsciousness.

When I awoke it was broad daylight. In the first few seconds as the sun struck through my closed eyelids I had to make a conscious effort to orientate myself, to remember where I was. So, I was in Don Miguel's house—in Don Miguel's bed. My eyes flicked open. The space beside me was empty. Then I realized that Miguel was standing at the foot of the bed, fully dressed, looking down at me.

"Ah, you are awake!" he said. "I am just going out. Shall I have coffee sent up to you?"

"If you please."

I stumbled out the answer, and with a quick *"Hasta luego"* he left me.

A few minutes later a maidservant brought me coffee. As I drank it I thrust to the back of my mind the remembrance of the previous night, and let my thoughts drift on. Now everything in my life would be different. Position, relationships, attitudes—all had changed. Even with Tía Amalia, for to her I would no longer be a girl: already that was obvious. By now at any other time Tía Amalia would be tapping at my door; now I was mistress of the house, to meet people when I chose.

Today I would explore the house, I decided; I would get to know the servants, enquire after Señora Ruíz's routine, perhaps consult Miguel about changes, and about his future plans. I must supervise the unpacking of my linen—and check the linen cupboard as I did it; inspect the store cupboards—yes, once I started I could certainly keep myself busy.

I got up, washed—the maid had brought hot water —and dressed. Now what? Beside the unmade bed was a long bell-pull; if I tugged it someone would come and clear my tray and tidy the room. I was about to do so when my eyes glanced on the dressing-room door. Before I rang I would look inside and see what attention was needed there. I was suddenly eager to see Miguel's room, as if the inanimate objects it contained could tell me something about the man. Lightly I stepped across the room and opened the door.

I started back with an abrupt shock, then, quite subdued, I slowly walked inside. To my astonishment I had seen that the room was not empty. Sitting on a chair by the one narrow window, sewing at something white which lay across her lap, was an Indian girl. Up to now all the servants I had seen both here and at Doña Sara's house had been *mestizos*—part Indian, part Spanish; dark-skinned, with more or less of the Indian in their features. They were nevertheless not unduly strange to me: they were conventionally dressed; they seemed "civilized." But this girl was pure Indian.

She was wearing a blouse of pale yellow, against which her skin shone like copper; her long hair, black and coarse and straight, hung about her shoulders and shadowed her face. I saw the long slanting eyes, the high cheekbones, the small straight nose, the soft red lips, and it was a face so alien in its looks and in its complete impassivity that I had at that moment no impression of its beauty. I saw a slender bronze neck circled by strings of polished beads; slim rounded arms—the girl was probably younger than myself by a year or so—billowing many-colored petticoats above slim ankles and bare brown feet; but only two things registered strongly with me, overwhelming everything else. One was, that the girl was mending one of Miguel's shirts; the other, that she was undoubtedly heavily pregnant.

As I stood and stared, the girl stopped sewing, fixed her eyes on me with a long unblinking look, and slowly rose to her feet.

"Who told you to do that?"

It was not the first question I should have asked, but somehow it seemed the most important. I waited, but the girl did not answer; she simply stood quite still, holding the shirt which rose whitely over her distended body.

"Why are you here?"

The Indian stared and made no reply. Then I realized that the girl might not understand Spanish. I tried once more.

"Did Señora Ruíz send you here?"

The girl's chin lifted with a hint of pride, and then she spoke in clear intelligible Spanish.

"Don Miguel is my lord, and master. I serve him."

I knew I must assert my authority. I had an irrational repugnance to this Indian handling Miguel's things, doing the tasks that I myself would do as of right. That she should mend his linen was not only incongruous, it was offensive.

"But only as I tell you," I heard myself saying firmly. "I am the mistress of this house."

"Don Miguel is my lord, and master," the girl repeated.

Was that all the Spanish she knew? I held out my hand for the shirt, and although the girl must have understood the gesture she did not attempt to relinquish it. I felt frustrated, helpless. I could not fight for the garment—so must I admit defeat, find Señora Ruíz? That was the last thing I wanted to do.

"Yes. So I am your mistress."

As I made the last attempt I heard the clack of footsteps, and Miguel himself appeared at the open door. He stopped short, then looked quickly from me to the girl in utter amazement.

"India—what are you doing here?" he asked sharply.

The girl turned to him and began to speak swiftly, softly, incomprehensibly—it was some Indian dialect, I realized, but there was no guessing what the girl was saying as her face stayed as impassive as before, the eyes as inscrutable as a lizard's. When she stopped Miguel answered, to my amazement in the native tongue. He looked displeased. I would have given a lot to know what he was saying. Then he ended in Spanish.

"On my orders you will do as Doña Marta says. Now go to Señora Ruíz."

The girl folded the shirt, placed it on a small table, and without another word she left the room.

Miguel turned to me, and for the first time he seemed a little at a loss. "I am sorry, Marta, I should have warned you—"

"She gave me a surprise. I thought the room was empty. How much Spanish does she understand?"

"She understands and speaks it quite well."

"She behaved as if she did not comprehend a word."

"Probably because she did not know you. You will have no more difficulty with her."

"Who is she?"

"I'll tell you her story later. Just now I am very hungry—will you join me at breakfast?"

It was impossible to talk about the incident while there was a servant in the room, so our conversation was confined to small-talk until the meal was in progress. Then, at last, he dismissed the servant and I was free to question him.

"The Indian girl, Miguel—tell me about her, please. What is her name,"

"Something very long and quite unpronounceable by most Spaniards. She refused to adopt a Spanish name, so she became known simply as the Indian girl. So 'La India,' or simply India, she has remained."

"Has she been here long?"

Miguel put down his cup and leaned back in his chair.

"I will tell you what happened. When I last returned

from Spain I decided to prove beyond legal doubt
the boundaries of my land. By the northern frontier
there is an area where Indians live; they are a tribe
which has had little contact with Spaniards. It happened that I did the chief of the tribe a service. It
was nothing to me, but it saved the life of his eldest
son. The *cacique* was embarrassingly grateful, and
wanted to recompense me. If I had refused what he
had offered it would have been an unpardonable insult, and would have made the whole tribe my enemy.
You understand what that would have meant—constant harassment to Valdoro, theft, damage, fighting—
I had no choice but to accept graciously."

"I understand," I said, and waited. He did not at
once continue, so I asked, "What was his recompense?"

Miguel took another bread roll, and answered without looking at me, in a manner that was matter-of-
fact, almost casual.

"He gave me one of his daughters, as a personal
servant."

"Gave you—a servant—that girl?" My instincts
rose against it. "But you have taken her away from
her tribe!"

"I had to. It was expected."

"And to keep her here—it's like slavery! She
couldn't have wanted that. And her husband—what
of him?—she must have been married then—"

"Marta, this is not Spain! Things are different here.
You must adjust yourself to that. Please understand
this. India is not a slave, and in fact considers herself
in an honored position here. She was happy to leave
her tribe, and was not bound to any man at that time."

"So she married after she became your servant. Is
he one of your men?"

"Indians do not marry as we do." I was not quite
sure what he meant, but felt it was a reproach to my
ignorance. "Do not worry about her pregnancy. I know
her man, and you need not concern yourself."

"But I thought it was my business to concern myself about the servants?"

"India is not a servant—not as the others are. She is a chief's daughter, a princess in her own opinion, and many people, white as well as colored, would rank her above *mestizo* servants. She serves me personally, and must not be given menial jobs. I intended her to stay at Valdoro; her loyalty brought her here against my instructions. Now I have spoken to her, she will be obedient provided you are tactful. Leave her her pride and you will have no difficulty."

Miguel sounded more confident than I felt about my ability to handle the situation. I made one last effort.

"Now the baby is coming, wouldn't she be better off with her own people?"

"She would never agree to that. She was given to me, a life for a life, and she must stay. She will choose her own help when the child comes."

And with that Miguel closed the subject. So this was one of the things I had to learn. I remembered Doña Sara's advice; this was tied up with Miguel's ambition for Valdoro. He was not going to let any friction with the Indians endanger the peace of his *estancia*.

Now, at last, I was hearing about Valdoro. The architect had arrived and Miguel had invited me to join their conference. I had been shown the plans, and there had been a progress report. When finished the house would be more like a palace, I thought privately, and was relieved to know it was going up in stages, some wings were not scheduled to be built until a few years later. The first stage, I considered, would be grand enough to satisfy my dreams, and would provide accommodation for a fair-sized family and servants. But there was no time to consider the fitness of enlarging it, Miguel expected me to follow the discussion and make myself familiar with everything. The interior of the main block and one wing would soon be ready for furnishing, and while he and the architect were deciding on the kind of doors, the wood to be used for panelling, even the plastering of the ceilings, I must acquaint myself with the size and number of windows and work out quantities for curtaining.

"And the tiles for the hall floor cannot be obtained in time?"

"Regrettably, no, Don Miguel."

My husband swore under his breath. "In that case you must lay it with stone flags. I want those tiles precisely as I have ordered them. When they are ready they can be laid and the flagstones used else-where—probably in the stable courtyard."

"That would be a practical solution."

"Doña Marta will make a list for you of everything she requires—you shall have that tomorrow—there may be some additions."

"Yes, Don Miguel."

"I hope we are not far behind schedule?"

"Not as far as I had feared. Most of the damage has been made good. It was lucky the fire did not reach—"

"Quite. Keep the men going. I do not want a delay."

It was not like Miguel to interrupt so brusquely, almost as if he wanted to silence the man who had mentioned a fire. What fire? Whatever it was it had apparently not been serious—due to a careless workman, I supposed. So I had to make out a list by to-morrow, and what a list! Everything from the kitchen stove and fire-irons to curtain poles, not forgetting the rings! Some things could be made on the spot, but as little as possible must be left to be done there, and if I missed something which the workmen could not make, once we had moved in it would mean doing without for weeks, perhaps months. It was plain that the list must take precedence over the linen cupboard.

It was as well that I settled to my list and gave it all my concentration for some hours, for I had barely finished it when Doña Sara arrived to take me on a round of visits. I had to meet Varena society before I could give my own reception, she told me, and that I must do as soon as possible in case Miguel took it into his head to be off to Valdoro again.

The next few days were an ordeal for me. I knew how to behave in society, but I had little sophistication, and the ways of the *hidalgas* of Varena were as different from the ways of Torillo ladies as a wolf differs from a mouse. When the ladies were alone together reputations were torn to shreds, barbed remarks were exchanged as if the intention of meeting was to wound, and all other talk was superficial and artificial to a degree I had never before encountered. It was soon plain to me that what I had considered normal standards of propriety were ridiculed and mocked at. I found it best to hold my tongue as much as I could, and to be as non-committal as possible.

One incident I remember clearly. One young lady had announced, not with pleasure but with great distaste, that she was pregnant. Another asked her, with malice in her tone, whom did she hope the baby would favor? To my horror the girl replied casually, "I hope it is not too unlike my husband, ugly though he is, for I shall insist it is his. But I doubt it very much."

Something must have shown in my face, for another remarked, loudly enough for all in the drawing room to hear, "Be careful, now! You have shocked Doña Marta! You forget she is newly wed!"

The young *hidalga* was quite shameless, for she laughed and retorted, "That's no excuse for prudery! No doubt she'll soon learn married ways." Then she spoke directly to me. "We married women believe that since one is obliged to comply with one's husband's wishes, no matter how little to one's taste he may be, it is perfectly reasonable to find compensation and pleasure elsewhere. The great thing is not to let him know. As for you, you have no reason to be proud or priggish, because you're lucky enough to find duty and delight in the same bed."

I could feel the hot flush on my cheeks, and could find no words to answer her in my embarrassment. I realized that silence was my best policy; I must try to

appear indifferent, to pretend some kind of confidence,
for if I let them provoke me into talking about Miguel
their shrewdness would at once penetrate my inno-
cence. They would know that I was still unhusbanded,
and totally ignorant besides.

"Oh, the cat's got her tongue!" someone else snig-
gered. "Don Miguel must be twice the man she expected—he's quite exhausted her!"

"Yes, indeed!" another voice broke in. "I'd wager
he could satisfy a dozen women—and for all we know,
he does! Think of all the times he makes mysterious
trips inland—and as for Varena—"

"Varena!" another voice still cut in. "As for Varena,
you should keep your remarks to yourself. We know
they will be prompted by envy and disappointment,
since he has never looked at you."

The voice was as crisp and downright as the words.
The intervention was most welcome to me both from
its meaning and for the fact that it drew all the attention from my miserable, silent, squirming self. All
heads turned toward the door.

The newcomer was someone I had not met before;
this I knew at the first glance, for her appearance
would not have passed unnoticed or been forgotten.
The other women in the room all had some claim to
good looks or elegance, a fine figure or a piquant personality; she, alas, had none. It was a kindness to call
her plain. Her only good feature was her eyes, which
were large and bright. Her skin was poor, her hair
thin and dull, and her face was dominated by a nose
too long for her small narrow skull. To make things
worse, no care in dressing could disguise the fact that
her slim body had one shoulder higher than the other,
and when she moved she walked with a slight limp.
But my pity for her was soon tempered with admiration, for I found that Doña Isabel could hold her own.
Her remarks, though not malicious, were as tart as any
and wittier than most. I noticed that while she was of
the company the women made no improper admis-
sions or outrageously scandalous remarks, but con-

fined themselves to more general gossip and back-biting.

When we were introduced we exchanged a few words, but after that she did not single me out for any attention. Miguel's name was not mentioned again, but I would not have been human had I not wondered if any in the company had received his attentions. I was not such a fool as to think such a man as he would have reached his thirties without experience of women. But I preferred not to know about it.

No sooner had Doña Sara satisfied herself that I had met Varena society than she had to start arrangements moving for my reception. It was much more hers than mine, for though it was to be held in my house that seemed to be the sum of my involvement. She drew up the guest list—naturally, she knew everybody—and told me what refreshment should be provided. She engaged the orchestra, and she instructed the servants how to rearrange the furniture. Her authority irritated me, for I am independent by nature, but I knew my own limitations and was grateful for her help. But you may be sure I took note of everything so that next time I should be self-sufficient.

The day before the reception she went over the guest list with me, giving me advice.

"You have met Doña Isabel, of course. You have enough sense to realize you must not show her any pity. You have not met her husband."

I hid my surprise that Doña Isabel was married, and listened as she went on: "Alfonso Sánchez would not be invited to this house if he were not her husband. Be careful to be absolutely formal with him if you do not want to displease Miguel."

"I am formal with everyone at present. May I ask why he is unpopular with Miguel?"

"He is *unpopular,* as you put it, with everyone that matters. He is an ill-bred little upstart, an adventurer who has crashed into society by marriage.

"You may as well know the story. You have seen Doña Isabel. She would never have been good-looking, but a childhood illness left her crippled, and though her father is of very good family and extremely rich the girl was virtually unmarriageable, and knew it. Then Alfonso Sánchez appeared. Oh, he was clever, the way he handled her. He talked with her, complimented her on her intelligence, said heart and mind counted, not looks and age—she's older than he by a few years, incidentally. She soon imagined herself in love with him, and her father, who in other circumstances would have booted him off the doorstep, let them marry.

Then, of course, everything changed. Now he has control of her money he does just as he likes. He's barely civil to her even in public, and lives like a bachelor, having affairs with all sorts of women. Her father made over one of his mines to the fellow as dowry, and he's exploiting it and frittering away all the money he handles on his women and his gambling. She will never admit to being unhappy, but it must have been a bitter experience for her, for she's good at heart and worth ten of most of the women here, who sleep with her husband and smile at her sweetly. She's got a tongue like a knife, but only uses it when necessary."

I remembered how the women had been implying a possible rakishness to Miguel, and how she had cut them off. In view of her own experience I was more grateful than before.

Of Miguel himself I had seen very little, for while I was busy meeting society and preparing for the reception he was eternally involved in matters about Valdoro. Instead of becoming more at ease with him I seemed to grow more awkward, more gauche; it was as if some barrier were making it impossible for us even to become on friendly terms with each other. If we had spoken different languages we could not have understood each other less.

Each night at bedtime I was struck with a kind of dumb and agonized trepidation. In my mind was the knowledge that he had married me to have a son, and that sooner or later I would be forced into intimacy with him. But he did not touch me; he hardly spoke. I would lie in bed thinking, how can you like a man, far less love him, when he has bought you in the way of business? Yet he was attractive to women, and I could see why, for he was handsome and altogether charming. I wished that he would try to charm me; it would show some personal interest.

I wondered what affairs he had had in the past, how serious they had been, and who had been disappointed when he married. Doña Sara had made it quite plain that he had taken a wife to get an heir and a housekeeper for Valdoro, and these I must provide, perhaps nothing more, but certainly nothing less. It was a cold-blooded marriage, and I disliked him for it. I dreaded the time when he would decide on a businesslike mastery of my body.

The evening of my supper reception arrived, and with Tía Amalia's help I did my best to make my appearance do Miguel justice. I was wearing my wedding dress from which we had removed the long undersleeves and bodice top to convert it into a décolleté ball gown. I remembered what a to-do there had been when it was in the making. My mother had wanted blue satin, but the dressmaker from Madrid had insisted that heavy materials had been out of style for some time, that everything was now for lightness, for soft and delicate fabrics made in what she called the "classical line." In France, she said, the ladies carried the vogue to such extremes that the transparency of their gowns was positively indecent. But this delicate silk gauze—white, of course, white was the rage, and so becoming to a bride—could be made on a foundation. . . .

I looked at my reflection in the long mirror. Yes, it was a becoming gown. Now the tiniest of puff sleeves clung to the edge of my shoulders, the little bodice fitted snugly into a wide band encrusted with silver embroidery and tiny pearls, which was set high up beneath the bosom, and from which the gauzy skirt

fell straight and full to the ankles, with a deep embroidered hem.

It was time to go downstairs. Miguel came in from
his dressing-room and I stood still, searching his face
for a look of approval. His eyes scanned me from top
to toe, widened and looked again intently. I was then
acutely aware that the short bodice clung closely to
my breasts, and the embroidered band seemed to focus
attention on that part of my anatomy which until now
I had been taught should be modestly covered. Now,
it seemed, it was correct to show one's figure, and ball
gowns such as this disguised nothing; they half revealed and wholly suggested the form beneath. When
I turned to the dressing-table to pick up my little pen-
dant I knew the soft material swung and clung around
my hips and thighs.

"You do me more than credit, Marta," he said
quickly. "Tonight you are quite beautiful."

I was grateful for the flattery. It boosted my confidence, especially as he had managed to say it with
such sincerity. I murmured my thanks, and made to
clasp my chain about my neck.

"One moment." He opened a small leather case
which I had not noticed he was holding. "Will you
please me by wearing these?"

In the velvet-lined case lay a necklace and matching
earrings which sent out a thousand brilliant sparkles
as the candlelight caught them. Diamonds. Never before had I seen such magnificent diamonds—and I was
speechless at the thought of wearing them. He took
out the necklace and laid it about my throat, clasped
it for me like a strand of white fire, and handed me
the earrings. My fingers trembled as I put them on;
why should I be so excited at the thought of wearing
diamonds . . . at the knowledge that Miguel was standing close behind me, was putting his hands on my
shoulders, holding me there to gaze at my reflection
in the looking glass? This time I did not flinch from his
touch. His mirrored eyes and lips smiled at me, and I
returned his smile in happy amazement.

"How different I look! If only my hair was black—"

"Black!" he exclaimed. *"Dios,* no! It is lovely as it is—the color of mahogany wood."

I was even more surprised that he should seem to like it and to find such a comparison.

"Come, it is high time we went downstairs," he said, and opened the door for me.

"My fan!" I exclaimed, and went to take it, but it was not on the dressing-table. I hurried to the chest and opened the top drawer—but there was only my plain everyday fan, which would never do for this occasion. I rummaged further. Where could it be?

"Come, Marta!" Miguel's voice was authoritative. "Send the maid to find it "

I joined him and we went into the corridor. Señora Ruíz met us at the stairhead.

"The guests are arriving, Don Miguel."

"Yes, I know. Would you be so kind as to find Doña Marta's fan and bring it to her?"

She dropped a curtsey and we went downstairs.

"Marta, I hope you have learnt discretion in this society," Miguel was saying. "You will meet very few people you can trust. The women are scandal-mongers and most of the men are predatory. Be careful how you speak, in order not to encourage their little pastimes."

He spoke lightly, but I felt that he meant his words to be taken seriously. I already knew about the women; of the men I had no experience.

We took our place in the *sala,* the orchestra was playing, the reception began smoothly. With a new feeling of assurance engendered by Miguel's manner and the knowledge that my appearance, thanks to the magnificent diamonds, could rival any of my guests, I greeted each arrival without shyness, in the way Doña Sara had instructed me. In a brief pause Miguel gave me a look and a nod of approval. I felt happier than I had done since I set foot in South America.

I looked up at the next guest to be greeted, and saw coming towards us the young man who had tried to

make my acquaintance in Buenos Aires. And then I
heard his name.

"Don Alfonso Sánchez . . ."

So this was Doña Isabel's husband, about whom
Doña Sara had been so condemnatory! Now I could
understand Miguel's disapproval.

He was bending over my hand as I greeted him
automatically. Then he turned to Miguel with a smile.
"This is delightful. We have already met, the señora
and I. You knew, of course, that we were passengers
on the same ship from Buenos Aires. A most enjoyable voyage."

I was speechless at his effrontery. He was implying
an acquaintance which was non-existent. Then someone behind me touched my arm; it was Señora Ruíz.

"Your fan, Doña Marta."

I took it and whirled it open, giving myself a moment to collect my thoughts. But thoughts became
chaos again, for I saw I was holding not my own best
black fan which Mama had given me, but the gray
and silver one Alfonso Sánchez had twice tried to press
on me, and which against my gown seemed chosen for
it. He looked at the fan, he looked at me, and smiled
again. There was triumph in his eyes. I could not imagine how it had happened, but the fan was there in my
hand, and Sánchez was taking this as a signal that I
was prepared to accept his interest.

"I congratulate you, Don Miguel, on your choice of
of a bride." His voice was smooth, a little too enthu-
siastic. "She will be a great asset to our society. You
have kept her to yourself far too long. Doña Marta,
I hope to improve on our acquaintance."

His eyes were on the fan again. I snapped it shut,
gripped it between my hands, and struggled to find
words.

"Don Alfonso, we really do not know each
other . . ."

It sounded like the lying disclaimer of a silly girl
caught in an act of folly. I knew that as I spoke, but
no other words would come.

"Then I have a pleasure to anticipate," he rejoined; he bowed, and moved on.

Miguel's face was like a mask. I had already learnt that he could hide his feelings, wiping them out of his face like someone closing the shutters over a window, and now behind that nothingness his mind was a room full of black thoughts, of which, I felt sure, he considered me the major cause of blame. I wanted to catch his arm, to say, "I don't know him; he tried to scrape acquaintance, that's all——" and to blurt out the whole story, but at that moment there was nothing to be done.

Guests were still arriving, and I had to go on greeting them, murmuring set phrases like an automaton, nodding and smiling with Miguel beside me, with those shuttered eyes and that frozen face. Then I had to mingle with the guests. With my new assurance completely dissipated this was fresh torture, but I pulled myself together enough to act a confidence I did not feel. As I spoke to them it seemed to me in my unreasonably sensitive state that every remark held a hidden barb, that each *hidalga* did her best to wound me.

As I tried to ignore their remarks—and also to take calmly the attitude of the men, now I knew why Miguel had called them predatory. Whenever one of them spoke to me he made some fulsome remark, while his eyes unashamedly devoured my face and figure. Devoured is not too strong a word; I had never known that men could openly look at a woman with such rapacity. I did not flatter myself that I was particularly attractive; but I was young, inexperienced, and a newcomer, someone fresh on whom to practice their seductions. With my marriage barely a week old I was fair game; it was good sport to them. A sophisticated woman might have relished it; I found it humiliating in the extreme.

During the whole evening while I was making the correct non-committal remarks and smiling the correct small formal smiles the back of my mind was a turmoil of thoughts, all centering on the fan. I simply could not explain its reappearance. At first I thought that Señora Alvarez had not wanted the trouble of returning it, and had put it into my luggage; but all my boxes had been unpacked by Tía Amalia or myself; it could not have gone unnoticed. The only other possibility was that Sánchez had brought it with him and bribed Señora Ruíz to hand it to me at the moment of his presentation. It must be that—but why? Out of sheer malice?

Even so, two things remained unaccounted for. One was, that I could have sworn I saw a flash of surprise in Sánchez's eyes as he saw the fan; the other was, how did my own fan disappear? Was that just a coincidence? How could it be anything else?

It is said that to succeed in life every woman needs to be an actress. I was certainly one that evening, for sheer self-preservation. I think I put up a good performance and disguised my torment and misery. But when the last guest had left I felt near to collapse, utterly drained of physical and nervous energy. And my ordeal was not over; I was sure Miguel would have something to say to me, and I had to give him some sort of explanation.

We went upstairs together in silence, and instead of going into his dressing-room he came into the bedroom with me. He closed the door, and stood beside me as I sat at the dressing-table and took off the diamonds I had so happily put on.

"How could you do that to me!"

He was no longer concealing his anger; it flamed in his face, vibrated in his voice. My heart thudded in my chest and no words would come.

"I suppose you thought it wiser not to tell me that you had spent three days with a man who is a profligate, a lecher, and my worst enemy!" he went on.

"I did not know him—I did not even speak to him!" I burst out.

"How can you expect me to believe that? Do you think I am a fool—and blind?" He picked up the fan from the dressing-table, held it under my nose and then threw it down. "I saw his look when you used this—and yours! This fan, which I had not been allowed to see—it wasn't the one you expected—of course, you'd keep his token out of the way until you could easily explain it—"

"It wasn't like that!" I cried. "I don't know how it got here—or how my own disappeared—"

"You don't know! It was *here!*" His voice was scornful; he went to the chest and pulled out the top drawer. "Disappeared!" His hand plunged in, and came out holding my best black fan. "This was only pushed to the back—behind the one you didn't want me to know about—"

He broke off and pulled something else out, something which he unfolded and held in front of me. It was the wrapping of the gray fan—and a crumpled sheet of writing paper.

"Permit me." His voice was heavy with sarcasm. With set face he read the note aloud, and now the implication was horrifying to me. *"Accept the gift; forgive the giver who only wishes to adore you.* I know Sánchez's writing. Forgive him for what?"

"For nothing," I whispered. "I have done nothing to deserve this."

Frantically I tried to collect my thoughts, to find a way of explaining it. But how could I expect him to believe what had happened in Buenos Aires, when the fan was now apparently in my possession? And if I had accepted a fan from Sánchez, was it credible that I would have spent three days on shipboard with him without exchanging a syllable? Even the words "I don't know how the fan got here"—that repetition stuck in my throat, for I could think of only one explanation, and to accuse Señora Ruíz of being hand in glove with Sánchez was impossible; she was a trusted servant, and it would look like the last desperate lie of a little coward. Even I could hardly believe it, much as I disliked her. So I sat there miserably silent, my throat

aching and my eyes stinging with tears I was determined not to shed.

"Is that all you can say?" His voice was icy.

"Yes. I can only tell you I have done nothing of
which I am ashamed."

"Then our standards must be very different. I must
ask you in future to come a little nearer to mine."
This his anger flashed out again. "God knows how
many people saw and heard you both! I have not
asked you for love, but I thought you would give me
loyalty!"

Holding the note between thumb and finger he held
it in a candle flame. When it was well alight he
dropped it in the grate. Then he picked up the fan,
held it shut in his lean brown hands and cracked it
across his knee, dropping the pieces with a small clatter in front of me on the dressing-table.

"Tomorrow that will be packed up and returned to
Sánchez. Should you require a fan I will see that you
have one."

He strode into his dressing-room and shut the door
behind him.

By the time he returned I was in bed. I did not pretend to be asleep, but he said nothing, and I had still
not found a credible way of explaining to him. He put
out the candles and got in beside me. At last I could
release my tears. I lay and wept silently in the dark
before falling at last into an exhausted sleep.

4

The great ox-wagons had creaked and rumbled away from the house soon after daybreak, and two hours later we were following, Miguel on horseback, myself and Tía Amalia in the carriage with two light mule-drawn wagons behind us. With us rode half the detachment of soldiers relieving the garrison post beyond Valdoro on the fringe of Indian country. The other half was escorting the wagon train, which our horse and carriage party would overtake during the day.

Since the evening of our reception Miguel had pushed his plans ahead with even greater urgency. On hearing that a relieving party was due to set out soon Miguel had decided to join it rather than wait for the next chance of an escort. Miguel, though his manner had been cold since the incident of the fan, was careful to reassure me that we were travelling with the army group for mutual convenience and help, not because there was any danger. Army arrangements were settled, so somehow everything had to be ready, and I fervently hoped I had not forgotten anything.

The journey to Valdoro would take ten days or more, travelling at the speed of the ox-wagons, and each night we must camp, for there were only two settlements on the way, neither of which had suitable accommodation for us. So much Miguel told me, and to me he was like a general considering his plan for an important campaign; thoughtful, critical, but above all forceful and confident.

I did not bother him with domestic details, they were my province, and he expected me to deal with them; so I was not surprised when Señora Ruíz referred to me in the matter of the Indian girl. She came up to me smiling that thin-lipped smile which I increasingly disliked.

"Doña Marta, can you tell me whether India is going to Valdoro or staying here? I should like your opinion as to the advisability—it is a long journey over rough roads, and she must be near her time. Of course she expects to go, and perhaps she should, to save—difficulty."

It was a decision which had been in my mind, and which, I admit, I had been avoiding. Now I thought of the journey, of the rocking, jolting bullock-carts and their effect on a girl in the last stages of pregnancy. To have her giving birth on the way would be a greater problem than insisting to her that she must stay behind.

"I think it would be madness for her to go, don't you?" I replied. "The journey might bring on the birth, and we wouldn't be equipped for that. It would be too dangerous. She must stay here until the baby is born, and come to Valdoro as soon as it is safe and convenient."

Señora Ruíz nodded agreement, and her face for once showed approval. "Yes, Doña Marta. I am sure you are right. I will tell her."

The decision made, I put it out of my mind. I had a great deal of stores and equipment to check and pack. A few hours later, having supervised some packing, I was returning to our rooms along the corridor from the kitchen quarters when India came out from the still room and stood before me. Normally her face was emotionless, but now I could not mistake the anger in her down-drawn mouth and staring eyes. The corridor was narrow enough for her in her condition to be effectively barring my way. I waited. She moved closer, and thrust her head forward.

"You say I stay here!" she almost spat at me.

I controlled my temper; she was an ignorant girl, and could not be expected to understand my reasons.

"For your own good, India, until the baby is born."

"I know what you do!" she went on, and I could hear hate in her voice, though I had given her no cause. "You try to keep me from Don Miguel—you, who are his wife—*and not his wife!* But I go with my lord—you will see!"

She aimed the words at me like a shower of poisoned arrows, then turned and left me. I stood there, feeling my heart thumping, trying to regain my composure. The Indian girl had utterly defied me; she was determined to disobey my instructions, but that was as nothing when I considered what she had said. She was jealous of me, that was suddenly plain, and had gloated over the fact which she had guessed and which I thought no one could possibly know. "You who are his wife—and not his wife—" she had said, and her meaning was unmistakable. *Madre de Dios,* was my virginity the subject of coarse gossip in the servants' hall? Or was it, as I could only hope and pray, that being pregnant she had some extra perception to guess my situation? I felt hot and cold, and sick at the thought. It was as if Miguel had rejected me, and this young Indian girl in the pride of her motherhood had thrown it in my face.

I hurried to my sitting room, wondering what to do. If I gave in to her I lost all authority; if I insisted she stayed, what then? But I did not have to do anything, for a little later Miguel appeared, his face dark with displeasure.

"Marta, I told you that India was my personal servant and must stay with me. Now I find you

have given instructions for her to remain here when
we leave. What possessed you to do that?"

Indignation made me bold. "She is pregnant!" I
burst out. "The child must be due soon. Do you want
her to have the baby by the roadside?"

"She will have the baby wherever she happens to
be, in her own way. These primitive people can usually
manage, and I imagine you and your aunt know
enough about childbirth to care for her. Can you not
understand that if she is left here she will follow me
on foot, alone, with nothing but what she can carry,
and the result will be infinitely worse?"

I digested this in silence. I was a fool not to have
thought of that.

"I am sorry. That hadn't occurred to me. I will tell
her I have reconsidered."

"There is no need. I have explained to her your reasons, and told her she may come if she takes care. I
have also told her that she must do her best to obey
you."

"Thank you," I said, and could not quite keep the
sarcasm out of my voice. "I do not enjoy being defied
by an Indian servant."

He looked at me sharply. "I have told you
that India is a special case. You must learn to cope
with her devotion to me without upsetting her."

"I will do my best," I answered, as coldly as he had
spoken, and the subject was dropped.

And so, when we set out, India went with us, riding
on a mule. I had expected her to travel in one of the
ox-wagons, but said nothing when I saw her, and on
considering the matter I decided she might well get
much less jolting on muleback that she would in the
great clumsy cart.

There was one new addition to our party, whom I
would have expected to travel in the carriage with us.
This was Father Marcos. I had heard he was young,
but I had expected a studious, dedicated, aesthetic
young man. Father Marcos was well built and vigorous, obviously of a practical turn of character, who

rode a particularly fine mule and looked as if only the humility of his cloth prevented him from taking to horse. So there we were, leaving Varena for our unknown *estancia*.

Miguel rode ahead with the officer of the relieving party; next came our carriage, Father Marcos beside it, followed by India, then the mule wagons and the soldiers. Whenever possible the soldiers rode beside the wagons to avoid the dusty wake, for the earth road was dry, the surface loose, and ochreous clouds rose at every wheelturn and hoofbeat. The first stretch of road outside Varena was reasonably level and we kept a good pace, driving through open country, the river on our right. My spirits began to rise. It felt like a delightful adventure to be bowling along with an escort of soldiers all with guns slung on their saddles and swords at their sides.

Everything, I thought, was very well organized. The journey had been divided into stages and we knew roughly where each night's camp should be. The carriage party would leave each day after the ox-wagons but would pass the train and arrive at the night camp ahead of it. The men of our party would select the camp site, draw water, start fires, and prepare a hot meal. This would be welcome, for although the weather was warm and cold food and wine would be all we would need during the daytime, with sunset the temperature dropped. Long after the carriage party was settled the ox-wagons would creak out of the dusk to join us.

How open and bare the country was away from the coast! If I turned back Varena would now be only a blob on the horizon. Varena, the compact little town, still showing signs of the way it was once stockaded against the hostile Indian tribes. But there were no marauding Indians now; those left after the fighting had all been absorbed as laborers and servants or had drifted back to live far inland. Yes, the warlike tribes had been put down a long time ago, all that was over, and now the Indians had a free choice of working for and with we Spaniards or living in their own way where we had not penetrated. The fort to be relieved, some days' journey beyond Valdoro, was no longer there to keep the Indians in subjection, but to see that the tribes lived at peace among themselves, and to keep Varena—and the Viceroy at Buenos Aires—in touch with Indian matters.

There were some signs of cultivation near the road, and here and there I glimpsed a few huts, but on the whole the countryside looked much more deserted than I had expected. But it was beautiful, richer and greener than my part of Spain, dotted with clumps of trees and divided in my view by the broad silver river.

At mid-day we stopped, ate bread, cheese and cold meat and drank some wine. Then the journey restarted. Tomorrow, I thought, I will ask if I can ride part of the way. It would be a change from driving, and I might have a chance to talk to Miguel. Surely he could not continue to remain so cold with me? I would have to ask tactfully, for he might not consider it correct for me to be the only woman riding with officers and men.

There were so many conventions I still had to learn. I consoled myself with the thought that there would be fewer rules at Valdoro—and, thank heaven, no Señora Ruíz to give me critical glances. I had not dared to ask whether she was coming, and it did not even occur to me that I should have decided the matter, but before we left she had told me that, although she had expected to do so, there was no one she trusted to leave in charge of the Varena house at present, and so she would join us later.

"I am sorry not to be able to help you settle in," she said. "I will see this house arranged for as soon as I can."

Her voice had been sympathetic, but her eyes had not looked at all regretful. She believes she is well out of it, I thought.

The day passed, Tía Amalia chatting with me when we felt inclined; for the rest I sat watching, making plans, dreaming. I tried to picture Valdoro, tried to imagine myself free of Señora Ruíz and truly mistress my house at last, surrounded by servants and workers who were part of an organization of which I was as yet completely ignorant. I must make a success of it to justify myself with Miguel. I must live down the bad impression he had of me. Not even Tía Amalia knew about the fan.

As the day wore on I became increasingly aware of a subtle change in Miguel. His cold withdrawn manner had faded. He was not only alert and interested as I would have expected, he had a quick and lively air. He was enjoying every moment, and from the way he talked to the lieutenant he knew exactly how our journey should be arranged, as if he had planned it from a fund of experience to the last detail.

There was a spell of excitement when we sighted the wagon train ahead, caught up with it and passed it to a chorus of shouts and cries from the soldiers of both parties; but the wagon drivers, who were Indians or *mestizos,* took the event calmly and considered a sign of recognition was enough. On we rattled, leaving the wagons behind, and once more the road was deserted. In the whole day we could not have seen more than half a dozen people on the road, and these were Indians on foot, apparently come from nowhere and going nowhere.

It was still light when we reached our first camp site and pitched by the river bank. A pannikin of water was brought for me to wash in, and as I did so I could smell meat roasting and coffee brewing. Yes, it was a delightful adventure, away from the formality and stiffness of town. After the meal I was able to stroll about, taking note of the way things were arranged. There was a general bustle when the wagons arrived and took their allotted places so that the camp was a compact and organized group. It was dark by the time the wagon personnel had eaten and the camp was tidied; people began to settle down for the night, for the wagon train would start off again at first light. The two large mulecarts had been loaded with flat chests of equipment and linen, on the top of which had been placed mattresses and blankets. In one of these Tía Amalia was to sleep, in the other myself and Miguel.

Tía Amalia bade me good night and climbed into her wagon, but I lingered, drawing my shawl about my shoulders and sniffing the cool air which smelt of trampled grass and burning wood. I had hardly passed a minute's conversation with Miguel all day, and still he was moving to and fro, talking to the men in uniform and his own servants. As I was climbing into the wagon he came over and bade me good night.

"I shall sleep outside tonight," he told me. "I prefer to be with the men on the first night of a journey; so I will not disturb you."

He spent the night rolled in a poncho, his head on his saddle—a curious and un-hidalgo-like proceeding, I thought—and then remembered Doña Sara telling me that Miguel had fought with the army on the frontier with Portuguese-held land. I did not know why, but it seemed he was used to campaigning; perhaps he found the contrasting way of living piquant now and then? What other reason could there be for him to sleep that night in the open on the hard ground?

The officer in charge of the relieving party was young, and treated me with a deference which would have been amusing if I had not reminded myself that Miguel's social position was responsible for most of it. The army detachment consisted of about thirty men, equally divided between the two trains; two corporals, one with each group; a case-hardened sergeant in charge of the ox-wagon escort, and the lieutenant who rode with Miguel. As we sat over our mid-day meal the following day Lieutenant García did his best to entertain me and I was grateful. Was the journey too hard for me? he asked. Too dull?

"Oh, no, Lieutenant, I am enjoying every minute!" I answered. "I suppose you know the country well?"

"It's not my first spell at the fort, though I wouldn't say I know the land as well as I would like. That takes years. It's a vast territory, and though the pampa looks the same for mile upon mile it's a deceptive simplicity."

"What does that mean?"

"It will sound fanciful to you, but the pampa can change its character suddenly with weather, wind or season; it has moods, and you don't know it until you've seen them all. Then there are the people. The pampa looks deserted, but that's deceptive too. People do live there. They live with the wild cattle and horses, and how they live is their affair, as long as it doesn't touch us. They'll never own a roof, and they don't want one; anything they can't carry on their saddles is value-less, an encumbrance. Such people are mostly *mestizos*. The Indians beyond the forts still live in their tribes, making their own little huts and keeping themselves apart. Sometimes they cause trouble, but usually they avoid us, unless it suits them to come and trade. But they have little that we want, and if they won't work for us they must go their own way."

"What did you mean when you said the *mestizos'* life was their own affair as long as it didn't touch us?"

He laughed. "Simply that they must behave them-selves! Out here we are the law, and when people like El Alacrán start making trouble they must take the consequences."

El Alacrán—the Scorpion—I had heard mention of him before.

"Who is El Alacrán?"

"Why, Doña Marta, hasn't your husband told you? I thought the man had paid some attention to Valdoro?"

In surprise I glanced across at Miguel, to see he was staring at the lieutenant with a slight frown.

"El Alacrán is a small-time bandit," he went on. "It amuses him to hold up unprotected travellers and re-lieve them of their money."

"And—at Valdoro?"

"Living as he does I suppose he is jealous of people who build houses. He has tried to cause delay in ways too trivial to mention."

"But what did he do?"

"Oh, he tried to scare superstitious workmen, he started a small fire—that sort of thing. You can put it out of your mind. He won't bother us any more. He would not attack a party as large and well-protected as this one, besides which we expect him to be well away beyond Valdoro, perhaps in Indian country."

The lieutenant looked as if he might have said more, but Miguel took him to inspect the wagons.

Each day my respect for Miguel was increasing. He was no idle nobleman who expected everything done for him, whose servants bore the burden of arranging for his comfort. More and more I saw that Miguel was an organizing and a driving force, and that even the lieutenant deferred to him as if he were his superior officer. That was most unorthodox, and I could only put it down to the close friendship between Miguel and the colonel, Don Gaspar. Miguel rode as long and slept as hard as any of the men; he ate the same food —though as far as that was concerned we all had the same provisions; the only extra delicacy furnished for myself and Tía Amalia was a plentiful amount of goat's milk supplied by a lugubrious looking animal which travelled in one of the ox-wagons and grazed complacently at every stop. How fortunate she was so docile, I thought, and had visions of making goat's milk cheese at Valdoro. . . . Miguel spent the second night under the stars.

By the third day we were well into the country, and about mid-day we reached a small settlement of adobe huts—half a dozen or so clustered by the roadside, with a cultivated patch of ground and a few tethered animals. Some half-naked children came out to stare as we passed, and the last I saw of them as I looked back was their immobile little figures still turned in our direction, watching our disappearing cavalcade. That night, and the next, I slept alone.

Each day saw a slight change in the countryside. The road we travelled was most of the time a gentle, almost imperceptible gradient, and with the gradual rise the country lost a little of its flatness, the trees, never plentiful, became more sparse, the river, a constant factor, still had wooded banks but the bed deepened so that the road ran higher above it. On the fifth day Miguel seemed in no hurry to overtake the wagon train, letting it keep its place ahead at mid-day, and stopping for a meal a little earlier than usual. Then he seemed to have second thoughts, for before I had finished eating he got up, saying, "I shall ride ahead in a little while with a few men, but I shall be back with you before long."

I had no chance to ask anything. He walked away, and was out of my sight behind one of the mule carts, rounding up the men he wanted, I supposed, to catch up the wagon train. He had his own reasons and I could not expect to be told everything. The lieutenant, too, excused himself from us and followed Miguel; either he knew of the change in the system or wanted to find out.

I finished my meal and got back into the carriage with Tía Amalia, regretting I had still not made the opportunity to ask whether I might sometime ride a little way with Miguel. I must find a chance to ask tonight, then if he agreed I could put on my riding habit when I got up tomorrow and ride with him before the sun grew hot.

There was a thudding of hooves in the dust and four horsemen swept past. Miguel, intent on pushing ahead, did not slacken speed or speak as he passed the carriage window. His wide, flat-brimmed sombrero was pulled well down on his head and his gloved hand obscured his face as he waved, so I could not see if he was smiling or grave. I looked back for the lieutenant whom I expected to ride in front of the carriage, but could not see him. He must be somewhere behind with the corporal, for he was not with Miguel; he and Miguel were much of a height, and I could see that the other three riders were all shorter than my husband. Then the command was shouted from the rear, the drivers slapped the reins and with a chorus of shouts the carriage and mule wagons moved out.

For the first time as I looked ahead the land ceased to be an even rolling green; there were rocks, huge and reddish-brown, thrusting themselves through it, towering skywards in the heat haze. They were still a long way ahead; the wagon train, like a tribe of beetles dragging their spoils, was almost level with them. Each time I thrust my head from the window I saw wagon train and rocks and the four horsemen some way behind; then the wagons disappeared round a huge outcrop while Miguel's group was halfway between them and us. Now the road was rising a little more steeply and the river bank was falling away; we were perched high up above the water which must be flowing deeper through its narrower bed. This was a pleasant change of scenery.

Miguel's group was swallowed up by the rocks; then some minutes later our carriage reached them. They were very high, and it was impossible to judge how extensive they were due to the way the road curved about them. As the clatter of the carriage wheels echoed back from the rocky walls I wondered whether by now both the wagons and Miguel would be in open country again. At close quarters the rocks were not very interesting; I turned round in my corner and gazed through the far window at the river. Tía Amalia was nodding; I too began to feel drowsy.

The attack when it came was so sudden, so unexpected, that at first I did not realize what was happening. I was only aware of the carriage jolting and swerving, of the horses snorting, of a creaking of shafts and a rattle of harness. Clutching at the window tassel to regain my balance I saw that a man was holding the horses' heads, pulling them sideways and thus bringing the carriage to a rattling halt. I could not think why the driver was allowing it—until I saw, above what had been a line of bare rocks, a series of dark blobs which resolved themselves into heads, and beside each head the long barrel of a gun.

Tía Amalia, jolted awake, opened her eyes and said, "What's happening? Why are we stopping?"

"I think, Tía Amalia, we have run into bandits," I told her, with a calmness belied by my thudding heart.

"Throw down your weapons, and don't try to be clever."

I could not see who gave the order, but I could hear it being obeyed. A fat lot of good these soldiers are, I thought; the first moment they're needed they let us walk straight into an ambush, and throw their guns down like a parcel of frightened pedlars. And where was the lieutenant? There was no sign of him.

Now a man strolled out of the rocks and up to the carriage door. I looked at him and found him unpleasing. He was short, stockily built, very swarthy, with a broad face and small deepset eyes. His lank, black hair hung about his shoulders; his shirt and baggy trousers were an indeterminate color due to the grime and sweat on them. The broad smile which he gave me showed a set of stained and irregular teeth and was certainly not as charming as he thought it, while the hand which he raised to his sombrero was engrained with dirt and furnished with a bunch of broken black-rimmed nails. The other hand held a long-barrelled pistol which was levelled at the carriage window, and the most striking thing about this repellent specimen of Riquezan manhood was the amount and variety of weapons he carried, his torso being festooned with pistols, ammunition slings and pouches, and an assortment of sheath-knives of various sizes.

"*Buenas tardes, señoras!* Allow me to introduce myself. I am El Alacrán, and delighted to meet you."

"I cannot say the same. Kindly let my carriage and wagons pass."

I choked down my fear, told myself I would show nothing but contempt to this horrible man, and wondered how long it would be before Miguel turned

back to join us. I could not see Father Marcos, but I
heard his voice, strong and firm.

"Have the decency to let the ladies pass, and do
your business with us!"

El Alacrán roared with laughter. Unfortunately his
amusement did not prevent him from keeping his pistol pointed steadily in our direction, and from my
place at the window, with the carriage slewed across
the road, I could lean out and look down the escorting line to see what help might be forthcoming. There
was nothing to give me hope.

Father Marcos sat astride his mule, blazing with
rage, but the man holding our horses was covering
him with a pistol. The soldiers were all disarmed, and
some were dismounting; of the accompanying *mestizos*
all save one had their hands in the air, and that one,
in the driver's seat of the nearest mule wagon, was
lolling back and singing slurringly to himself. He was
not mad, as I thought for the first second, but rolling
drunk. When prodded with a gunbarrel he giggled,
collapsed against the back of his seat, pulled his poncho
about him, pushed his sombrero even farther over
his eyes so that all which could be seen was a foolish
yet seraphic smile, and prepared to go to sleep.

"Quiet, priest! In good time, Doña Marta," the
bandit replied, still chuckling. "I have not come simply to make your acquaintance. We have business to
transact, you and I. Money business."

"How dare you stop us, you blackguard!" Tía
Amalia burst out.

"Shut up, old one! I'm talking to the lady! Now,
señora, what about it?"

"I don't understand you. Are you offering me
money—compensation, perhaps, for this inconvenience? Or are you begging from me?"

I wanted to hold him talking; the longer he stood
there the greater the chance of Miguel coming back.

This time El Alacrán did not laugh. "Don't put on
airs with me, señora. You can't afford to. Just give
me the money before I lose my temper."

"What money?"

"Don Miguel's money, of course!"

"It is not my husband's habit to let his wife carry his cash. You must ask him for it."

"You're a saucy one! Don't waste my time! I want the money he's taking to Valdoro—he'll have a lot of wages to pay there. Then there's the matter of some diamond trinkets. I imagine it's all stowed in your carriage. You can give it to me now, or watch my men take the carriage apart, and your fancy wagons, until we find it."

It had not occurred to me that Miguel might be carrying wages. As for the diamonds, they had been returned to Miguel's safe keeping. I had no idea where they were.

"You surely don't think my husband would risk my safety by letting me travel with anything of value?"

This provoked another roar of laughter. "A fat lot of trouble he's taken over you! He rides off and leaves you with a handful of cloth-headed soldiers and a few drunken peons as escort, while he has a gay little gallop to the wagons! And that in the one place for miles around where you could be ambushed! He's too cocky by half, that husband of yours! He thought I was the other side of Valdoro, that I wouldn't show my nose around here! He won't be so proud of himself when he finds I've got his money—*and* his wife, perhaps—"

He looked at me with a slow, assessing grin. My throat tightened and I felt sick.

"I don't advise you to lay a finger on me," I told him firmly. "You might get away with taking his money, but if you touch either of us, Don Miguel and the whole garrison will make you pay very dearly for it."

"I don't think so. You see, I have a splendid plan. If the money isn't here I shall take *you*. I'll leave the old one to give your husband a message. I won't touch you—well, not very much—provided he ransoms you for a good price and the army gives me safe conduct to

Portuguese territory. If he won't pay up quickly, you'll be rid of a mean husband and I shall have a pretty woman to amuse me. Now let's stop wasting time. Where is the money?"

For a moment I was too sick to answer; but Tía Amalia, who had been listening tight-lipped and tense, could stay silent no longer.

"There isn't any money, you wretch—or if there is, neither of us has seen any! There's nothing in this coach."

In the brief silence which followed, the drunken waggoner could be heard gently snoring and whistling. Below the level of my fear I was furious with him— where could he have got so much liquor?—dead drunk while I was left to cope with this only too literally stinking bandit. . . .

"So you say! Step out and we'll search. And first of all, I'll see whether you're wearing those diamonds under your dress. . . ."

He leered at me as he spoke. This horrible suggestion made me even sicker but more determined than ever to delay, and I sat back stubbornly. Tía Amalia did likewise.

"Oh, so you want my assistance! It'll be a pleasure!"

I could not bear his hands on me. I would fight him, in or out of the carriage. He put his pistol in its holster, and wrenched the door open, when I heard a faint click and a voice, quiet, and calm, and heavy with authority.

"Don't touch her, or move, unless you want a bellyful of lead."

It was Miguel's voice, but it came from the waggoner, who now looked most alert as he perched on his seat, the blued muzzle of a pistol gleaming beneath the edge of his poncho.

"Yes, El Alacrán, it is I, Miguel Moural. Tell your men to throw down their guns." He waited, then smiled coldly. "Come, do you really want a bullet in your guts?"

El Alacrán's hands came slowly away from the

carriage door as he turned cautiously around. His face, at first incredulous, then wary, was suddenly swept by fury as he took in just how completely he had been tricked. With his hands at shoulder height he stood in baffled silence, head swivelling as he looked from me to Miguel, and back, and back again.

"My trigger finger is getting tired of waiting."

El Alacrán swallowed. "Men, throw down your arms," he ordered. "He's got me at gunpoint—he's ready to shoot—"

Along the ridge of rocks men rose to their feet one by one and sent their guns clattering down. The soldiers were quick to retrieve them, and to repossess themselves of their own weapons. I heard the corporal detailing men to round up the bandits and bring them down, to secure their own horses and to find where the bandits' mounts were hidden. And all the time Miguel sat up on the wagon, dirty-faced behind the betasselled mules, watching the proceedings, and I felt waves of relief and amazement succeeding each other. Now I understood. It was the lieutenant wearing Miguel's clothes who had ridden ahead, to let El Alacrán think the carriage and my valuables were unescorted, to temp him out into the open. Meanwhile Miguel, dressed as a peon, had taken over the wagon—and everyone, including myself, had seen what they expected to see.

When the bandits were secured Miguel handed the wagon over to the real driver and ordered his men to mount. By this time the lieutenant had returned with some men, and they escorted the bandits out ahead of us. As he passed the carriage window Miguel looked in, smiled reassuringly and said, "We will talk later."

That was all.

If I had been dying of shock it would be no different, I thought. So being his wife also entailed being used as bait for bandits. It was plainly my husband's scheme—the young officer would never have dreamed of it, or if he had, he would not have dared to suggest it. It was typical of Miguel to use me for his

own ends. I had been useful, and that was that. I did
not even merit a word of thanks or apology. And
what was going to happen to the bandits? I wondered.
Would they go on with the wagon train or be sent back
to Varena?

We were out of the rocky area, and we made camp
where the river bank was a fairly gentle slope. I felt
hot and sticky, and very tired—a reaction from being
scared, probably—and I thought I would cool myself
with a little more water than a pannikin would hold.
So I took a towel and clambered down the bank. There
were several clumps of bushes, and no one drawing
water, so I quickly undid the high collar of my dress
and took off my shoes and stockings. I washed my face
and hands, then sat on the bank and dabbled my feet in
the cold clear ripples, leaned back and ran damp fingers
into the roots of my hair. For a few minutes I revelled
in the coolness. Then a sound made me turn, and I saw
Miguel, himself again, coming down the bank.

I scrambled to my feet, and standing on the grass
I shook my skirt about my wet ankles and started to
button up my collar.

"Stay as you are. We are not in Varena now."

That was not a dignified way to treat me, I thought,
and went on fumbling with the buttons.

"Let's call a truce, Marta, and try to understand
each other."

Now he was beside me, and as always I found his
nearness disturbing. I told myself it was simply because
I was not used to men, and I remembered my anger.

"I understand one thing," I retorted. "That is, you
are quite happy to use your wife as bait. I made a fine
piece of cheese in your mousetrap."

"I was there all the time. I would never have let
him touch you."

I forgot my nervous respect of him and looked at
him squarely. "It was arrogant of you to assume you
could prevent it. Anything could have happened if
your plan had gone only slightly astray."

"But it did not!" he said, and caught one of my hands in his. "And you were magnificent!"

Still holding my collar in one hand I retorted, "I would have been more magnificent if I had known I was part of your trap."

"I couldn't risk telling you. And I had to catch El Alacrán and break up his band, for Valdoro's sake. *Dios,* woman, leave your collar—you have a beautiful neck, and I am your husband."

He was still holding my hand, and a strange shiver seemed to run from his fingers into my body.

"I thought you had forgotten," I said tartly.

"Indeed?" he replied, and smiled.

I blushed—I could feel it. He was misinterpreting me.

"I meant . . . I was not consulted . . . I am treated like a servant, expected to get on with my work—no more. . . ."

I was stammering, uncertain of myself or of what I wanted to say.

"That is not what I wish you to be, and if you have felt that, I apologize." He took me by the shoulders and held me near to him, so that my hands were resting on his chest, and his head bent down to mine. "I apologize as a husband should."

His head came lower, his face was over mine, and his mouth pressed down upon my lips in our first true kiss. I was so surprised that I could make no resistance. Indeed it seemed to flood me with new sensations and send my thoughts spinning in confusion. My anger evaporated. It was all I could do to stand, I was trembling so.

"*Ay,* Marta!" he whispered against my lips. "We must sink our differences. This is too good to lose."

I tried to still my pounding heart.

"I think there are no real differences between us, Miguel," I managed to say at last, as calmly as I could.

"Only the essential ones between man and woman, for which God be praised," he said, with mock seriousness.

In my prudishness I was shocked, and turned away, finished fastening my collar and went to pick up my stockings. I hesitated, conscious that he was watching me.

"Your feet and ankles are as beautiful as your neck, and I've no objection to seeing them," he went on.

I did not know how to take him, how to answer such a remark, so I spoke the truth.

"You are a different man since we left Varena."

"Not a different man—sit down and dry your feet—the same one, but free of town conventions. We must leave them behind; it's time we got to know each other."

I did as he bade me, keeping my head down as I plied the towel so that he could not see my face. How could that one kiss turn my world upside down? For this was still the man I resented for his *hidalgo* arrogance, and feared for his flashes of cold anger. What had happened to me, that a few minutes' conversation and one tender embrace was enough to make me fall in love with him?

After our meal I saw the bandits being taken to one side of the camp.

"What will happen to them?" I asked.

"There is going to be a court-martial," Miguel answered. "I must go."

Tía Amalia and I kept well away—it was not our idea of entertainment—and I went to enquire how India was feeling. Daily I kept an eye on her, and made sure she was well. I would have done so out of humanity, but in addition I felt responsible for her. It was a thankless task, for she seemed to resent any interest. This evening was no exception.

In answer to my enquiry she said, "I am well," and staring at me with eyes like large black berries she added: "And so is the child. He moves strongly."

It seemed to give her satisfaction to tell me this, and I smiled and said, "I am glad."

To my amazement she looked at me with open hostility, and flung two words at me, "You lie!"

I controlled my surprise and anger. "I am a truthful person, India. But if I were not, it would still be impertinent of you to tell me so."

"You—Don Miguel's wife!" she said, and her voice held scorn as well as hate. "I shall have a son—you will see!"

"For your sake I hope you do." I countered; then briefly reminded her that there was goat's milk for her whenever she wanted it, and left her.

I hated such exchanges with the girl. It was a difficult relationship, for it seemed she almost considered Miguel her private property and me an interloper. He had done a lot for her, I knew. He could have kept her about him doing menial jobs for his comfort, but he had had the girl taught sewing and other accomplishments, including civilized behavior, by the nuns in Varena. She was intelligent and had been a good pupil, and that, I guessed, had fed the girl's natural conceit. At present she was almost insupportable to me; I could only hope the arrival of her baby would give her an absorbing interest and sweeten her temper. Knowing the Indians' views I hoped for her sake that it would be the male child she seemed so sure of—a girl would certainly be unwanted and a blow to her pride.

I walked about for a little while and then went to my sleeping wagon. I was ready for bed, tired by the excitement of the day. The tail board was up and the back canvas laced. I climbed in at the front and lowered myself over the seat, lacing up the front canvas part of the way.

Once inside the wagon it was like a little room—or one huge bed, for the mattresses filled it completely over the luggage below. It was dark outside, and the rising moon gave no light. I needed none; I undressed and put my clothes aside, slipped into the shift which lay ready, and unpinned my hair. I then unlaced the top part of the rear canvas so that a current of air would blow through, and lay down, pulling the blankets

over me. Although physically comfortable, I found my
head full of stray thoughts, and was mentally unset-
tled, more so than I had been since I decided on marriage. Why had I not realized that I had been half in
love with Miguel from the first? That was why I had
so resented his impersonal request for my hand, *Your
second daughter, then?* and his businesslike attitude
throughout. But now I knew. . . . If I could learn to be
a loving wife, perhaps he would love me? Then I remembered Doña Sara's words, and they were a hard
blow to my rising spirits. Miguel had married me for
Valdoro; I must help him in his ambitions, not distract
him with lovesickness. I recalled how he had said this
very afternoon, "This is too good to lose," and my
hopes rose again.

The mattresses rocked beneath me—someone was
climbing on to the wagon. Before I had time for more
than surprise I heard the words, "Marta, it is Miguel,"
and heard him opening the front canvas wider. Turning my head I saw him silhouetted against the night
sky as he swung himself inside, then it was dark as he
drew the canvas together.

"You were not asleep?" he asked.

"No, Miguel," I replied.

"Good. I had hoped you would be awake."

I could hear the sound of his movements as he undressed.

"Am I quite forgiven for not warning you about this
afternoon?" he went on.

"Yes," I said with a little laugh. "There's no point in
harboring annoyance when it's all over and done."

I felt him lift the blanket and lie down beside me.
His voice was close as he murmured, "That's how a
woman should be—fiery but forgiving. I think we can
agree, you and I."

A little wind lifted the canvas and a shaft of moon-
light stole through, revealing Miguel's face above me.
His dark eyes gleamed; I lay as if hypnotized gazing
at them, then his hand came up and stroked my hair. I

did not move; his fingers glided down my cheek and around my chin.

Excitement stirred within me. His face came closer, and his lips began to drop gentle kisses on my cheeks. His hand rested on my bare shoulder, his mouth sought mine, and his kiss, no longer gentle, made my heart throb chokingly in my throat.

"Put your arms about me, *querida*," he said softly.

To obey seemed the most natural thing, and as my hands slid around I could feel the muscles of his back moving under the warm smooth skin. He leaned over me. I thought: He has never called me "dear" before. . . . His hand moved caressingly, his mouth pressed my shoulder, following his touch, and inside me a sweet tumult surged. I forgot everything else, all my preconceived notions of love-making, my fears of inadequacy, my doubts of its delights. I was only aware of Miguel and of the way my whole being was yearning to him.

"There—you are not shy of me in the dark."

It was true. Perhaps the shared danger of the day had made me more at ease with him; whatever it was, now we were invisible to each other, wrapped in the gloom, my self-consciousness had slipped away. His firm, warm fingers eased the shift from my shoulders and I did not protest, and though his caresses and his kisses became intimate and searching beyond anything I had imagined, I did not want to draw away. Even surprise was drowned in wonder. His mouth returned to mine, parted my lips with sensuous kisses which I knew were passionately desiring, which told me this was the night he would possess me. This was the hour —the moment. Now it had come there was no distress, just a suffusion of rapture as I yielded utterly to him. I was no more a maiden, but a wife, and gloried in it.

I had not realized I had slept; languorous and loving I must have dozed without awareness into a hazy dream; but suddenly I was wide awake at the sound of a sharp, slightly muffled crack. There was enough light inside the wagon for me to see Miguel asleep beside me, the blanket pushed down from his bare chest. Then he opened his eyes.

"What was that?" I asked.

"It is dawn," he said, irrelevantly.

"Yes, but what was that noise? There it is again."

"Dawn. The firing party," he said.

"The firing party?"

"The court-martial condemned El Alacrán and three of his men to death."

Another crack.

"You mean they are being executed?"

"Yes."

"How horrible!"

My happiness had soaked away like water on dry earth. I could only think of the terror of lives ended in bullets and blood.

"So were their crimes." Miguel was completely calm, his voice held no emotion. "They were all murderers. El Alacrán had killed at least a dozen people, and not in fair fight. Some were women. I'll spare you the details, but death is rather less than he deserves." Another report. "That will be the last. They knew what to expect."

"But to shoot them here—out of hand—" I cried.

"What would you have? Their crimes were known. The result would have been the same for them if they had been sent to Varena. This is better than weeks of prison, with a hangman's noose at the end of it."

"You are so calm! And that was the man who—"

I had a vision of El Alacrán outside the carriage, about to lay his hands on me, and shuddered.

"You were always safe, Marta. I did it to secure Valdoro, but I would not have let you come to harm, I swear it."

"I want to believe you," I said, and lay looking up at him, hoping he would convince me with a kiss.

"I had considered everything," he answered, and reached for his clothes. There were no kisses, and no more words. He dressed quickly and left me huddled under the blankets in the wagon, trying to recapture last night's magic but feeling only a depression of spirit and some slight aches in a languid body.

But, I told myself bitterly, it is all for Valdoro. I am put in a trap—for Valdoro. El Alacrán and his men are shot—for Valdoro. And I have been seduced by my own husband—not for love, but—for Valdoro.

5

At the first sight of Valdoro my heart sank. We had
been travelling for five more days, past the little settlement at Puenterojo where the river divides and
where we took the easterly fork which is still the Rio
Oro. The north-westerly branch is its tributary, the
Rio Rojo, which runs past a settlement or two and the
mines at Platinas. Always ahead of us we could see
the river, flowing towards us in its wide and rocky
channel; on the other bank the ground rose a little
and in the far distance were mountains. On our side
of the river the country was flat and grassy, the bushes
and trees became fewer and fewer. We were on the
fringes of the pampa.

Then, on the fifth day after the ambush, I saw
buildings. They were still far away, and as I looked I
picked out a large shape with a collection of small ones
around it. As we drew nearer I saw it was not newly
built; it was roofless and seemed to be almost a ruin,
and the other shapes were adobe huts radiating from
it. Then I saw beyond this another gray blob, paler and
clean-cut—that must be Valdoro. I remembered then

that Miguel had told me of a ruined church and settlement which had been abandoned at the expulsion of
the Jesuits. The Indians had drifted away from the
settlement and it had been totally neglected, but he
intended to restore it so that it would be the Moural
chapel and an "open" church for our Indian workers.
As the carriage rattled on I saw it clearly, an old stone
church where a bell still hung in a roofless arch, and
I looked beyond it to the slightly higher ground. Yes,
that was Valdoro, the gray blob which was becoming
the rectangular shape of a house.

I watched as we drew nearer, and with each turn of
the wheels my excited anticipation flagged and a depression settled on me. I had called it a house, but
to me it looked more like a fortress—or a prison. The
huge flat façade was broken only by a series of windows and one enormous doorway, and topped by a
roof of pink tiles—no ornamentation, nothing to break
the austerity.

The house had two stories. The windows on the
ground floor were tall, narrow and high-set, not much
better than slits, only the first floor windows approached reasonable size. How could I have been so
unprepared for the look of it? I had seen the plans
but I had paid little attention to the elevation. I had
been concerned with the inside, with the lay-out of
rooms and how they would be furnished. Miguel had
told me to buy curtain material by the bale, and make
curtains as we needed them, and I began to understand why. I could see one of the wings which ran at
right angles to the main block, and the end was roofless, the walls only one story high. What sort of a place
was I coming to?

We were now quite near Valdoro, and Father Marcos turned his mule towards the church. I resisted the
temptation to join him in inspecting it and delay my
discovery of Valdoro. So the carriage swayed on for
another mile, and Miguel spurred his horse as if impatient to be there. The place had looked deserted, but
as Miguel drew near it, a few figures appeared and the

great door swung open. It was in two halves, and the
opening was a good fifteen feet wide, large enough to
admit the biggest of our bullock wagons. It was enor-
mously thick, banded with metal and studded with
nails, like a castle doorway. Always the words "castle
—fortress—prison" recurred in my mind. The house
looked dead because the windows were closed inside
the wooden shutters; we drove through the arch of the
doorway and stopped in a dark tunnel; beyond was the
sunlight of the courtyard.

Miguel appeared at the carriage door, holding out
his hand to me. As I stepped down I saw Baltasar Ruíz
standing there. He greeted us with respectful formality,
and Miguel responded adding, "I have brought you a
letter from your wife. While you are reading it I will
show Doña Marta the house. Then you can give me
your report."

Ruíz bowed and pushed open a door in the left-
hand wall of the tunnel-like entrance. Miguel led me
inside.

"Welcome to Valdoro," he said.

It was as well he did, for me there was nothing wel-
coming about it. To me it looked in a hideous state of
unpreparedness. The plaster was in places not dry
upon the stone walls; the floor was stone-flagged (with
the paving stones intended for the courtyard, I remembered), and above us to our left were the high shuttered windows. Outside they were twelve feet from the
ground, inside somewhat less, with stone steps leading
up to the sills which widened from back to front, the
windows being set in a V in the thickness of the walls.
Thankfully I saw that on the opposite wall large low
windows gave on to the courtyard, and of these the
shutters were open, allowing plenty of light and air into
the room.

The room occupied the whole length of the left side
of the façade from the gateway and seemed enormous.
The impression was due at least in part to the fact
that one's eyes travelled up and up, past where the
ceiling should have been, to see the windows serving

the second story and beyond them the beams of the great roof. A huge barn—an unfinished church—a castle—any of those; but a house, a home . . .?

"This is the main hall," Miguel was saying. "It is a pity the building isn't farther advanced, but we shall manage. The room on the other side of the hall will be a dining-room—the kitchen is in the wing on that side. You couldn't see it as we drove up, but that wing has both floors and its roof."

A door at the far end led to the other wing. We went inside. This room actually had a ceiling.

"We had better take this for our bedroom at present; your aunt can have the next one. The upper rooms and the end of this wing are not finished, but these are quite habitable."

He turned to me, his eyes bright and questioning. "What do you think of it? I'm sorry, *querida*, the delays have held things back, but now we are here we can get the men moving, and it won't take long to settle down. This is only the beginning. It will be the finest *estancia* in Riqueza, I promise you."

I racked my brains for a reply, for I felt bereft of speech.

"It's rather overwhelming like this," I said lamely. "You must give me a little while to sort things out."

He took me literally.

"You haven't long," he said. "You must decide what you want unloaded from the mule wagons, so that they can be moved out of the way before the bullock carts arrive. Don't unpack more than you need at present."

"No, I won't," I said. There isn't anywhere to unpack anything, I thought desperately; then forced myself to a calm consideration of things.

So I reconnoitered the rest of the finished rooms, had the floors swept and the necessary boxes brought in. I had fires lit, and a meal started in the kitchen before we had a table to eat from. There was a well in the courtyard and sacks of charcoal and some wood in a section of the long adobe building which at present made the south side of the square. In these hutments the house servants would live for the time being; the workmen, I discovered later, were sleeping in and around the old settlement by the church.

I was thankful that a few of our *mestizo* house servants had come with us temporarily from Varena, for they understood Spanish and could take my instructions. That evening the task ahead of me, to turn Valdoro into a comfortable well-run home, seemed formidable indeed. Nor did I relish the presence of Baltasar Ruíz. His manner was so reserved as to verge on the intimidating, and his eyes were often coldly critical in spite of his respectful manner.

I prepared for our first meal at Valdoro. There would be five of us regularly at table, for Father Marcos and Ruíz would eat with us. I could only find a trestle table, but I had it spread with a linen cloth, and decorated with lighted silver candlesticks. The meal was about to be served; four of us were ready to take our places; then Ruíz entered. He spoke to Miguel, but loud enough for us all to hear.

"I think you would wish to know, Don Miguel, that the Indian girl is in labor."

This, I felt, was my concern.

"I will go to her," I said at once. "Please show me where she is."

"I will come too," said Tía Amalia.

Miguel nodded and we left the room.

I was grateful for Tía Amalia's support, for I had only been present at one birth, helping my mother with one of our servants, and felt too ignorant to cope by myself. My aunt, I knew, had considerable experience as a midwife.

India was established in a small room near the kitchen. She was walking up and down the room, making small crooning noises to herself as we came through the door. At the sight of us her manner changed, her face contorted, her eyes blazed, and she poured out a flood of Indian phrases; although I could not understand a word it was quite plain she did not want us there. I started to reason with her in Spanish, but she refused to understand or to answer me, and each moment became more excited and angry. We were doing no good by staying.

"We had better tell Miguel," I said to Tía Amalia. "He's the only person who can reason with her."

Already I have to admit defeat, I thought.

When we returned to the hall Miguel seemed unsurprised by India's reaction. "Start your meal," he said to us. "I will see if I can persuade her to accept your help."

Although I was very hungry, I found myself—quite unfairly—annoyed with India for coming between Miguel and myself on what should have been our first meal together at Valdoro. However it was not long before he returned.

"There is nothing wrong," he said. "An Indian woman is with her, and will let you know when she needs help. It seems India has taken an unreasoning dislike to you, Marta, and in the circumstances it would be as well to pander to her. She will excite herself again if she sees you, so I suggest you do not go to her. But she has agreed to let Doña Amalia be present later on." He turned to my aunt. "I should be most grateful if you would supervise the birth and see that she has proper care. I am not familiar with the Indians' ideas of midwifery, but . . ."

"Of course, Don Miguel. Shall I go now?"

"No, no. We will be told when you are needed."

Was it cowardly of me to be relieved that I was not going to have the task of delivering India's child? I had the feeling that if anything went wrong I would be blamed. As it was, it was not a difficult birth. Late that night Tía Amalia came and told us that India had the boy baby she had been so sure she was carrying.

"The first birth at Valdoro," said Father Marcos. "The child must be baptized as soon as possible—a good beginning to God's mission here."

I did not see the baby until the baptism, and it seemed to me that India avoided me, although she refused to rest in bed. I had no time to bother with her fanciful dislike of me, but I was mildly surprised that she acquiesced in Father Marcos's arrangements. It would be some time before the church could be rebuilt and reconsecrated, but the child was named after its patron saint, and baptized Juan Bautista in Valdoro's courtyard with all the house servants and many of the workers crowding in as spectators. Father Marcos no doubt saw it as an opportunity to remind backsliders among the Indians of the obligations and the benefits of Christianity. Some of the formalities were dispensed with, and one godparent would be enough, he had said. But who? It must be a good responsible Christian.

Father Marcos had his own ideas. He said to Miguel, "Don Miguel, forgive me for this request. You are the *patrón* of all these people, and this is our first baptism. Would you consent to stand as godfather?"

After a moment's hesitation Miguel had agreed. That will please India, I thought sourly, and increase her notions of her own importance. *Dios,* am I being resentful of an Indian servant? I asked myself. That would be ridiculous. At home it was not unusual for a *patrón* to be godfather; the girl's race should make no difference.

The baby was a lovely boy; quite small, but as healthy and vigorous as one could wish. On first sight the pale golden color of his skin surprised me: I had expected him to be as dark as India, but on reflection I thought it possible that Indian babies were paler at birth than they later became—and besides, it was equally possible that the child's father was a *mestizo.* I reminded myself to ask Miguel whether the father knew about the baby's birth.

At last I was able to ride a horse again. I had got some order into the household arrangements, and could make few improvements until more rooms in the house were fit to live in. Since Miguel divided his time between supervising work on the house and riding on the pampa I asked whether I could sometimes ride with him.

"Of course," he said with a quick smile. "I shall be glad of your company, and I want you to love the pampa as I do."

Quite early in the morning, while it was still cool, he ordered our horses to be saddled. The day was sunny with a light breeze; it would be perfect for riding. As I joined him in the courtyard he gave me an approving look; the family's sacrifices to equip me with good riding cloths had been justified, much as I wished they had not been necessary. Everything fitted beautifully, from the crown of my flat-brimmed Cordovan hat to the sleek soft riding boots. A *mestizo* groom helped me to mount and I settled my wide skirt comfortably about me. Miguel was still on foot, exchanging a few words with Ruíz.

From the servants' quarters I saw India emerge with her baby on her hip and cross the angle of the courtyard towards us. She stood as near to us as she could, only a yard or two from my horse's flank, watching us. To me it seemed a kind of dumb insolence, and I felt my hackles rising. She stared at Miguel, then she stared at me. Miguel was turning away from Ruíz; the baby kicked and made a little crowing sound; deliberately India pushed her blouse from her shoulder and set the baby to her breast. Miguel had to pass her to mount, and his eyes rested on her momentarily. I gritted my teeth, not knowing why I felt sick and angry. It was the most natural thing for an Indian woman to suckle her baby at any time and place, whenever the baby cried, but I knew in my heart it had been done deliberately to affront me. I said nothing. Together Miguel and I rode out of the courtyard.

Miguel was speaking, and I turned my attention to him.

"One thing you must remember, Marta, and that is, never ride alone. When you wish to ride you must have either myself or Ruíz with you, and for any distance, a groom as well."

I looked at him questioningly.

"Oh, there is no danger, but it is a rule I make in case of accident. The pampa is wide, and the grass is high. If your horse should miss its footing and throw you, it would be very difficult to find you if you were lying injured. Look about us now, and you will see what I mean."

I did see. The great grasslands stretched ahead and around us, apparently limitless, ruffled into light and shade by the breeze, giving up sweet odors in the sun. Here and there was the darker speck of a tree, and to one side was the silver ribbon of the river edged with richer green, and the gray scar of an *arroyo*. Right on the skyline at one point was a stretch of purplish-mauve under the blue—a ridge of mountains.

"How much of this is Valdoro?" I asked.

He threw back his head and laughed. "All of it! You know my land starts this side of Puenterojo, and all you can see from here is mine, until you reach the foothills of those mountains. You can ride all day and still say, "This is Valdoro!"

The sounds of the workmen around the house had faded behind us; I could only hear the soft thud of our horses' hooves, the creak and jingle of harness and somewhere in the distance a bird calling a plaintive and repeated cry.

"Look!" said Miguel, and pointed.

There was a brownish blotch by the far upper reaches of the river, a blotch which became separate dots.

"Cattle," he said "My cattle."

"How do you know they are yours?" I asked.

"They are wild cattle," he answered. "On my land the wild cattle are mine. But don't worry, I shall establish rights of ownership. I need more *vaqueros* —and some must live near the boundaries. Then I can get all the cattle branded with my brand, and there can be no disputes, as there might be, for instance, near Puenterojo."

"I see," I said. "But why is it important?"

He turned to me in astonishment. "Did you not realize? This will be our way of living. I have cattle to sell. My beef will go all over Riqueza, to the *saladeros,* through the Viceroyalty, and some, perhaps, to Portuguese territory. I shall keep the best stock for breeding. My cattle are going to be the best in the country—my horses, too."

"And are they wild as well, the horses?"

"Most of them start that way. We shall break in the best stallions and mares. Some will be for breeding, some for sale, and some for work-horses for the *vaqueros.* I told you this will be the best *estancia* in Riqueza."

"I am beginning to believe you!" I laughed, but thought to myself: I am still only guessing at the strength of that ambition Doña Sara had talked about to me. At last, at Valdoro, it made sense. Here there was something worth living and working for. And I had been chosen to help. Riding with Miguel stirrup to stirrup in the fresh-gold vastness of the pampa I felt proud and glad to be a part of it. Suddenly I was happier than I had ever been. I loved Miguel. He never spoke to me of love, but why should that matter? By day I did the duties of the house, and he treated me with unfailing courtesy and more consideration than one might expect from so single-minded a man. By night he taught me the excitement of physical love, and his passion was a wonder, a delirium which left me adrift in unreasoning ecstasy. Doña Sara had said, "He knows how to keep a woman happy" —was that what she meant? In his turn he seemed happy with me. I was being a good wife to him, I was doing all he wanted—perhaps for him that was love: men were physical creatures and had such different ways of looking at relationships.

"*Ay,* Marta," he was saying, "I have such plans for Valdoro. I shall see it established."

Our eyes met and I smiled. He put his gloved hand out and caught my wrist.

"You do understand?"

"Yes, I understand."

Still his hand held me, and his face was serious as his eyes scanned mine.

"Marta—for Valdoro I want one thing more. An heir."

"I know," I said, with a momentary flutter of the heart.

"Are there—no signs yet?"

"Not yet. It is—very early . . ."

"Of course. I am impatient. Forgive me."

That night he possessed me more passionately than ever, and such was my love for him and his charm for me that it was not until afterwards I thought: That was for Valdoro and an heir. Why could it not be for love?

During the next few weeks I found myself often in the company of Father Marcos. In spite of our preoccupation with domestic matters he seemed to consider Tía Amalia and myself as good Christians whose faith needed little reinforcing, and it is true that I was glad of the regularity of services and confession, which he held for us in the great hall. When the church was restored we would of course worship there. He already held outdoor services for the Indians, and later they would congregate outside the church which was constructed so that a crowd could stand before it and participate in the service within.

Father Marcos was eager to reach the Indians and to help them. I discovered that he spoke one Indian dialect well, and had a smattering of two or three others. I asked him to teach me; I wanted to learn and hoped to surprise Miguel. As I said to Father Marcos, it would help me to control the servants—and India would have less excuse for misunderstanding my orders.

"Certainly I will teach you," he said, and paused. Then he added: "This is a personal matter, I know, but as your pastor I must commend you for your Christian attitude to the Indian girl."

I accepted gratefully his words of praise, but even then I was such an innocent fool that I did not comprehend their full meaning.

For a few weeks everything went smoothly. Of course there were minor difficulties—India's obstinacies, the inconvenience of having workmen everywhere—but I was able to ignore them, and the work progressed. I was sure that construction was moving faster now that Miguel was on the spot all the time. We still could not use the great hall, for even when the floor of the upper rooms had been laid and the hall ceiling plastered between the beams the men were constantly using the staircase as they worked on the rooms above. Since these were to be the main bedrooms I was eager for them to be finished so that I could get them furnished and put into use. The courtyard was still cluttered with loaded wagons, for Miguel refused to have them put outside while they still held goods—to discourage theft, I supposed. I had the kitchen fairly well equipped and managed to get the housekeeping running smoothly. When Señora Ruíz deigned to arrive, I thought, she will find this place under my authority. Try as I might, I had not been able to conquer my dislike of her and her husband, and though I believed them loyal to Miguel I did not trust their attitude to me.

Then came a particular day I shall never forget.

When my immediate morning work was done I was balked by the workmen from setting a room to rights. I had a strong desire to get into the open air and ride, but I suspected Miguel had already left the house. I remembered Miguel's instructions, and knew if it was so I should ask Ruíz to accompany me. I knew too how much he would silently resent it; to have him with me would take all the pleasure out of the ride.

I found Ruíz in the courtyard. He seemed to have just finished saying something to India who gave me a long look and walked away. I asked Ruíz if he knew where I could find Don Miguel.

"He has left for the *arroyo,* señora. There was a report of a large herd of cattle moving down it."

I stood irresolute.

"Did you wish to ride, señora?"

His blank look implied he hoped I did not.

"I had thought of it," I admitted.

"In that case . . . well, it is not far."

Now he allowed me to see his reluctance. I had no wish for his company; as he said, it was no distance; the *arroyo* was hardly out of sight of Valdoro, and I could expect to meet Miguel there. I made my decision on impulse.

"I am sure you are busy. I can ride there by myself and meet Don Miguel."

"I will accompany you, Doña Marta."

His words were stiff and grudging; he would be a silent martyr all the way.

"There is no need. If Don Miguel is not there I shall ride straight back."

His eyes gleamed as he bowed his head. "If that is your order, señora."

We both knew that was what he wanted.

"Please have a horse saddled for me. I shall be ready directly."

I changed and was back in the courtyard in a few minutes' time. Ruíz was standing by as I mounted.

"Are you sure you do not wish me to accompany you, señora?"

"Quite sure."

I touched up my mount and cantered off. How I enjoyed that ride! All the delightful sensations of the sun, the air and the exercise refreshed me, and were increased by the feeling that at last I had exerted my authority over that disagreeable man. I felt for the first time truly the mistress of Valdoro. A canter; a short gallop; a slackening to a canter again, and then a steady trot which I held for some minutes, and there in the distance was the *arroyo.*

To my surprise there was no sign of Miguel or of any cattle. But the *arroyo* was on the far side of the river—which was, at this time, though broad, very shallow and easily forded—and cut through some higher, rocky ground; after a little distance there was a bend in the *arroyo* which quite obscured its upper reaches from view. It was likely that I should find them there. I encouraged my horse down the river bank and it splashed its way across, the water never reaching my stirrups. We climbed out and started up the *arroyo*, the horse picking its way delicately among the rocks to reach the grassy dusty verge. And there I saw figures.

To my amazement they were not what I had expected at all. I watched as they all came into view, a group of people on foot, about twenty of them, all Indians, and with them three men on horseback. The Indians, both men and women, were walking with every appearance of tiredness and dejection, and a dreadful feeling crept over me at the sight. The horsemen carried guns across their saddles, and long whips; it looked as if they were herding the Indians like cattle. It could not be true. But I must know what was happening. I quickened my horse's pace and rode up the *arroyo* toward them. On seeing me coming one of the horsemen rode out in advance of the group.

"*Buenos días, señora!* How nice to see a white woman around here!"

I did not like the look of him; he had piggy, calculating eyes and a wide false smile. He seemed to me part Indian and all scoundrel. I could now see that besides his long gun he carried a brace of pistols —an unnecessarily large armory, I thought. And I had the odd feeling I had seen him before.

"*Buenos días.* I am Doña Marta, wife of Don Miguel who owns this land."

If he did not tell me what they were doing I intended to ask.

"What a pleasure to meet you, Doña Marta. My name is Moreno. We are just riding through."

"Some of you are walking," I said pointedly.

He laughed. "*Ay,* that's true. They don't qualify for horses."

"But they are with you, no?"

"Verdad. You could say they are my responsibility."

I looked at them as they dragged themselves toward me. Indians, I knew, had much endurance, but these looked exhausted. Poor creatures, they were hollow-cheeked and dull-eyed. One woman had a tiny baby on her hip; it sagged in its sling of cloth and whimpered as if it was too weak to cry.

"Then you should do something for them. They look tired and hungry."

"Are you telling me my business?"

"I am suggesting they need rest and food. Without it they won't be able to go much farther."

"They'll get it when it suits me. And they'll go as far as I want."

"Where are they going?"

He folded his lips and looked at me insolently. Then: "Look, señora, it's none of your business."

He turned around and waved the others on. He would have ridden past me but I moved my horse across his path. I was sure the Indians were going against their will.

"Where are you taking them?"

He laughed roughly and stared at me in defiance. "Where do you think? To the mines at Platinas."

"To the mines?" With a flash of disgust I remembered vague remarks I had heard in Varena. "You mean you are taking them to work there?"

"Of course. There's always a demand for mineworkers."

"But surely they don't want to go?"

He laughed again. The Indians had now reached us, and, on seeing us talking, two of the women—one of them with the baby—sank wearily to the ground. Moreno turned on them with an oath, and to my horror raised his whip and lashed at them.

"Stop that!" I cried, and moved my horse toward him.

"Get on! Get moving!" he shouted at the miserable group, and the other riders lifted their whips menacingly. The Indians huddled together and started to walk again.

"That's it! And you keep your nose out of my business, señora!"

I controlled my fury as best I could and snapped at him, "On my land this is my business!"

My horse was barring his way. He put out his hand and snatched at my reins to pull it aside. Without a second's thought I raised my riding whip and brought it down smartly on his wrist. He let go, but red rage leapt into his eyes. Suddenly I knew where I had seen him before. It had been at a distance, and weeks ago. He had been one of El Alacrán's men.

"You bitch! Do you want a lesson? Get out of my way!"

I would not give ground, though I admit I was beginning to feel frightened. I was one woman against three rogues. If they chose, I was at their mercy. I hoped I would have time to warn them of certain retribution from Miguel if they so much as touched me.

"Do you want to go with these men?" I called to the Indians.

Moreno sneered. "They can't understand you!" he said exultantly. "But they know my language!"

"Yes, the gun and the whip!" I retorted.

I think at that moment he was about to force me out of his way, but he checked and looked around. Then I too heard the sound which had attracted his attention, and as I gazed into the distance, around the next bend in the *arroyo* came two riders—and one of them was Miguel.

"Here is my husband!" I told him. "We'll see what he has to say."

Then, as they drew nearer, I saw Moreno's men raise their guns to cover my two deliverers. At this Miguel and his man came on with right hands raised to show they intended no force. My heart began to sink. Miguel ignored the men and rode straight up to me.

"Marta! What are you doing here?"

His brows were drawn together and anger was in his eyes.

"I came to meet you," I said hurriedly. "But look at these poor creatures. They are being taken to the mines. I'm sure they don't want to go—please make these men release them."

Moreno smiled and did not lower his gun. "He may own this land, señora, but he's in no position to make us do anything."

Miguel looked at Moreno, and when he replied his answer and the correct politeness with which it was delivered amazed me.

"My wife does not understand the situation. But I do. I do not approve of this, but, as you say, matters have gone too far for me to alter them. I would suggest that in future you find some other way to make money, preferably not on my land."

"So—you've more sense than your wife!" Moreno turned to the others. *"Arriba!"*

"No, Miguel!" I cried. "Oh, please—look at this poor woman with a baby—"

His face was set. "There's nothing I can do, Marta."

But there was something. I turned to Moreno. "Do you get paid for this?" I asked.

"You don't think I do it for nothing, señora?"

"Then I will pay you for this woman—and have her for my servant."

A cunning look crept into his eyes. "Mineworkers come expensive, señora. She looks strong. I'd get good money for her."

"Marta, do not interfere," Miguel said sharply.

"But look at her! The baby will die if she goes on—"

Moreno sneered again. "What a fuss over a little animal! That's all they are—but if you want the bitch—"

He then named a price; Miguel refused to treat; he offered to reduce it, and I still pleaded, while the Indians, uncomprehending, apathetic, simply stood and waited, not even daring to sit down.

"It's all the same to me," Moreno said, and prepared to move off yet again. I caught Miguel's arm.

"Please, Miguel, I've never asked you for anything before—just save the mother and her baby. Do it for me—"

Miguel stayed silent; he was still angry; how could he be unmoved? Then with a sudden movement he fished in his belt. "You're lucky I have some money on me."

He handed some coins to Moreno, then spoke to the Indian woman in a native dialect, pointing at me. To my surprise the woman turned to a man beside her and clung to him.

"Oh, Miguel, take the man as well!"

"Oh, no, you don't!" Moreno interrupted. "He's young and strong—he's the fruit on the top of the basket!"

I know my horror showed in my face, but Miguel's look was stony. "It's no use, Marta. You're lucky to get the woman."

The Indian man spoke to his wife, then pushed her toward me. The woman looked pleadingly at him, then at us. I smiled and held out my hand.

"One thing, *señor!*" said Miguel to Moreno, with cold sarcasm. "Do not try this again. Another time the situation will be different."

Moreno fingered his gun. "It could be different now. But we shall see. *Buenos días!*" he retorted insolently, and waved his troop on.

I had to sit there helpless, watching him and his men urge the Indians on, down to the river and along the bank, to what I now guessed would be slavery and inevitable death in the mines. The Indian woman watched them all the way. Miguel turned to his *peón* and told him to bring the woman to the house.

"We will ride ahead," he said to me.

"Have you any food with you?" I asked the *peón.* "A bit of bread and meat, señora," he answered, surprised.

"Please give it to her. I'm sure she is starving. Let her sit and eat by the river."

He shrugged and felt in his saddlebag.

Miguel spoke two words to me. "Come, Marta."

I followed him to the river and we forded it in silence. Our horses had clambered up the bank and we were on the level grassland heading toward Valdoro before I dared to speak.

"Thank you, Miguel. I wanted to save them all, but even one—"

He turned on me in anger.

"Marta, what did you think you were doing? I considered you responsible, sensible, obedient—but *this. . . !*" For a moment he was speechless, as if mastering his rage, then: "In the first place, you ride out by yourself in defiance of my order. Then you run yourself into danger, you jeopardize everything with your tender-hearted sentimentality, and you turn a weapon against me which I could have used against my enemies—*Dios,* I had thought better of you."

I was dumbfounded; I didn't even understand half of what he said, and his furious accusations wounded me to the heart. I had to defend myself.

"I knew where you were. Ruíz said you were at the *arroyo*—he offered to come—"

"And you refused his company! He would have had the sense to keep you out of danger!"

"I told him I would come straight back if I didn't meet you. I didn't expect those men—oh, Miguel, I recognized Moreno—"

"Yes," he said grimly. "You were lucky he didn't put a bullet in you."

I had never considered myself in such danger, and looked at him astonished.

"They must have been very tempted. But he knows he would be hunted down, and would follow El Alacrán. For pity's sake, Marta, why did you interfere?"

"Those poor people! Don't you care?"

"Yes, I care! I don't want slave traffic on my land. But your life, and the peace of Valdoro, are worth more to me than the lives of a handful of Indians."

"It's not right to weigh one against the other. Surely you could have stopped them—"

"Stopped them? When the leader had a gun at your head—and there was another at my back? I had to let them go—but you—you went one better. You put me in their hands!"

I stared at him.

"Don't you understand? How can I inform on a slave-runner—when I've bought a slave from him? How can I prove I'm not manning my *estancia* with slaves? Do you think there won't be rumors now? My enemies know I must have peace here—and a rumor like that is enough to start an Indian rising!"

Still not comprehending the full situation I was sick with horror at what I had done.

"But why should there be? She won't be a slave—we are helping her."

"Try to prove it!"

"You talk of enemies—but who—? And why should anyone want to make trouble here?"

Now his anger was overlaid with disbelief. "You must know who—and why."

"Indeed I do not."

"Then you have less sense than I gave you credit for."

"Perhaps you will enlighten me."

He answered with weary patience. "The less land I have, the less power I have. The less power I have, the more there is for other people."

"The less land? But no one can take your land—"

"Didn't you know? I thought Doña Sara had told you how things are."

"She told me nothing."

"Then I will tell you now. The original title to my ancestor defines only the boundaries to the south and east, where the land was beginning to be settled. For the rest, the wording is "such land that is not covered by another title and remains at peace"—in other words, where the Spaniards were not in conflict with Indian tribes. The territory has been accepted as belonging to my family for generations, and I have petitioned the crown for my boundaries to be confirmed. But until they are, if there is fighting on my land anyone can start a legal process to dispute my title."

I let this information sink in, and found it explained a lot.

"But who would want to do that?"

"Your friend the mine-owner," he retorted sarcastically.

"I have no such friend."

"No? When the biggest mine in Platinas is owned by Sánchez?"

"Sánchez! He's no friend of mine!"

"I'm glad to hear it. I thought that little ship-board interlude—"

"How can you speak like that! I refused to allow him to be introduced to me, after he'd done his best to scrape acquaintance—"

Miguel's face lightened into surprise. "Refused? Then why his remarks—and the fan—?"

The whole incident was now so far in the past and seemingly so unimportant that I was able to tell Miguel in a few quick phrases all about it. But I only told him what I actually knew, and kept my suspicions of Señora Ruíz to myself.

"And I suppose somehow he managed to get the fan presented to me through one of the servants simply to embarrass me and make trouble between us," I ended. "He succeeded, unfortunately. But all the interest was on his side, and it must have been pretence, prompted by sheer malice."

"Malicious, yes, but not pretence. He wanted you, and still does."

My heart sank, for I thought that even now he did not believe me.

"Yes," he said at last. "It was malice, and more than that. Trouble between us might have delayed or even stopped our establishing ourselves here. Sánchez would like to see me reduced to a few fields; then I would be a nobody and not in line for any office under the crown. He wants crown appointments; naturally, they can be very remunerative. In addition he wants an unlimited supply of labor for his mines. Indians on my land are automatically and legally my workers, so my presence is unwelcome to him for many reasons.

"He will make trouble for me, in any way he can. Well, I have the consolation that he didn't charm you with his bold looks; but I could wish your soft heart had not caused me to buy a slave from his runner."

With that, the matter was closed. I was glad he knew I had not encouraged Sánchez. I was still at fault; he had made it plain I had blundered badly.

At Valdoro work had gone well that day, and I found that the bedroom over the great hall was finished, clean and ready for me to furnish it. I bustled the men to move the furniture. Tía Amalia and I hung the curtains at windows and bed, and by evening everything was settled there. As I went down to dinner India came up to me in the hall.

"Now you have moved, señora," she said to me, "is it not time I had a better room, in the house, instead of being in the servants' quarters?"

I was astonished by her impertinence, but she looked at me coolly, waiting for my answer.

"I think you are very well where you are, India," I replied. "I see no reason to move you."

Her black eyes flashed anger. "Reason! I have good reason!" She smiled arrogantly and held out to me the golden-skinned baby she was carrying. "Is not this a reason? I have borne a son, and now I am strong my master will wish to visit me again. You have no son—perhaps you are barren? Do you wish Don Miguel to come to the servants' quarters to get another?"

In that instant my stomach churned, my head swam with nausea. I was overwhelmed at the revelation which I had been too much of an innocent even to suspect. Sickness and humiliation prompted one immediate reaction—I raised my hand and slapped her face.

She gazed at me like a snake about to strike. "You—his wife!" she spat at me. "I was his Indian wife before you came!"

In one swift movement she tossed her black hair back from her face, turned, and was gone.

I stood there trembling from head to foot, my heart pounding so much that I felt it in my throat. I believed her. I saw now that everything pointed to her story being true—her privileged position, her possessive attitude to Miguel, the fairness of the child more Spanish than Indian . . . And so many little remarks made in my hearing in Varena . . . even Father Marcos . . . She called herself his Indian wife—just what was that? Frantically I tried to think. I could not believe that Miguel would have married her by Catholic rites. I must be his true and legal wife. And I had been legally married in Spain, before her child was conceived—but not married by the Church until afterwards. He must have taken her as his mistress while waiting to marry me. . . .

Then, still shocked, I pulled myself together and thought: I won't give in to her! She will not take my place. Yet in fresh anguish I knew she had already supplanted me—and knowing that Miguel had loved her, and still desired her, how could I bring myself to be a wife to him? We are supposed to accept a husband's infidelities, but surely not in the very house . . . If he thought he could come from her bed to mine—

Ruíz came in, and looked at me shrewdly. I determined to show nothing of my feelings. Still he looked at me. I went to the dinning-room and sat through an interminable dinner, forcing myself to eat food which stuck in my tightened throat and nearly choked me, and tried to make conversation in a normal manner. By the time I could go to bed I had a racking headache, and knew I had little prospect of sleep that night.

I was wearily brushing my hair as Miguel came in.

He stood looking at me in the mirror, then came and placed his hands on my shoulders. His touch always made my heart leap—now I felt a fluttering inside and shivered.

"Marta, promise me you will never ride alone again."

"Very well, I promise. Though I hardly see why it is so important to you."

Anger and jealousy made me add the comment. His mirrored eyes gazed at mine intently.

"You must know—I need you, Marta."

I should have realized what it cost so proud a man to say that. I could have guessed that he meant more than was put into actual words. But jealousy blinded me, and I only thought: Yes, you need me—as you need a good servant, no more. I stared back at him, said nothing, and went on brushing my hair. If only I had been tender at that moment, how different matters might have been. But as I sat there coldly, his hands dropped from my shoulders and he turned away.

He took off his coat and began to untie his cravat.

"By the way." His voice had a studied carelessness. "Now that more rooms are finished I think India had better be given a room on this side of the courtyard."

My body went cold. "Is that what you wish?" I asked.

"Yes. It will be better for her to be here."

I put down my hairbrush. "And better for you, too, I suppose."

He looked at me and did not speak. The first remark which had leapt almost involuntarily from my lips breached a dam of pent-up thoughts and feelings, and now words flowed through like a torrent.

"So—not only am I obliged to accept your Indian mistress, I have also to arrange her lodging so that you can visit her without passing through the servants' quarters. I know you married me for your own reasons, but I did not expect to be so humiliated by your lack of regard. Very well, since one bastard is not enough for you, I will arrange for her to be moved to the nearest wing."

Still he stared at me, a muscle in his jaw working, his face otherwise expressionless. Then, at last, he said: "I can see that apologies or explanations will be useless. I am sorry you think so poorly of me that you can interpret my intentions in that way."

"What other way is there? It's all too obvious."

"Is it? Oh, I'm partly to blame—I've mishandled the situation."

"On the contrary," I broke in, "you have handled it very well. You have had everything your way, and now I know everything. I am to be the complaisant wife. I understand what Doña Sara meant about taking you with your faults as well as your virtues. Don't worry. I'll keep my side of the bargain."

I stood up, turned my back on him and moved to the bed.

"If that is your attitude there is no point in saying more. I shall leave you to your self-righteousness."

He picked up his coat and left the room.

I climbed into bed and burst into tears, a violent storm of sobs which only made my headache worse. I pictured him going to India's room in the servants' quarters, to forget my angry reproaches in her arms. He should be with me, but now his actions and my reactions had driven him away, perhaps for ever. By now he was being welcomed. India would be eager to console him with her body; his head already would be on her brown breast.

I forced myself to stop crying and steel myself with my bitterness into some sort of strength. In that moment I resolved not to be supplanted. He preferred India to me, but I could not stop loving him though love was mingled with hate; and I would cling to my nominal position as his wife. I must accept that India was Miguel's mistress, but I was and would remain mistress of Valdoro.

Hours later Miguel came silently to bed.

The next day India was established in a room away

from the servants' quarters, and I had to bear her arrogant ways and triumphant glances when we met. You can be arrogant, I thought, but I can be strong. We shall see who wins in the end.

6

The very day after the incident of the slave-drivers Miguel left on an expedition. The atmosphere between us was cold. Miguel merely told me in a curt fashion that he would be away for a few days visiting the Indian tribes.

"It is absolutely necessary for them to hear from me that I was not concerned with the slave-running, and that I will do all I can to prevent it in future," was the sum total of the explanation he gave me.

India did not miss her opportunity to wound me. There was a look of triumph in her eyes as she glided up to me during the preparations for departure.

"You see, I go with my lord," she whispered. "You cannot help him. You are no good—for anything."

She settled her baby on her hip. There was no need further to stress my inadequacy.

How surprising that I should be left in charge of Valdoro, I thought. But I knew my position was only nominal: Ruíz was the one who really had control. But Ruíz, however, was not quite up to that responsibility.

The morning after Miguel's departure, as I moved

about my bedroom, I noticed that everything seemed very quiet. When I went downstairs and into the courtyard I could see the reason—no one was working at the building. I stopped one of the house servants and asked where the men were. She rolled her eyes up in contempt as she answered me.

"Those stupid country Indians!" she said. "Something frightened them in the night. They say the spirits around the old chapel are restless, and they have left their cabins. By now they may all have run away."

I could have wept with frustration. My first day in charge and all the work-force disappears! What a situation for Miguel to find on his return. Was there nothing I could do? I thought hard for a few minutes, and remembered what Miguel had said about previous scares—that they had been attempts to stop the establishment of Valdoro. I sent for one of the *mestizo vaqueros*.

"I want you to get some of the men and take a message to the Indians who have run away," I said. "Be careful not to frighten them, or to look as if you are intending to bring them back by force. Tell them that if they are leaving they will need food for the journey. If they come to the house I will have enough cows slaughtered to give them all beef. When I have talked to them they can decide freely whether to go or stay. They get the beef in any case. Is that understood?"

The *vaquero* looked surprised, but agreed and went off to collect his men.

Next I sought out Father Marcos. I explained the situation to him.

"I don't know what frightened the Indians," I said, "but I strongly suspect it was not spirits, as they believe. I want you to perform a service of exorcism by the chapel and the cabins."

"Doña Marta, I cannot do that unless there is real evidence of evil there!"

"Father Marcos, I thought you had come here to give the Indians the comfort of our religion."

He looked shocked. "And so I have."

"You do not believe in their spirits, but they do. Here is your chance to prove that our God is stronger."

"We shall prove nothing!"

"Father, the Indians no longer worship their gods, but although they are now Christians the old superstitious fears are still there. Their Christianity needs strengthening. The most important thing to you at this moment is that they need your help and encouragement. A service of exorcism will give them the spiritual strength they need; and tonight the *vaqueros,* who are not so superstitious, can stay on guard against anything more substantial than a spirit."

It took some more argument, but at length he agreed.

The *vaqueros*—with the promise of the extra meat—brought most of the labor force back to the house. When they were all together I told them how Father Marcos would exorcize the spirits, and they would then have nothing to fear. I hoped they would return to work. They took their meat and trooped off to the service. Father Marcos made a good impressive job of it, and eventually most of them decided to stay and see what happened that night.

I told the *vaqueros* what I wanted them to do, and they agreed to watch through the hours of darkness, turn and turn about, for a bonus.

This was quite effective; no spirits or apparitions manifested themselves. There was something else, though.

During the night I was restless, and could not sleep. I tossed in bed, then I got up and went to my window, pushing it wide to the cool night air. It was then that I smelled burning. In the darkness I went on to the balcony and looked around. As I did so I saw a little tongue of flame licking the thatch of one of the temporary buildings.

"Fire!" I shouted, rushed back into my room and dragged on a robe, then seized a poker and a copper jug and ran along the corridor banging them together.

It had the hoped-for effect and I carried on into the courtyard, for there were servants sleeping in the temporary buildings and I feared for their lives. The house servants managed to rouse them, which was as well, for the fire was gaining hold, running through the thatch like a live thing.

The courtyard presented a macabre picture. Amid the darkness, fitfully lit by the leaping flames, servants in various stages of undress rushed to and fro, fear written on their faces. Those who were trying to do something were balked by others more frightened who were rushing purposelessly about. I started to bully some sense into them, pushing them to make two lines from the well to the seat of the fire. Ruíz, apparently still dazed with sleep, made a totally ineffective attempt at drawing water. I ordered him sharply to go and get more buckets, and set two of the strongest men to raise the water. Once the human chain was established, full buckets going up one line and empty ones down the other, the panic died down. Luckily there were no animals in the buildings; even our best riding horses were corralled at that time, and *vaqueros* were with them; my few precious hens were in the far corner building of the courtyard, where I thought they would be in less danger than squawking about beneath the servants' feet. Now the flames were being systematically doused I set some men to beat out the spark-caught thatch with brooms or drag it off. Ruíz came up to me just as I hopped away from a falling mass.

"Señora, you must go back to safety! Leave it to the men."

"Nonsense!" I snapped, annoyed at his helplessness. "This is my house, and I'm going to see it doesn't burn!"

Tía Amalia was organizing the removal from the nearby buildings of anything inflammable or subject to damage by water. It was a mercy I had seen the fire when I did; another quarter of an hour and the tale would have been very different; as it was, we had a hectic time fighting it, but we caught it and put it out before it did appreciable damage. As I limped off to bed I reflected that this, as well as last night's to-do, might be attributed to angry spirits; but the next morning the *vaqueros* told me they—and the Indians—had heard three horses being ridden away from the house. If they had not promised to stay at their posts on watch they might have stopped them. But I told them they had done well.

And whatever Miguel might think, I had done my best. It was only then that I remembered India's old room had been close to the place where the fire began.

By day the courtyard looked a mess, and so far Ruíz had given no orders to clear it. It was almost as if he wanted the place to look at its worst when Miguel returned. Difficulties and frictions were trying my patience and I was running out of tact, so instead of suggesting to him what should be done, I put on an air of authority and gave my orders direct to the servants. Inwardly I was very nervous, but all was well. The previous night might have helped; at all events they accepted me as mistress, and soon the litter of half-burned thatch was being swept up, the damaged building cleared, the courtyard cleaned and tidied.

I inspected all the straw-thatched buildings, and had anything inflammable or of any value stored elsewhere in the finished wing of the house. A fire might happen again; better to have less rooms in use and one's belongings intact. There was one large wagon piled high with goods, which I inspected as I had it unloaded. To my surprise I found among some furnishings a magnificent portrait of Miguel. My new-found power must have gone to my head, for I did not wait to consult him. I gave my instructions and watched while it was hung over the great fireplace in the main hall. There, I thought, the spirit of Valdoro's founder will preside over the *estancia*. Each time I passed through, there he was, looking at me with that characteristic expression, not smiling, yet not completely grave, his eyes dark and brilliant as in life.

Everything was clear and the builders back at work again. Ruíz, coldly formal, was, I thought, trying to take my measure. For what? I had thought that extreme loyalty to Miguel had made him antagonistic to me, but now I confessed myself quite unable to understand him or his motives.

I was considering this as I smoothed my hair, having washed and changed after supervising the morning's work. Glancing out of my window I saw riders approaching from the Puenterojo road, coming towards the *estancia*. There were three horses, one a packhorse, and as the group came nearer I could see from their dress that the two men were master and servant. I went downstairs ready to offer hospitality.

I expected a stranger, for I knew no one outside our distant capital with the exception of one or two officers at the garrison post, so it was a complete surprise to me when the servant announced Don Alfonso Sánchez.

He came forward with an eager effusiveness more suited to a Varena drawing-room, and kissed my hand.

"Doña Marta! How refreshing to see you at the end of a dusty ride! Country life must agree with you; you are more beautiful than ever!"

"*Buenos días,* Don Alfonso. This visit is a surprise. Let me offer you some refreshment." I signed to the servant, who brought wine. "You have, of course, come to see my husband. I regret he is not here; he is not returning, I believe, until the day after tomorrow at the earliest."

If I had any illusion that this would make him pack up and ride away it was swiftly dispelled. He explained that he had been visiting his mines at Platinas, and intended returning to Varena with the next detachment. He hoped we would extend him hospitality until then. Naturally, since there was not a habitable house within forty miles, it would have been impossible to refuse even if the code of hospitality had not been

so strict. It was as well, I thought, that I was chap-
eroned by Tía Amalia. The date of Miguel's return
was uncertain, and as the relief detachment had not
yet come through on its way to the post Sánchez would
be here for nearly a week by the time the relieved men
arrived.

Tía Amalia soon had a room prepared, and he
changed out of his riding clothes. He reappeared,
dressed to perfection in a pale green brocade coat,
ivory waistcoat and dark green breeches. I expected
to find him insufferable as usual, but instead he presented us with a much more agreeable side of his
nature. He chatted pleasantly; he even complimented
me on the conditions at Valdoro.

"It is so extraordinarily civilized here. And it must
be difficult for you, living here with the building work
still in progress. And did I not see some signs of
a fire?"

"Yes," I said. "Due to carelessness, I think. But
there was little damage, and that only to a temporary
building. The grass thatch is wretched stuff."

I was not going to admit to Sánchez that Miguel
might have enemies, even though I personally thought
the trouble-makers must be old associates of El Alacrán, who would be nobody's friends.

Later that evening when we were temporarily alone
he took the opportunity to say, "Doña Marta, I owe
you an apology. I have behaved to you quite repre-
hensibly in the past. I did not realize how different
you are from most of the ladies of our society—" I
began to speak, but he went on: "No, pray, let me
finish. That does not excuse me, it only explains why I
thought I could give my inclinations full rein without
causing offense. I am old enough to have more sense.
I should have known an honorable lady the moment
I met her."

He took my hand and kissed it, but this time not
formally, but lingeringly, flashing up an ardent look as
he did so. I was at a loss for words, so unexpected

was this contrition, but thought, you are still too forward.

As if he read my reaction he went on: "Doña Marta, I ask nothing more—simply to be forgiven, and to be allowed to touch these pretty fingers. Surely that is not too much? I shall be desolate without it."

He gave me such a tragical look that against my will I laughed, a laugh in which he shamefacedly joined, and ended all chance of my being stern. "Pretty fingers" indeed! My hands are not long and slender, but inclined to squareness. But they had improved since leaving home; there, in winter, looking after the hens made them so rough that sewing was a trial.

Sánchez behaved astonishingly well that evening; he drank little, he chatted, he even sorted the colors for the embroidery Tía Amalia and I were working on a bedspread; and later, before we retired, he took a guitar and played and sang tolerably well. I was thinking I must have misjudged him, until Tía Amalia muttered to me as we walked with our candles upstairs, "Now we know how he got round Doña Isabel."

Perhaps it was being so unhappy about Miguel that made me more tolerant to Sánchez; for whenever I thought of my husband I saw him in the company of the Indian girl who rode beside him, their child slung on her back; or, worse still, at night, I imagined him couched on the pampa, his head on his saddle, and India lying close, covered by the same poncho. Then I could not sleep for the bitterness which rose within me.

Sánchez seemed happy to spend as much time as possible with me, though he never overstepped the bounds of propriety. However he once did begin to make more excuses for himself.

"Doña Marta," he said seriously as we walked back from inspecting some horses in the corral, "You know that I have behaved badly in the past. My reputation is not—perfect."

A delicate understatement, I thought.

"I have one trouble," he went on. "I need to love and be loved. Is that so dreadful?"

Without going into his definition of love I answered pointedly, "You know very well the *need* is not dreadful."

"Then would it be wrong to seek some satisfaction, provided I injured no one?"

"That is a very vague question, Don Alfonso. Only you can answer it in your particular situation." This, I thought, was treading on swampy ground and I did not want to be drawn in. "But since you have a wife, Don Alfonso, surely you can have no questions?"

"A wife, yes." He looked down, and then shook his head. "I must admit my marriage was a mistake. I thought her love for me would be enough, but it was not. It is my fault; she is in no way to blame. You know her; she is a good woman, a clever woman. But I look at her; I used to feel pity; now I feel revulsion. I cannot treat her as a wife."

"You should not be saying this to me. I like to think Doña Isabel is my friend."

"Friend? Has she any, with her tongue? No, I must reserve the right to love where my heart leads me." He gave me a look the meaning of which was plain. "When I see someone who meets the difficulties of her own marriage with courage and pride I am humbled into admiration. That admiration leads to affection which is all the sweeter for being unexpected."

We reached the house and I did not need to reply. I was smiling to myself at the romanticization of his predatory instincts, and at the same time I felt myself blushing at the thought that he knew I had difficulties in my marriage—I supposed by now all Varena had heard of Miguel's Indian son.

Miguel returned just after sunset. I was in the great hall, and heard the sound of riders outside, heard the massive door to the *zaguán* being opened. He must have dismounted at once and handed his horse to a groom, for though I hurried across the hall he met me just inside the doorway. He smiled on seeing me and my heart lightened.

"Miguel! Did everything go well?"

"Yes, it was satisfactory." He pulled off his gloves. "And how was everything here?"

"It could have been a lot worse!" I said jokingly. "We had a little fire."

"A fire? Where?" His brows drew together in the old danger signal.

"In the thatch of the temporary quarters. We soon got it under control."

He started towards the door leading to the courtyard, then stopped and turned on me. *"We?* What do you mean?"

"I saw the fire first and organized the servants, that's all."

"Where was Ruíz?"

"He was there, but—he was quite useless."

I said it impulsively and regretted it at once. I saw that Miguel hardly believed me. We went out into the courtyard; by the afterglow and the light of torches he could see the damage.

He stopped the chief groom and asked him quietly what had happened. I stood aside and tried not to listen, but I felt much happier when the man said, ". . . and it was the señora who told us what to do, put some of us in two lines from the well, passing the buckets up and back, and told us how best to fight the fire."

When Miguel came back to me I saw approval in his eyes.

"You acted well, Marta," he said. "How did you know what to do?"

"There are some advantages in being a country girl," I said wryly. "I remembered what happened when one of our barns caught fire, but then we were short of hands, not hampered by too many."

"You took risks," he said gravely. "Are you sure you were not hurt?"

"No, not a bit. I ruined a pair of slippers, that's all."

"You shall have ten pairs!" he said warmly. "It will be cheap at the price!"

This time as he re-entered the hall he saw his portrait over the fireplace.

"*Dios!* You found that! Have I to see myself every day?"

"It seemed the right place for it. You are the founder of Valdoro."

"So you and my father think alike. It was his present to me; he intended it for this house. I suppose it had better stay." He put his hands on my shoulders and looked kindly at me. "May I think that your putting it there means there is a truce between us?"

"Has there been war? I hope not."

He bent his head and put his lips on mine. His kiss was brief, yet tender, and to me inexpressibly sweet. Then the courtyard door clicked open and India came in. She looked at us standing together, and then pointedly ignored me.

"Master," she said. "It is well I live in your house. My cabin was fired—you saw it."

"Yes," he replied. "But you were not there—and will not be there."

My heart sank again. Then I remembered Sánchez. Miguel must be told of his presence. It would annoy him to walk in on Sánchez unprepared.

"Miguel," I said, "I must tell you. We have a guest."

"A guest? Who?"

"Don Alfonso Sánchez."

"*Sánchez!* What is he doing here?"

"He intends to join the force returning to Varena. I could not refuse him hospitality."

"No, you could not. I am sorry I was not here."

And still he frowned. That is enough bad news, I thought. You can hear about the building workers later.

That all came out over dinner, but by then, bathed and changed and rested, he was in a better mood, and since we had only lost a day's work it was nothing to be concerned over. When everything had been explained he looked at me, then at Father Marcos, and began to laugh.

"You mean, you persuaded Father Marcos to exorcize non-existent spirits?"

I nodded. "We weren't certain they were non-existent. It seemed the most reasonable thing to do."

"You have achieved more than I would have thought of—or if I had, I doubt whether I would have had the nerve to propose it to the Father! I must congratulate you both!"

"It seems you have a jewel of a wife, Don Miguel," said Sánchez, and even his approval did not reduce Miguel's amusement.

I thought the precarious goodwill between Miguel and myself might improve now he had returned and found that I had tackled the emergencies. I told myself I must try to ignore the things that troubled me. But it was not easy.

As I left the men to their brandy and went to bed that night I found India setting out Miguel's things in his dressing-room. I had the feeling she was waiting there to emphasize her presence.

"You have finished, India," I said. "Thank you —you may go."

Her slanting eyes held a hint of malice. "You do not wish to know what happened on the journey? I was with my lord—all the time with my lord." She paused, then went on: "I tell him what the tribes say, and speak for him to the tribes. I make him happy. He cannot do without me."

"I know you help him with Indian tongues."

"We met two, three tribes. They all know me as his Indian wife. And I see my father, the *cacique*." She tossed back her long loose hair. "He is pleased with me that I have given my lord a son. He wishes me many more sons, for joy for my master and peace between him and my father."

She brushed past me and left the room.

Madre de Dios, what can I do? I thought, knowing there was nothing I could do.

But a few days later I had a ray of possible comfort. I began to suspect that I might be pregnant. Let it be so, I prayed. Let it be so. And send me a son for Valdoro.

7

Two days later Valdoro was buzzing with excitement. The relief detachment for the army post was coming through, and would spend the night with us. The men would set up camp by our corral, and I had tables erected in the courtyard so that they could have their evening meal there, while the officers—there were two of them—would have beds in the house and dine with us.

On their arrival only one thing dampened my pleasure. It transpired that a small group of civilians had travelled from Varena with the military party, all save one having left them at Puenterojo to go on to Platinas; the one remaining was Señora Ruíz. I found that I liked her no more and trusted her even less than I had in the past, but one thing surprised me about my attitude to her. Previously she had always made me feel nervous, unsure of myself; now I found myself meeting her with the confidence of mistress to servant, no longer intimidated by her subtle airs of disapproval or disdain. It may have been because I had tackled the organizing of Valdoro single-handed and had so far succeeded; but on reflection I feel that my determination to hold my position in the face of Miguel's infidelity had brought out some steel in my character of which I had not until then been aware.

Of course Tía Amalia and I were eager for all the news from Varena, and we did not leave the dining table until we had heard all the gossip the men could remember. Then Señora Ruíz excused herself and my aunt and I went to sit by the fire in a withdrawing room, while the men finished their wine in the great hall and discussed politics and Bonaparte.

The next day the detachment set off again, and we knew that in four or five days' time the men they were relieving would arrive. That morning Miguel seemed thoughtful, and later in the day when we were alone he said, "I hope you feel inclined for a jaunt back to Varena. We are going back with the returning detachment, so you will have just a few days for packing."

"Back! So soon? What made you decide?"

"They said last night that a big mail ship is due in Buenos Aires in a couple of weeks' time. It may have the royal confirmation of Valdoro's boundaries. In addition, it is time for the Viceroy to make crown appointments for Oro province. If he should visit Varena I would wish to be there."

"Of course."

"It is fortunate that Señora Ruíz has arrived. With both the Ruízes here we can leave Valdoro in their charge."

And I hope they'll manage it properly, I thought.

Miguel was still lost in his plans. "You may as well pack all your better clothes. It's just possible we may need to go on to Buenos Aires."

Buenos Aires, with Miguel! Oh, how I hoped so! It would mean a chance for society, excitement, perhaps a few weeks of gaiety and high living before I returned to the seclusion of Valdoro. Now I was going to be busy; there would be plenty to organize before our departure.

First I had to exchange information with Señora Ruíz.

She reported to me that she had found an excellent woman to act as housekeeper in our Varena house.

"And how have you engaged her? On a temporary basis, I hope?" I said, determined not to be saddled with her appointee if I did not like her.

"Naturally, I told her that her position was subject to your approval."

There was a glitter in the black snake-eyes which I ignored. I told her that Tía Amalia and I, with Miguel, would be paying Varena a temporary visit.

"And India?" she asked.

"India is going with us."

Miguel had made that plain.

"I hope she is giving satisfaction—to both of you?" she went on with offensive sweetness.

I knew what she meant, and there was no way of answering without betraying this, so I said nothing. But she knew how to wound without saying anything one could take exception to, and I needed all my new determination not to flinch when she continued conversationally, "She has a fine healthy baby. It looks as if it will be an attractive child, and pale-skinned. *Some mestizo* children are quite handsome, don't you think?"

Por Dios, I thought, she is telling me she knows. And that child will grow up here—the Indian bastard and my child together: everyone will know—and Miguel doesn't care for my humiliation. I'm here to give him an heir and ask no questions.

"I assume you are familiar with the kitchens, Señora Ruíz?" I said firmly. "Now you must get to know my routine for the rest of the house. There are matters I wish you to put in hand while I am away."

I moved the interview firmly back to a business footing, and by implying the kitchens were her province I felt that was one point I had scored.

When the detachment arrived nearly a week later it was like meeting old friends, for it was the one we had travelled out with, headed by Lieutenant García who, with his unaffected good manners, true feeling and modest speech was a welcome addition to our dining table.

The next morning we made an early start, and it was annoying to find myself attacked by queasiness on rising. I fought it, drank my coffee and felt capable again. It was not until I was in the carriage that I realized I could consider my pregnancy confirmed. But I decided not to tell Miguel yet; I wanted to be quite certain before informing him.

The journey was uneventful, and was accomplished in a shorter time than our outgoing one, without the ox-wagons to slow us up. I saw little of Sánchez except at meal-times; only occasionally did he ride beside the carriage and exchange a few words, and at all times he behaved correctly. But I could not help noticing that when he did so, invariably before long Miguel joined us. I would have liked to think it was simple jealousy, but I knew it was due to his violent distrust of the younger man. I was grateful that my aunt was sharing my sleeping quarters as well as the carriage; she, of course, had guessed at my pregnancy, and with her help I was able to conceal my sick feelings on rising even from Miguel, who regularly came to wake me.

We reached Varena late in the afternoon and drove straight to our house. We were greeted by a flustered and effusive woman, over-genteel and over-polite in her speech, and I liked her garrulity as little as I liked Señora Ruíz's cold reserve. I did not want to condemn her out of hand, but I felt more and more strongly that it was in Miguel's interest as well as my own not to trust anyone who might be an ally of the Ruízes. If Señora Ruíz had been involved in the affair of the fan, which to me seemed most likely, then she must have closer contacts with Sánchez than anyone had so far suspected; and if there was nothing wrong with *that*, why make a mystery of it?

Miguel went to see Doña Sara that evening; I sent a message that I would call the following morning.

When I entered the *sala* Doña Sara greeted me with an air of restrained approval.

"So you've been looking after Valdoro satisfactorily? Well, that's something."

I did not wait for long to broach my own subject.

"Doña Sara, I want to ask your advice."

"What might that be about?"

"Do you know the woman Señora Ruíz has engaged to be my temporary housekeeper here?"

"I can't say that I do. She hasn't been employed around here before. Hasn't she come from Buenos Aires?"

"I've no idea. Doña Sara, I must take you into my confidence. I do not altogether trust Señora Ruíz—oh, I don't mean I suspect her of theft, or anything like that—it's a matter of . . . discretion and I would rather not have one of her friends employed in my house in my absence. Do you know anyone—someone you could really recommend—who might housekeep for me?"

Doña Sara looked at me shrewdly. "I may do. You don't strike me as the sort of girl who'd take this attitude without good reason. I think we need to have a talk, you and I."

The result was that Doña Sara found me a woman I liked on sight, and as Miguel had not been favorably impressed by Señora Ruíz's appointee I was able to pay her off and establish Señora Enríquez. That's one spy the less, I thought, then checked myself. Was pregnancy making me fanciful? I must be careful not to become as obsessed with the Ruízes as Miguel was over Sánchez.

Obsessed did not seem to be too strong a word when Miguel began questioning me about Don Alfonso. What had he seen of the house, where had he been, what had he done, had I ridden with him, what had he said? It was quite a catechism, which I answered as best I could, trying not to feel resentful.

"I think he is settling down, becoming less wild, and

better behaved," I told Miguel. "He said or did nothing to which I could take exception."

He shot me a swift glance. "I hope you are right," he answered. "I distrust the fellow when he behaves badly, but when he reforms I trust him even less."

The subject was beginning to bore me; besides, I had promised Tía Amalia I would not keep Miguel in ignorance any longer of our personal news.

"Let's not say any more about him," I said. "If it is convenient, Miguel, I should like to do some shopping tomorrow."

"That will suit. I will order the carriage for you. Is there much you need?" he asked casually.

"Quite a lot. There are things I must buy—now that I am pregnant."

As the words registered themselves his expression, for once unguarded, flashed his emotions to me. Surprise—delight—pride—and utter satisfaction. There was no doubt it was welcome news. He moved forward and seized my hands.

"Marta! This is splendid! You gave me no hint of it! How soon, *querida?*

"I am only just sure myself."

"And you are well?"

"Why shouldn't I be? I'm hardly aware of anything yet."

He was standing close to me, his eyes shining down into mine. My heart ached to love him. In any other circumstances I would have made this the opportunity to move into his arms, to hope that he was beginning to love me; but the face of India came before me, and the knowledge that mine would not be his first-born was bitterness in my soul. I could not stop my heart beating quicker at his touch, but no warmth came to my face and I began to draw my hands away.

"Marta, surely you are pleased? Don't all wives long for babies?"

"That I don't know," I said. "I suppose I am glad. I am hardly used to the idea yet, that is all."

But it isn't all, I was thinking. I will not invite fur-

ther humiliation by asking you to send India away, but
if only she and her child were gone we might still have
a chance of happiness.

Although Miguel had only left Don Gaspar that
morning he went off to Doña Sara's house as soon as
possible, trying not to look as if he was rushing away.

"He's gone to tell them the news," said Tía Amalia.
"Doña Sara would have to be the first to know."

"It's just like having a mother-in-law here," I com-
mented.

"She'll certainly assume that position," my aunt
agreed dryly. "As for Don Miguel, he's as proud as
a peacock."

"Proud for Valdoro, yes. He wants a legitimate heir."

My aunt came toward me and placed her hand
on mine.

"*Querida,* I know you're not happy. I didn't think it
was my business to say anything before, but now I
must. Don't let India spoil your marriage."

"There's very little to spoil," I answered.

"Oh come, Marta, you must be a woman, not a silly
girl. Men can do these things without considering them
important, and then regret the consequences. You
should be glad he is honorable enough to treat her
fairly."

"*Treat her fairly!* He does more than that, bringing
her into our part of Valdoro, taking her on his expedition, bringing her here—*caramba!* I wish he would
treat *me* fairly!"

"You must give him a chance. If you won't show
him affection, how is he to know you care? I am sure
he is fond of you—or why would he be so jealous?"

"It's Valdoro again, and his position. They mustn't
be threatened. I'm just a machine to do what is expected of me."

"No, *chica,* I don't believe that. He wants *your* child,
not just a legitimate heir."

But I was unconvinced.

The next day before going shopping Miguel said I

must call on Doña Sara again. "She wants to congratulate you," he said.

She wants to give me her instructions, I thought, remembering how she had exhorted me on the eve of my marriage.

When we entered the *sala* Doña Sara greeted me more warmly than she had ever done.

"So you've succeeded, child! You may kiss me. When is the baby due?"

I kissed the wrinkled yellow cheek and told her all she wanted to know.

"Now take my advice. Don't do anything silly, but don't overcoddle yourself either. Don't you agree with me, Doña Amalia, that the women who lie on a couch for six months are not the ones who have the easiest childbirth or the best babies?"

"I have always believed gentle exercise to be beneficial," my aunt answered.

Doña Sara nodded vigorously and showered me with advice and admonishments.

For a few days, while Miguel renewed contacts with the army officers and important civilians of Varena, Tía Amalia and I busied ourselves with shopping. For a first baby there would be so much to make, it was not too early to begin. And then Miguel told me, as I had secretly been hoping, that we would be going to spend a little while in Buenos Aires. I was glad it was early in my pregnancy; apart from slight morning sickness I was feeling fit, I could enjoy myself and no one would know. . . .

At first I could not believe Miguel was serious when he told me that from Buenos Aires he was sending me back to Spain. Even when he gave me his reasons I found it hard to credit, but such were his sober and considered intentions.

"You know, Marta, my plans for Valdoro," he said.

"For which you need a wife on the spot," I interjected.

"Indeed, yes. But everything I do is planned for the

future. You know, too, that I want an appointment under the Viceroy."

"Yes, though I am not sure what or why."

"Marta, I believe in this country, and I am working for it as well as Valdoro. I want power because I know how it should be used—and I want to keep out men like Sánchez who will abuse it."

"How does this concern me?"

"I am coming to that. Sánchez is one of a breed of self-seekers who come out from Spain with the sole intention of making money. With a man like him in office justice will be bought and sold, ability will count for nothing, men will bribe their way into posts, or any rank, and the *mestizos* and Indians will be treated as laboring animals."

"So you *do* care what goes on in the mines?"

"Of course I care!" he answered hotly. "But to try to do anything now would be like firing a pistol at half-cock. When I have office I shall know what to do. But the future is not built in one generation; my sons must carry on after me."

"Miguel, isn't it enough to plan your own life without trying to settle the lives of children not yet born?"

"In building a country one must look ahead. That is why you must go back to Spain until the child is born."

I was utterly bewildered, struggling to stifle the thought that now I was pregnant he was shuffling me off. *He has India. Always India.*

"But why? I see no connection."

"My son must be 'Peninsular-born.' Don't you realize the prejudice that exists? *Criollos* are never appointed to the highest offices."

I knew that *criollos* were people born in South America of Spanish parents, but it had never occurred to me that their birthplace could be a bar to preferment.

"I have never heard of that," I answered.

"I assure you it is so, and not only in civilian posts. Why do you think Don Gaspar with all his service and ability has got no higher than Colonel of Varena garrison and the Oro detachments?"

"I'd not considered it. I'm as ignorant of army matters as I am of politics."

"Well, that's how it is. And that is why my son must be born in Spain, so that he will have the best opportunities."

Miguel's single-mindedness, if that was what it was, seemed to me totally impractical.

"And you want not one son, but several, I gather?" I said flatly, as if producing them was like buying a box of tin soldiers.

"Yes, Marta, with God's help."

"And mine!" I flashed, with a tartness that seemed to surprise him. "I am astonished that you can be so drunk with your ideas that you cannot see facts."

"What facts?"

"If I am to produce sons for you I shall be spending all my time sailing to and fro between here and Spain. The result will be that I shall know every wave in the ocean and nothing of Valdoro. Who is to be in charge there? And do I leave children there while I sail off to produce another, or do they have to become little sailors as well?"

"Oh, *querida,* all that can be settled when the time comes!"

He took my hand and smiled at me. The thought of a family seemed to have made him tender.

"I thought we had to plan ahead," I retorted. "Besides, you have ignored the most elementary thing that can upset everything for you."

I drew my hand away and he stared at me, concern growing in his eyes. He thinks I am going to refuse him another child, I said to myself—and I would be justified, since he has an Indian bastard.

"And what is that?"

"If you insist, I suppose I must go to Spain to have the child. But then, what happens if it's a girl? You will have me going to and fro each time I'm pregnant—and they may all be girls—and you'll have no wife to organize Valdoro and no sons to succeed you. You might as well have left me here, producing *criolla* daughters for you to ignore."

He stared at me in silence. *Dios,* I thought fearfully. I have said too much. I have tried his temper too hard. It was foolish to strike out because he has hurt me.

"I am sorry, Marta. I have put matters badly. You must think I see things out of proportion." He began to walk about the room. "It isn't like that—I shall love and value them, sons or daughters. Give me one son born in Spain, one to work for this country for me, then we will see how to arrange our lives. Of course I don't want to send you to and fro, never to have you with me more than two or three months in the year. Of course I need you at Valdoro, but we are building a new land, a new life, and sometimes I look so far ahead that I don't see what is near me. So you must bring me back to earth. Very well, at the moment we must consider which is more important, the child or Valdoro. I want the child born in Spain— and when you come back with my son we'll work together on Valdoro."

I could have gone into his arms and said, "Yes, we will be a family, living and working for a new life." But at the back of my mind was the knowledge that, even at that moment there was waiting for him in my house an Indian mistress and a *mestizo* son. And all the time I should be away she would be there—and if I came back with a daughter . . . I could imagine her gradually taking over my place, myself returning to find in my room the colored petticoats she loved, her beads and peacock finery—and a little brown boy with black eyes staring while she laughed and jeered at me. "A girl—only a girl—a *daughter*—when I have given him a son!"

A wave of nausea turned me giddy. I must have paled and swayed, for Miguel suddenly put his arm at my back and said anxiously, "Marta—are you ill?"

"No—just a little faint—some water—"

He handed me to a chair. "Some wine will be better. Shall I call for your aunt—or send for the doctor?"

"No, no, it's nothing. It's passed already. I'm perfectly all right. I'll go to Spain—to have this baby."

And if it's a girl, I thought, perhaps I won't come back.

8

In no time at all, it seemed, we were on the ship for Buenos Aires. Doña Sara was of our party, and with two more *hidalgos* and their womenfolk all the passenger accommodation of the small vessel was taken. All the coastal traders available were sailing full, for the arrival of the mailship which brought us news, fashions and overseas supplies was a good excuse for the aristocracy to visit Buenos Aires.

During the three-day voyage I had time and opportunity for thought. Only now was I beginning to understand the man I had married. Doña Sara had been informative, and I now knew that Miguel's grievances against Sánchez were not imaginary. It was he who had started the rumor that the legality of Miguel's title to the Valdoro land was doubtful, and for more than a year he had been conducting a subtle campaign. If he could oust Miguel from the north-western part of our territory Sánchez stood a fair chance of buying enough influence to get title to it himself; then the *caciques* would be obliged to furnish him with a quota of Indian labor. At present he relied on virtual

143

kidnapping; if it caused trouble with the Indians or if Miguel tried to prevent it by force Sánchez would be well pleased, as he would then have reason to say the land was not at peace.

Miguel was in a cleft stick until his title was confirmed. It was easy for Sánchez to buy the help of unscrupulous men who had probably been responsible for all the delays and accidents at Valdoro before our arrival and since, for our presence there to hold the estate together was plainly unwelcome to him. It had been a great stroke of Miguel's to plan and carry out with army strength the arrest of El Alacrán, for once we were established at Valdoro with all our goods and supplies a raid would have been irresistible to him. I now saw the reason for the fortress-like appearance of the main building. I wished that Miguel had taken me into his confidence; but I realized not only his natural reserve but his unwillingness to alarm me prevented him from doing so. He needed to give me an impression of complete stability, his pride could settle for no less.

I was glad I saw the situation clearly at last, for emotionally I was in a turmoil. I am pleased to say that I did not seriously think Miguel was sending me to Spain in order to have complete enjoyment of his Indian mistress—that was not in his character—his reason was the one he had given me. But I was practical enough to see that it would give India opportunities she would be ready to take, and I knew Señora Ruíz's dislike for me was such that she would not attempt to restrain or discipline the girl. Sometimes I felt so hurt that I determined, once in Spain, nothing would induce me to return. I would hide in a little village and do the most menial work in order to keep myself and my baby from discovery. I was certain I had no real affection for a man who, although he could arouse in me such raptures of physical delight, was so calculating in his love-making, that he could swiftly transfer it to an Indian girl. It was nothing but a mockery of love. But when Miguel came and stood beside me at the ship's rail, to talk quietly of his plans to entertain me in Buenos Aires and of his hopes for the future, I would feel my love for him rising up within me, making the thought of separation quite unbearable. In spite of everything I still loved him.

The more I knew Miguel, the more I found his character full of strange inconsistencies. He seemed completely insensitive to my feelings where India was concerned, yet he could remember and redeem a promise lightly and jokingly made.

As soon as we were settled in Buenos Aires he sent for one of the best shoemakers.

"I wish you to make ten pairs of slippers," he said, then turned to me. "Choose exactly what you want; they are to be of the best—and do not forget that we hope to go dancing."

Ten new pairs! I had never dreamed of having so many at one time. I revelled in the luxury, decided for once to be quite unpractical, and chose to have four pairs of white satin ballroom slippers, three pairs of black kid for the house, and three pairs of *babuchas* for the bedroom. When everything was decided the shoemaker measured my feet and promised the first pair of ballroom slippers in two days' time. I do not think I had ever felt so frivolous before.

Buenos Aires was noisy, bustling, as gay as I remembered it, and to my delight we did not stay with Señora Alvarez but in a fine house in one of the main *avenidas*. This time my aunt and I were able to enjoy ourselves to the full. We were introduced into society and had invitations galore. But after several days two things still eluded us; the mailship had not reached the port, and we had not yet been requested to attend the Viceroy.

The mailship was overdue; it became quite a habit for the *hidalgas* on their morning drives to order their carriages to make for a spot in the *campo* outside the city where they could enjoy the fresh air and at the same time have a view of the sea and keep watch for incoming ships. Since Miguel usually spent part of the

morning at the Viceregal Palace, Doña Sara, my aunt
and myself were frequently among the carriage parties on the *campo;* my only regret was that I had to
drive rather than ride. Some of the ladies rode, but
without my husband to accompany me it would have
been considered improper behavior on my part, even
if Tía Amalia had been sure of its wisdom in consideration of my pregnancy. The latter did not bother me;
I would have loved to be on horseback, but for Miguel's sake I could not flout convention. Even so, without Doña Sara I might have found some of the mascu-
line attentions embarrassing.

Miguel had taken me riding once or twice in
Varena, formal rides at a time when exercise largely
gave way to the social occasion. There all the other
women riders had been middle-aged; officers' wives,
with something of the air of old campaigners about
them, who contrasted markedly with the delicate or
sensual-looking creatures in the carriages. These ladies
were fashionably dressed, and were busy shielding their
complexions from the sun with frilly parasols from
under which they darted curious or seductive glances.
In a short while Miguel had been surrounded by
riders, and although the men gathered round and
talked they spent most of the time looking at me in a
way that belied the formality of their greetings. Here
in Buenos Aires the carriage company was of the same
mold as in Varena, against whom I did not expect
nor wish to compete. And yet, as I sat with Tía Amalia
and Doña Sara, a succession of young men rode up to
greet us and kiss our hands. Dealing with my hand
seemed to take them longer than saluting the other
two, but I did not give way to vanity because I knew
it was their curiosity rather than their admiration.
They all wanted to know what sort of woman Miguel
Moural had married.

Inevitably, Sánchez appeared. On the fourth day
after our arrival he was one of a party of gentlemen
who rode up to greet us, but it was not until two days
later that I actually had any conversation with him.

The carriage was a roomy landau, yet with Doña Sara's stiff legs covered by voluminous petticoats and accompanied by her long walking stick like a series of ramparts in front of me I had no room to move, and I was feeling cramped and uncomfortable. (Doña Sara had insisted that I sit in front of her instead of Tía Amalia, so that she could talk to me more easily.) We had been stationed at our favorite vantage point for some time, and I could tell that if I did not move soon the chance would be gone and I would be condemned to an uncomfortable drive back.

"I have cramp, Doña Sara. I think I will get out and walk by the carriage for a few minutes."

With great indulgence Doña Sara, instead of arguing with me, called her little Indian page, the carriage steps were lowered and I was able to get down. With my parasol over my shoulder I strolled a few steps, better able to enjoy the light breeze which lifted my hair and cooled my cheeks. Doña Sara insisted I carry a parasol in case the direct rays of the sun affected me—at any moment I expected to hear her deep cracked voice ordering me, "Carry your parasol elegantly, Marta! You are not shouldering arms!"

A single rider came up to the carriage, greeted the old tyrant and my aunt, and then, dismounting, joined me.

Sánchez bowed low over my hand.

"Doña Marta, if you are walking a few steps, may I be permitted to join you?"

As I strolled on the short dry turf he moved beside me, his horse's reins looped over his arm, and made small talk. Then, surprisingly, he said, "Doña Marta, it is not difficult to guess why your husband is here. What will happen if he goes back empty-handed?"

"Happen? Nothing, I imagine. He will merely wait."

Sánchez's eyebrows lifted. "For several years? Is he so patient? There are not likely to be more appointments free for a long time."

I had assumed Sánchez meant the land rights, but he did not. I recovered myself.

"My husband is not so anxious for preferment. Don Alfonso."

He looked at me closely. "You are a loyal wife, Doña Marta. For your sake I wish your husband deserved your loyalty."

"That is not true, he does. And if it were true, I would still refuse to have anything to do with a person who said he did not."

I began to turn away but he laid a hand on my arm.

"Then I must retract. Forgive me. I should not have criticized." His voice became low and hurried. "It is simply that, caring for you as I do, it wounds me to see his blatant liaison with that Indian girl."

I stood still, hoping he would not see how the blood had mounted to my face. Why must he remind me of that?

"Don Alfonso, escort me back to my carriage."

"I am sorry. I offend you more each minute, but I only wish to help you. Doña Marta, your husband may not get an appointment. Then, if he takes you back to your *estancia* you will be completely cut off from society. On the other hand, I may well be given a post. In that case I shall be in a better position to help you. Please remember that. Should the situation become intolerable I should like to think that you would turn to me."

I was too amazed to interrupt him. When he finished I said flatly, "You are making a great many suppositions. I do not agree with them, and I do not intend to discuss them. And I would remind you that, although I am a newcomer, I am not friendless."

He looked at me soberly. "I understand, and beg your pardon."

I was amazed at the difference between his manner now and that of our first encounters. Surely this was prompted by a genuine regard? Though what he, or any man, could do for me if my life 'became intolerable,' I could not think.

"I am too eager, I know," he went on. "But I see you so seldom, and—please let me say it—you have become very dear to me. I thought that if you were lonely as I am lonely, we could console each other. I could help you without any obligations on your part. Oh, I know, you don't think of me as a lonely man, but the society of other men, riding, gambling, all the easy pleasures are only time-wasters, a poor compensation for the lack of real love."

I began to walk back, and said nothing. I was quite at a loss. I could have sworn his full lip trembled; I had never expected to see him moved with emotion.

"So you see, Doña Marta, there it is. You can order me not to speak of it, but you cannot order me not to love you. And I shall hope to see you again—discreetly. We shall meet at one or other of the balls, no doubt. Remember I am always ready to serve you."

We had nearly reached the carriage. I had been too disconcerted by Sánchez's conversation to look in that direction, and it was only then I saw the man motionless on his horse beside the open landau. It was unfortunate that the first time I had walked with or spoken to Sánchez was the one time Miguel had chosen to join us.

Sánchez acknowledged him, handed me up the steps, mounted his horse and rode off, leaving me to be firmly shut up with the two other women and guarded by Miguel who rode silently beside us, ramrod-stiff with disapproval.

* * *

Then, at last, one of Miguel's desires was gratified. He was granted a brief audience with the Viceroy, and we were both invited to the great Viceregal ball. To me this would be as much an ordeal as a pleasure, for beside it the Varena receptions paled into insignificance. I was thankful that Doña Sara was with us to coach me in all the formal procedure and protocol, and it was a blessing that my white gown was still in the height of fashion and had not been seen in Buenos Aires. With that and the diamonds I felt I could hold my own as far as appearance was concerned.

The splendor of the Viceregal Palace astounded me, and I had to be careful to appear unimpressed, to look about me without gaping like a simple rustic. The huge, splendidly decorated rooms opened out one from another in vistas of color and light. The brilliance of hundreds of candles was multiplied a thousand-fold by the cut-crystal drops of the chandeliers, and gleamed on gilded walls and polished floors, bright uniforms, metal accoutrements, gay gowns and sparkling jewels. In the supper room the white damask cloths were covered with dishes of gold and silver plate, crystal glasses and bowls of exotic flowers. Servants in impressive livery were everywhere, their white-gloved hands offering food and drink, retrieving dropped fans and relieving the guests of empty plates and glasses.

I knew the formal dances, and so was able to stand up and acquit myself well enough. But I was always glad to see Miguel approaching me if we had changed partners; the touch of his fingers clasping mine renewed my fragile confidence. In due course I was presented to the Viceroy and made my curtsey; Doña Sara had coached me well, and his looks and manner told me I had passed muster. The possibility of letting Miguel down had been an appalling prospect, and I breathed much more easily when the brief interview was over.

It was plain that Miguel was popular among the officers, who seemed to treat him as one of them; but I could not help sensing a touch of resentment among the men who were not in uniform. This could well have been due to the fact that many a wife did not disguise her admiration for my husband, glancing at him with smiles and coquetry. There was no doubt that he looked splendid in his court dress; his tail coat was of somber black but heavily embroidered in yellow, white and gold, and enhanced everything else—the white stockings, the knee-breeches of yellow silk and the white satin waistcoat embroidered to match the coat, above which were the ruffles and folds of white shirt and cravat.

For me, reactions were reversed. While the men did

not hesitate to show approval and admiration the women, when not greeting me with false smiles, were giving me looks which were curious and critical, some even hostile. I realized that I had incurred some enmity by marrying a sought-after bachelor, and had compounded the offense by being young, quite attractive, and more stylishly dressed than most. But since I was unlikely to move in their circles it was of no consequence to me.

Miguel had been cold to me since seeing me with Sánchez, but had made no comment, and I had thought that to mention the incident would give it an importance it did not possess, and any remark that might pass as an excuse would be an admission of guilt. I did not feel guilty. I had not encouraged Sánchez, nor did I intend to do so. He seemed sincere; he wanted me to think well of him, but with such a man what was his sincerity worth? It might be as ephemeral as his love affairs were known to be. I wanted nothing to do with him; I only wished Miguel could be convinced of that. But my modest success at the ball seemed to be pleasing Miguel. He did not appear to mind the general admiration the men showed me, and as we danced he gave me an approving smile.

"The worst is over," he said to me. "Now you can enjoy yourself."

"And I shall, if you are pleased with me," I said.

He looked surprised. "Does what I think make any difference to your enjoyment?"

"It makes all the difference."

"I am glad," he said, and smiled again. "Yes, I am pleased with you."

At last the ball was over, and we were in our carriage, rattling over the roughly-paved streets, and in the light of torches which flared intermittently through the windows as we rocked through the night I could see Miguel leaning back and watching me.

"So Buenos Aires had seen my wife," he said smiling. "And half of Buenos Aires approves."

"Half?" I queried.

"The male half," he replied. "Most of the women are jealous—jealous of your youth, your freshness, your beauty."

"I am not beautiful!" I said, amazed. "And you have never called me so before, not in that way."

"Have I not? I expect I thought, in such a business-like marriage, you would not wish to be courted."

"Courted? That depends . . . not if that means paying flattering insincerities. But every woman likes a compliment now and then."

"I am sure you had plenty tonight. But you must not let them go to your head. The men here are very practiced at playing on a woman's emotions to get their own way with them."

His lips curved in a cynical smile, yet his eyes were still kind. The wine I had drunk had gone a little to my head, and I felt clever and daring, capable of much more sophistication than normal.

"You mean," I said, "that they might try to seduce me."

His look was stern and direct. "I mean precisely that."

I played with my fan. It was time he realized that even a wife deserved a little attention.

"That might be quite amusing. I think I should like to be seduced. Of course, I should not give in."

He leaned forward and deliberately cupped my face between his two hands.

"You are being a silly little girl," he said. "Don't you know the whole point of seduction is that the woman must give in, sooner or later?"

He was bending over me, his head close to mine, I could feel his breath on my cheeks and see the glitter of his eyes in the chiaroscuro of torchlight and dark.

"The conquest is important," he went on, "for it is the consummation of all the delightful and passionate preliminaries."

Then his mouth was on mine, hard and possessive, taking my breath away. I gasped as the kiss ended, and his voice was low but firm, almost harsh, as he said, "So

you would like to be seduced? Then remember this—
you are my wife, and no man touches you. You are
mine."

His hands slid down from my face to my shoulders,
slipped under my cloak so that they were warm on my
bare flesh. He was drawing me towards him, and my
heart was beating fast—but the carriage slowed down,
rocked to a stop, and we heard the coachman dismount
and hammer at the door. We had reached our lodging.

I still felt excited, even a little light-headed as I went
upstairs. So in spite of our outward coolness to each
other Miguel was not indifferent. I knew that in the
cold light of day I would suspect his reactions to be
mainly prompted by his personal pride; but tonight—
tonight I could let myself be deluded that he found me
attractive, that he cared a little.

My maid helped me to undress and was brushing my
hair when Miguel came into the bedroom. He was
wearing his dressing-robe, and without his splendid
clothes he still looked just as handsome, with a casual
charm.

He signed to the maid to leave; she put down the
hairbrush, curtsied, and went out. I heard the door
close quietly behind her as I gathered my hair together
ready to plait it. Miguel took my hands in his.

"Leave it loose," he said. "It is beautiful."

He shook it over my shoulders, then drew me to my
feet, put his arms around me and held me close to him.
His fingers ran through my hair, drawing it away from
my neck, and then caressed my throat, my shoulder; his
lips showered me with little questing kisses; as his
hands caressed me more intimately my blood began to
pound. I felt my limbs melting. My body ached with
longing as his kisses became more passionate. He lifted
me on to the bed.

"I am the man to seduce you," he whispered.

9

The very next morning we heard that the mailship had been sighted. But it was evening before it anchored in the roads, and we knew they would not begin to unload until the following morning. We spent the day in mounting anticipation, for apart from the hope of Miguel's title deeds there should be letters from home. It was nearly three months since I had heard from my family.

The next morning a servant was sent to the port office to find out when they expected the mail to be unloaded, and we all breakfasted and awaited his return. He came to say the mail would be coming off very soon, as there were important dispatches. Miguel sent for his horse and prepared to leave.

"I shall go straight to the port office and collect our mail from there," he said. "At the same time I can book your passage on the return sailing. It is a good comfortable ship, and the sooner you leave the better."

I knew it was my pregnancy he was considering, so it was foolish of me to suspect that he wanted to get rid of me, but I had a sudden feeling of desolation, and I knew I would rather live with him and accept his faults, even tolerate his mistress, than be parted from him.

Two hours passed, and at last he returned with a large package of mail.

"Is it there?" I asked.

His eyes were shining with hope.

"I think so. I couldn't open it there."

Of course, the mail would have to be accepted soberly and opened in private. But among the letters one stood out. It was large and sealed with the most elaborate seal that I had ever seen. Silently I handed Miguel a paper-knife. His face was pale as he opened it and began to read. Then I did not need to ask him— his look told me that all was well.

"It's confirmed, isn't it?" I cried. "Is it all the territory—all you should have?"

He put the paper into my hand. "Yes. All Valdoro. All that is truly mine. At last I have a title that no one can dispute." He smiled. He was satisfied, assured. "Now we can look at the rest of our mail."

It is strange how, when one's affairs are going well, one never visualizes the possibility of any set-back. So it was with me. I had the joy of letters from home; relations between Miguel and myself were warmer than they had been for some months; even our parting would have the compensation of reunion with my family; and when I returned with a child surely Miguel would welcome me with affection and put his mistress aside for good? I felt happy and confident.

That evening we were going to another ball, this time a private one. To add piquancy to the occasion our hostess had decreed it should be a masked ball, and this, I thought, promised to be delightful. Such affairs were touched with informality, and the anonymity of masks, however easily pierced, gave license to frivolous conversation and to statements of affection that would not otherwise be possible. One could say almost anything—and avoid the consequences if one wished. So the atmosphere was always particularly gay.

Miguel wore a dark blue coat and yellow waistcoat

and breeches, only slightly less splendid than his court
dress, and a small plain mask of black satin; I thought
he would be easily recognizable by his height even with
a more concealing mask. I wore a new gown, an under-
dress of ivory satin covered by fine floating silk in pale
apricot banded under the bust with crystal beads. My
mask was of apricot satin with little feather wings; only
the color of my hair would be likely to betray me, and
this I partly disguised with a scarf of silver gauze.

When we arrived everything was in full swing, and
we joined the dancers. Without introductions there was
freedom to dance with anyone, and one partner after
another led me on to the floor; some I was acquainted
with, others I was reasonably sure I had never met.
There was one of whose identity I was sure; I recognized Sánchez the moment he came up to me. His
curled hair and full lips betrayed him, although he was
wearing an elaborate mask of silver with a large gold-
sequinned teardrop on one cheek. He danced with me
and paid me the customary compliments. As was also
customary I replied somewhat coquettishly in a disguised voice. It was silly but amusing. Later in the evening he danced with me again.

This time he said, "What must I do to convince you
that I love you?"

"Nothing," I said. "I will accept your declaration tonight, and forget it tomorrow."

"That is not what I want," he replied. "Remember it.
It is true. That is why I wear a mask with a tear—to
show you I am weeping because my love is hidden and
unfulfilled."

"The teardrop, *señor enmascarado,* is as false as
your protestations," I retorted.

"No," he insisted. "Some day you will find the truth
of it. When you are alone and need a protector, I will
prove it."

I was startled out of my flippancy. *"When . . ."*

"Why should I be alone?" I caught at my self-
possession. "Señor, I will let you into a secret. I am a
married woman."

"Adorada señora, I am desolated."

We danced on. Then, he drew me closer to him and murmured, "At a masked ball one ignores marriages. You have been unattainable, but tonight I shall forget that. I shall delude myself that before the night is out you will be in my arms, and we shall be exchanging kisses."

"I have no control over your delusions," I said as the dance ended, "but I can govern the realities."

"I shall still hope, *bellísima.*"

Miguel was close by and I turned to him. Sánchez bowed and moved away.

"Was he bothering you?" Miguel asked.

"No. We exchanged the usual masked frivolities, that was all."

I was beginning to feel a little tired, and refused the next request to dance.

"I think it is time you rested," Miguel told me. "Come to the supper room and I will get you a glass of wine."

The ante-room opening off the ballroom was cooler, and I sank gratefully into a chair while Miguel went to the buffet. I sat fanning myself, thinking what a delightful evening it was, and hardly noticed at first that a group of men had strolled in to stand talking just inside the ante-room by the open ballroom door. Then I realized they were discussing the ladies—and not very discreetly.

I did not wish to eavesdrop, and was thinking of showing myself when one of them said, "As for your russet-haired witch, I agree, she is a charmer. I quite envy you. She's not long out from Spain, I believe? She has the freshness of one only just released from family protection."

With a dreadful sinking sensation I realized they were talking about me. Now I could not show myself. Instead I tried to hide behind a display of poinsettias. Another voice broke in.

"And the eagerness, too, I dare say. These young girls, when they're away from parents and priest, can be very rewarding—even when they have a husband. Two men are not too many."

Somehow I got to my feet although my legs were trembling. Then I heard Sánchez's voice.

"And I don't concern myself with husbands."

They all laughed.

"But you must admit," another voice went on, "that he's less of a fool than some. He'll keep a close eye on her. Tell me, how do you propose to manage?"

"Why should I tell you?" Sánchez retorted lightly. "There are always ways and means. I was with her not so long ago in ideal conditions."

"So you've done it! You sly devil—how *did* you manage it?"

I heard a step and turned. Miguel was crossing the room, and behind him a footman with a tray and glasses. Miguel on seeing me must have thought that I was near fainting, for he came quickly to me and gave me his arm. As he did so Sánchez's voice reached us, clear and lazily insinuating.

"I spent several days with her at the *estancia*— Valdoro—in the absence of her husband. It was fair enough, I thought. After all he was away with his Indian mistress."

Miguel handed me into a chair, strode to the doorway, caught Sánchez by the shoulder and dragged him round to face him. He snatched off Sánchez's mask, then his own.

The rest of the group fell silent and moved back, falling into a semi-circle behind Sánchez. In the background the music still played. I could see the moving colors of the dance, but here the deadly quiet became a palpable thing. From what I could see of Miguel's face he was very pale, while Sánchez's face was flushed with guilt and wine.

"You will tell these—*gentlemen*—that you are a liar," said Miguel in a voice that had an edge of steel.

It was a moment before Sánchez spoke, and then he was deliberately off-hand.

"I'll do no such thing. What I said was true. I stayed

at Valdoro in your absence. There's no deyning that.
Do you object to the mention of your mistress?"

Miguel's jaw clenched. "You made an implication
concerning my wife. You will retract it."

"*Caray!* Am I to be accountable for implications?"
Sánchez laughed. "You must have good reason to be so
sensitive."

Miguel's eyes blazed. Then he turned to the other
men. "See that this peasant does not leave. I shall be
back directly."

He brushed past them and walked quickly towards
the hall. I sat there feeling utterly lost in my isolation
and cold with the horror of it all. What was Miguel going to do?

"I do believe he's gone for his seconds," said one of
Sánchez's companions. "You'll fight, of course? He
called you a peasant."

"Of course," Sánchez said venomously. "He's a good
shot, but if he challenges me I can be a better."

"In your own way, *amigo*. A little anticipation, perhaps? Yes, I dare say you'll pull it off."

A wave of terror engulfed me. A duel—with an unscrupulous man like Sánchez, who, it seemed, was prepared to fire before the command. Miguel might be
killed, all for a few scurrilous remarks. How could a
man be such a fool to risk his life like that? Then, remembering what Sánchez had said to me, I wondered.
Had he planned this encounter? No, that did not seem
possible; but he was ready to profit by it.

At last one of the men turned towards the ante-room
and saw me. He had the decency to look a trifle shame-
faced, and I sat there, frozen, trying to appear brave
and confident. Then they drew together and whispered
among themselves. I could not move.

Quick steps clicked on the tiled floor and Miguel
came up to them and stood, his hands behind his back,
waiting silently for Sánchez to face him. Sánchez
turned and smiled insolently.

"Move in," Miguel ordered, and Sánchez strolled
into the ante-room as if humoring a child.

"I do not duel with my inferiors," Miguel told him icily, and raised his hand. It was only then we could see he held a whip.

Sánchez's expression altered in an instant to startled horror as the whip flashed up. He put up an arm but was not quick enough. The lash descended across his face and I heard him scream. Then he turned away, crouching, his arms over his head, and Miguel brought the whip down with all his force across Sánchez's back. Once—twice. The young man was groaning at each stroke. I counted eight blows before Miguel stopped.

The dancers by now were crowding round the doorway, and inside Sánchez was huddled, still groaning, with blood running down his face. Shocked looks, excited questions, each turning to the other in speculation. Our host pushed through the guests.

"Gentlemen, whatever is going on?" he demanded.

Miguel bowed to him. "I apologize, Don Lucas, for the disturbance. But when a dog misbehaves it has to be beaten—at once." He thrust the whip into the hands of a startled footman. "Give that back to the coachman. And order my carriage." He took me by the arm. "Come, Marta. We are leaving."

Everyone stood aside as we went out. My shawl was placed on my shoulders and we walked towards the main door. I was hardly aware that as we reached the head of the steps a young officer came running up them. He saw us there, with the guests talking excitedly behind us, and said with some surprise, "So you've heard the news?"

I was dazed, but not so Miguel.

"What news," he asked.

"About the war," the young man answered.

An elderly guest nearby asked sharply. *"What* war?" and the officer looked round at all the interested faces.

"So you *haven't* heard? The peace is finished—we're at war with England again!"

Miguel looked at me. "That's no concern of ours," he said, and handed me into the carriage.

* * *

Buenos Aires had plenty to talk about the next day. But only one thing was concerning me: I was dreadfully afraid that Sánchez, consumed with rage as he would be over last night's incident, would challenge Miguel to a duel. After hiding my anxiety for some hours I finally asked Miguel if he expected a challenge.

"No," he said. "Sánchez's friends will prevent him. He would not invite the further indignity of a refusal. An *hidalgo* does not duel with a peasant, and although Sánchez has married into one of the best families a peasant he remains. To have the reason for my refusal made public would be a further humiliation which he cannot afford."

He will be a worse enemy than ever, I thought, and a dangerous one since he has no standards.

During the day an officer called; and we all discussed the war news. It was no rumor; the peace was ended. Spain had joined with France in the war against England.

"I'm not sorry," said Captain Romero. "Personally I would welcome some action. Life's been dull recently. But I don't suppose we'll see any here. One is so remote in the Americas and I expect the English fleet will be tied up in European waters."

"Why does Godoy think we have to support Bonaparte?" asked my aunt waspishly.

"He's just over the Pyrenees—perhaps Godoy considers he'll make a better friend than an enemy," Miguel answered.

"Bonaparte is nobody's friend but his own." Tía Amalia retorted.

"The point is, why should we be drawn into war with England?" said the captain, to my surprise. "We should be able to choose for ourselves, and we should be governing ourselves, without reference to policies at home."

"*Caray,* captain!" my aunt exclaimed. "If you were not an officer I would be suspecting you of being a revolutionary."

"Oh, no, señora!" he replied. "I am as loyal as any

man. You'll find no treason or revolution in me. But
government from Spain is becoming impractical. We
have to wait weeks—months—for any change of policy, any instructions to reach us on international affairs,
and as for our own business, what do officials in Madrid
know of our life, our conditions out here? Of course
we owe allegiance to the King. I would not wish to alter
that, but I think we should be in charge of our own
affairs."

Miguel nodded. "There are many people who think
the same. I believe it will come, in time, but meanwhile
Godoy dictates policy, the King approves—and we
pay the taxes. A great deal goes to Madrid that could
be better spent here."

The men went on talking, but I paid little attention. I
had my own situation to consider. We were at war—
and I could use the fact to my advantage.

I waited patiently until the captain had left, and we
had dined. It was a good dinner, and I made sure
Miguel had a bottle of his favorite wine. Then, as he
sat sipping his brandy I brought out my sewing—a
gown for the baby—and started my campaign.

"Miguel, have you thought how the war will affect us
personally?" I asked, as casually as I could.

"In general terms, taxes will be raised again, no
doubt. There will be delays and difficulties over supplies from Spain, but that should not bother us—we are
well equipped."

"I wasn't thinking of that. Have you—have you
booked my passage to Spain?"

He looked surprised that I should even query it.

"I have reserved an excellent cabin for you and your
aunt."

"But is that wise, Miguel? Surely the English fleet
will be watching for our ships—and merchantmen
make good prizes."

A mere flick of his eyelids showed me the thought
was new to him.

"Our combined fleets should be able to keep the
English busy," was his comment.

He was delaying, considering.

"But there are always privateers, Miguel."

"True. But our merchant ships will now be going in convoy. There will be too many for a privateer attack."

His male ego would not allow instant capitulation, but I could see he was worried and pressed my advantage. A little womanly weakness would not come amiss, I thought.

"Miguel, I am nervous of going." I hoped Miguel would not see the incredulous leap of Tía Amalia's eyebrows, and hurried on. "Everything will be so uncertain. At best, there is bound to be a delay while a convoy of ships assembles, and we will be kept to the speed of the slowest ship. A few weeks here, with a slow passage, and I shall be in danger of having the baby on the high seas." He pursed his lips and suppressed a nod of agreement. "At worst, we might be caught in an engagement—a cannon-ball would be no respecter of passengers—and if the ship were captured and taken to an English port—if the shock didn't bring on the birth earlier, your son would be born, not in Spain, but in England."

I clutched the baby's gown in my hands and looked gravely anxious, as if suppressing a dozen fears.

His eyes were so full of concern that I was almost ashamed of my guile.

"You are quite right, *querida*. I should have thought of that. You must stay."

I told myself I had no need to feel guilty. Miguel was only thinking, Better a *criollo* son than an English-born baby. But even that was irrelevant to me, for I had achieved my object. I would not have to leave Miguel.

The next rumor that reached us was that the Viceroy was speeding up the settlement of Crown Appointments. In view of the war situation he did not wish to leave Buenos Aires on any tours of inspection, so it was most probable that the new appointments would be made quite soon. Miguel did not comment on this but I knew he greatly wished for a post so that he could put some of his ideas for the betterment of the province into practice. I myself was quite confident he would have some position, for how could they pass over a man of such outstanding ability and with such a knowledge of the Indian tribes?

But everything was topsy-turvy; I had another shock. When the appointments were announced there was nothing for Miguel—Sánchez was made Controller of Taxes for Oro Province!

10

There was no point in staying longer in Buenos Aires. We had the title deeds, which was the most important matter, and so we sailed back to Varena.

"After all," I said to Miguel, "if you had a crown appointment you would be torn between administering for the benefit of the public in Varena and organizing your own *estancia* affairs at Valdoro; and even you cannot be in two places simultaneously. As it is, you can establish Valdoro as you wish it to be run and then, in a few years' time when it is going smoothly, a post may come along for you and you will be free to give your time and thought to that."

I had never before ventured an opinion on Miguel's affairs. I spoke spontaneously and was then nervous of his reaction.

Miguel nodded slowly. "That is a sensible, practical way of looking at it," he said. "My trouble is, I am ambitious and impatient. I see things that need doing and itch to get my hands on them. And seeing fools bodge them rouses me to fury."

Until recently I had not thought of him as a man of

quick anger, but I now realized that normally he had such great self-control that he did not betray himself when a lesser man would do so. Constantly I remembered the scene at the private ball. Every detail would return so clearly, and I found myself shuddering at the recollection of the whip cracking on Sánchez's back and I could still hear his groans and see the blood on his face. It was a dreadful thing to have done—and yet —what man worth his salt would have allowed such insults to his wife and himself to pass? There was no doubt that by the standards of our society he was more than justified. It seemed extraordinary to me that the same man could be such a tender lover.

I guessed that once we were back in Varena Sánchez would take every opportunity to use the power of his new post against Miguel, but about this Miguel seemed unconcerned. He was too proud to discuss the appointments with me, but Tía Amalia, who heard most of the gossip, said that the general opinion was that Sánchez had bribed and ingratiated his way into the Viceroy's favor.

"In fact," she told me, "they are saying that coming after the beating the appointment is 'slave and court-plaster'!"

So it seemed we were to settle back into domesticity. Miguel had vetoed my return to Valdoro; he said that the baby was to be born in a civilized fashion in Varena, and that Doña Sara would find me the best midwife. By this time I was convinced the child would be a girl, and I dreaded the disappointment she would be to everyone save myself.

We had an uneventful passage in spite of the rumors of English ships approaching our waters, and I was glad in due course to be driving in our carriage from the harbor past the barracks to our house. Happily, I thought, I was free of Señora Ruíz. I had my new housekeeper, I was mistress in my own house, everything should go well.

As I entered the hall on Miguel's arm Señora Enríquez came forward and curtsied her greeting. We exchanged a few words. Then from the shadows at the end of the hall a figure moved out and came into the light. With the smoothness of a wild animal India rushed forward and threw herself to the floor, her black hair falling to the ground as she clutched Miguel's feet.

"My lord—my master—at last you have returned," she whispered.

In no time at all, it seemed, Miguel was off again. I had hoped that our relationship had improved, that he would keep aloof from India and spend more time with me, but I was wrong. We were hardly inside the house before he was closeted with her for an hour or more, and I grudged her every minute. I would not let myself think what was going on, but I had seen her look and her smile of greeting as he raised her to her feet, and that had been enough to tell me she desired him still and intended him to know it, in spite of her apparent humility. And what chance had I in my condition against a girl so exotically beautiful and with such unbridled sensuality? As far as I knew Miguel had no wish to resist her, and for him our happy time in Buenos Aires had been no more than an interlude. My fears seemed confirmed when he told me he was going inland with a military patrol, and that India was to go with them.

When the morning of his departure came I insisted on getting up to see him off, early as it was; they were leaving at first light. The room was lit with the ends of last night's candles as he came to say goodbye, and the desolation of parting swept over me.

"I hope not to be long away," he said. "A few weeks, no more. I must renew my contacts with the *caciques* after my absence in Buenos Aires. Meanwhile, I leave you in good hands. Your aunt and Doña Sara will look after you."

"I know that, Miguel. But . . . I wish I could go with you."

He gave me an indulgent smile. "You know that is not possible, *querida*. But I will soon be back, and then if all goes well there should be no more expeditions until after the baby is born."

"If all goes well? What does that mean?" I asked.

"Nothing at all! Just a superstitious proviso! Now, I must go."

I expected just a formal kiss, but to my surprise he put his arms about me, held me close and kissed me long and passionately. Love surged within me and my lips trembled and softened under his. I clung to him until he raised his head.

"Take care of yourself, *querida,* and of my son."

As he left the room a candle guttered and died in a pool of wax. How appropriate, I thought. He is the candle that lights my life, and however fitfully he burns, my life is dark without him. Then I heard the clatter of hooves and the clink of accoutrements, and hurried to a front window. I flung open the shutters and gripped the cold bars of the railing watching as the military rode past. Then I saw Miguel riding with a young captain, a couple of baggage wagons, and India on a mule, her baby slung in a poncho. As she passed, India turned and stared at me expressionlessly. Miguel had not seen me; my heart went cold again.

With Miguel gone I had little to do or think about beyond planning for my baby and waiting for his return. Out of courtesy I was obliged to spend more time than I cared for in Doña Sara's company—she visited me frequently and I had to return her calls. But there was some compensation; I found out that she was extraordinarily knowledgeable about general affairs in the Viceroyalty, and I learnt much from her which I hoped might be of use to me as Miguel's wife. She was scathing about Sánchez's appointment as Controller of Taxes.

"It will simply be another way of lining his pockets," she said. "People will bribe him to lower their assessments—he'll favor his friends and his enemies will be taxed to the hilt."

"But surely someone will notice if the taxes are not fairly applied?" I asked.

"What an innocent you are!" she retorted. "Do you think the real payments will be entered? There are plenty of clerks who will make false entries when their jobs depend on it. They get their cut as well. No, for Sánchez it's a golden opportunity to even a few scores and make a profit at the same time. Wait and see what happens when it's Miguel's turn."

"Can nothing be done about it?" I asked.

"With pretty-boy Sánchez in favor at the Viceregal Palace? Impossible! No, Miguel will have to grin and bear it. What we need is an *intendente* who'll root out corruption—and a fine chance we stand of getting that."

"Why do you say that?"

"Because *intendentes* don't care. An *intendente* must be Peninsular-born. So he runs the province for the benefit of Spain. We should be running our own affairs for our own benefit."

I was reminded of the officer in Buenos Aires.

"So you think we ought to be governing ourselves?"

"Of course we should! What do they know in Spain about our conditions? The best positions here are filled with *chapetones,* while the *criollos* who know the country are kept subordinate."

I noticed that she had used the contemptuous term "*chapetones*" for the Peninsular-born Spaniards, and remembered that her son was a *criollo,* and that even in the army his promotion had been inhibited.

"Miguel is a *chapetone,*" I said. (And so was I!)

"Miguel is different! He knows the country better than most of the *criollos.* He's the sort of man the country needs—he cares about the Indians, although they're no danger to us now; he knows the *mestizos* and the way they're educated enough and resentful enough to foment grievances—and he gets on with the *criollos.*"

"That's as well," I said. "Our child will be a *criollo,* thanks to Bonaparte."

If an *hidalga* can snort, she snorted.

"I don't suppose you'll suffer as I have for that," was

her downright retort. "Times are changing. They must change. The Crown can't make our policy and fix all appointments indefinitely. Another generation will be given a free-er hand—or will take it. Meanwhile men like Miguel must do what they can. And women like you ought to help them.'

"How can I help Miguel in such matters?" I asked, surprised.

"By being a bit more tolerant of his position, for a start!" she said sharply. "There's no need to stand on your dignity and look disapproving every time he goes off with the Indian girl."

Anger began to rise in me. "Isn't there? I consider I am quite justified in objecting to her, and her position in my household."

"Oh, hoity-toity!" the old lady jeered. "Can't you put your tongue to the word? It's high time you admitted he's like other men! Surely you know by now that married men have mistresses?"

My heart thumped and I gritted my teeth, pausing for control before replying.

"I did not think that a gentleman would keep his mistress under the same roof as his wife."

She did not turn a hair.

"For Miguel the situation is different. And for the wife, what's the odds, when she knows the facts?"

"At least one can ignore—at times—what is not constantly under one's nose. I can never get away from it," I responded, as coolly as I could.

"I suppose you wouldn't feel as badly if it wasn't for India's baby," she said shrewdly. "Though really it makes no difference—or won't, if you're sensible."

"What do you call 'sensible'?"

"Do you wish me to speak plainly?"

"I have no doubt you will," I retorted, with a sharpness I would not have dared to show a few months ago.

"Well, somebody must. *You're* going to give him a child; if it's a boy, don't use it as a weapon. Don't say to Miguel, 'There's the son you wanted, but you'll have no more unless you give up the Indian girl.' He won't be blackmailed."

I must admit that such a thought had crossed my mind, but I had dismissed it. All the same, surprise at her acuteness kept me silent.

"You might hurt yourself with that stroke more than you would India or Miguel. Perhaps you haven't considered that raising children is not always easy, and here there can be extra difficulties. One is not a good number to lose from; if you consistently refuse Miguel your bed you may find yourself through accident or illness without a son at all. It would be folly to estrange yourself from him." She fixed me with her sharp black eyes. "You wouldn't want him to legitimize India's boy?"

I must have gaped at her like an idiot.

"You hadn't thought of that? It's been done in the past, you know. Quite famous men have legitimized their Indian bastards without marrying their mistresses. There's no reason why it couldn't be done again."

"Your warnings are quite unnecessary, Doña Sara," I blurted out. "I am Miguel's wife, and I intend to remain so, in every respect. But you cannot expect me to tolerate the Indian girl."

"That is what you must learn to do. Then the more children you have the less of a threat she is to you."

Such talk sickened me. *Por dios,* let me have one child first, I thought, before planning a quiver-full for me.

"I respect your intentions, Doña Sara. But you must leave me to manage my own affairs."

"It's Miguel's affairs I'm concerned with," she snapped, putting me in my place. "He's not a man to lose his head over a woman, but I think he could be fond of you if you could learn to handle him. Then he might not always want India as a mistress. But he'll still need her for the *estancia,* which is why I'm telling you to tolerate her. You'll never get rid of her."

I was so amazed that Doña Sara could see the possibility of Miguel finding some affection for me that I did not stop to ask why he should need India for the *estancia*. She did nothing that could be called work, even in the house. If there was any chance of his caring for me, perhaps I had not quite lost the battle. Then I caught a gleam of such malice in Doña Sara's eyes that I wondered if she was making this up to unsettle me. But why should she? She had no reason to dislike me. No, she had given me a great deal to think about. If I stopped fighting, and gave India best, or took the wrong action, and Miguel legitimized Juan Bautista, how intolerable my station would be then.

On Miguel's return his first words were to enquire about me and the child. I asked him about the expedition and he said it had been satisfactory.

"I must go and see Gaspar as soon as I have changed," he said.

I hid my disappointment. I had thought that, for the first evening at least, he might be satisfied to dine with me. But no, he had to see the colonel. I said nothing, and sent servants to take hot water upstairs.

Some time later, when I knew he would have bathed and changed, I went to see whether his saddlebags had been properly unpacked and the dirty linen taken for washing. I entered the bedroom. The dressing-room door was open, and I could see and hear everything. Miguel was standing with his back to me, in breeches and shirt-sleeves. India faced him, her arms copper-brown beside the white cambric of his shirt as she held him in a fierce embrace.

"My lord!" I heard her say. "Come to me tonight. It is time we made another child—and I can please you, you know that well. Only come to me. . . ."

He did not answer at once, and in that instant India must have sensed my presence, for she looked over his shoulder and our eyes met. Quite shameless she did not move a muscle, but still clung to him. I came forward.

Miguel heard my footsteps and turned, drawing her arms from about him. His look was more of hurt than guilt; I suppose, I thought angrily, I am to blame for intruding.

"Leave us, India," he said.

Then I saw in the far corner her poncho was spread, and on it Juan Bautista was lying, kicking his plump coffee-colored legs. So now she brought him to my room. In a little while he would be running all over the place; while my child lay in her cradle India's boy would be everywhere, fussed and spoiled as Miguel's bastard. And India wanted more. . . .

"Do not concern yourself about me," I said to Miguel. "I can see that it is not enough that she has had you to herself day and night for weeks on end. If you both want more bastards do not hesitate on my behalf."

I turned and left the room, feeling that I was choking.

A little later Miguel ordered a fresh horse and left without a word to me. The butler told me Miguel had left a message that he would dine with Don Gaspar in the barracks, and would probably be late returning. Very late, I thought, and wondered in whose bed he would spend the rest of the night.

During dinner Tía Amalia informed me that, through Señora Enríquez, she had heard the servants were full of gossip that an English ship had been sighted. But there was now no sign of it, and when I asked my housekeeper about it she said the general opinion was that it had sailed off again. I dismissed it as a silly rumor; some excited girl had probably imagined the whole thing.

When the attack started I did not at first realize what was happening. We both looked up when we heard a distant booming sound, and when this was repeated we still gazed questioningly at each other with no thought of danger. A few moments later Señora Enríquez rushed in.

"Doña Marta! Doña Marta!" she gasped. "There is

an English ship in the bay, and it is firing on the town! You can see the flashes from the front window!"

"Caramba!" cried Tía Amalia, and we picked up our skirts and hurried to one of the outer rooms. There were several house-servants there—the maid must have called them from the servants' quarters—and they shamefacedly drew back as I appeared.

"I was just closing the shutters, señora," said the little Indian maid, "and I saw a flash out to sea, there—"

We looked in the direction she indicated. It was quite dark, but the moon was rising and no doubt the white buildings of the town would be visible from a ship beyond the harbor. The English must be attacking the fort: they would have to silence the guns before they could enter the harbor, presumably to plunder us. As I gazed out on to dark sea and sky there was a sudden orange glow, then another booming noise. I thought I heard something more—and then I saw a spout of water leap up in the harbor, catching what little light there was before it fell.

"That was a cannon-ball in the harbor!" my aunt exclaimed. "Let's hope they don't improve their range on the fort!"

There was a pause, another flash and boom, and this time I distinctly heard a strange whistling noise followed by a splintering crash somewhere in a street behind us. At last I came to my senses.

"Get downstairs, everyone!" I ordered. "It's not safe up here, we might have a ball through the roof. Señora Enríquez, go and tell the other servants. Tía Amalia, take them all down to the cellar. We must stay there until the firing is over. Go on, I'll follow you."

Now they had realized the danger they could hardly get down fast enough.

"I'll call them out of the kitchen wing," said Señora Enríquez, a little flustered but still self-possessed.

I took my time going downstairs, refusing her offer to stay with me. When I was half-way down she suddenly turned back from the bottom of the stairs.

"What is it?" I asked.

"The Indian girl!" she said. "I have just remembered —she is in her room in the attic."

I waved her back. "I'll get her."

"But, señora—"

"I'm all right." I had already turned. "See to the others and get them to the cellar. I'll come with India."

I hurried up the stairs, more aware than usual of my weight and clumsiness. I reached the top passage, and went along it, calling her name.

There was no reply. I had lost count of the cannon balls which were booming away with an intimidating regularity, and now, thank heaven, being answered by our guns. There was another boom, and this time a terrifying rushing sound which grew louder and louder. It could not have lasted long but it seemed interminable. Then there was a hideous splintering crash and another duller one. The house shook violently and there was a sound of falling debris. I rushed to the attic room which India had taken and flung open the door. It was a shambles.

A ball had crashed through the roof and found its way out through a corner of the room. The lamp in the passage gave enough light for me to see a gaping hole torn in the brickwork at the angle of two walls, while splintered roof timbers hung down crazily and the air was full of plaster dust, and held a smell of scorching. In the middle of it all India knelt, moaning hysterically, her hands to her head. There was a trace of blood—she had probably been struck by a falling tile which had cut and dazed her, for there were shards nearby.

I caught her by the shoulder and shook her.

"Get downstairs! It's safe in the cellar!"

She did not move, and I pulled her up and pushed her to the door.

"Get on! Get downstairs!" I repeated firmly.

She took a few steps while I looked about the room, then turned.

"My baby!" she cried.

"Yes, I'll get him," I told her.

I had only just seen where the boy lay in a dark corner near the window. Then, in one moment, it seemed we were at the mouth of hell.

The whole earth seemed to shake, the house rocked, windows blew in and the rest of the ceiling fell upon us. At the same time there was a tremendous roar and a brilliant red light which suffused everything inside and out of the house. I distinctly remember seeing through the hole in the wall people in the street below being lifted from their feet and flung to the ground. When the red brilliance subsided I heard over the dying roar falling masonry and cries from the street. I said to myself, "At least I'm still alive," and wondered at the faint orange glow which flickered in the distance. I ignored India moaning and screaming outside the door. Where was the baby? I found that I was on my hands and knees, and began crawling among the rubbish towards where the child had lain. There were roof joists criss-crossed in front of me, and when I moved one a shower of plaster fell on my head. Then I heard the child cry.

It was a wonderful feeling, to know that life, at least, was there. Gingerly I crawled nearer, careful how I moved anything in my path. It took a long time, but all the while the little boy cried, his sobs becoming louder and more insistent. Either my eyes were growing accustomed to the conditions, or the light was increasing in the room. At last I saw him between two beams, his blanket covered with dust and plaster, his face screwed up and his fists flailing—apparently unhurt. Then I could see that a roof timber and some laths from the wall were making a kind of tent under which he lay, and the timber was holding up heaven knew how much of plaster and tiles which at any moment might shift and fall. Somehow I had to get him out without disturbing the props above us.

He was more than six months old, and a thriving, vigorous youngster. I crawled nearer, talking quietly to him, put my hand out and stroked his brown arm.

He bellowed at me, his face clownish with white plaster-dust dark-streaked with rivulets of tears. I went on talking and worked my hand under his shoulders, trying to get enough purchase on his chubby body to draw him towards me. But there was too much rubble and wood in front, and with great care I began to remove the joists which were barring my way. I must have a clear passage, however small, to pull him out, there was no room to lift him anywhere. By now I was lying on the floor.

I heard my aunt's voice outside. "Marta! Marta! Where are you?"

"Here, Aunt," I answered quietly.

"*Ah Dios!* Are you hurt?"

"No, I'm not hurt. I'm just getting the baby. Don't come in—"

I could hear her draw in her breath as she looked through the door.

"*Ay, querida!* Come out. Let me do it—you must not—"

"Stay where you are," I told her. "Two of us going to and fro might bring everything down. I've got to pull him out slowly."

With the greatest care I tried to move a joist, but as well as supporting a great deal of rubble, it was wedged firmly, and would not give way. With the next one I had more success. I drew slowly on it and another pile of rubbish descended on the baby and myself. A lump of plaster had fallen on my back, weighing heavily on me, but it had to stay there. But now I could reach the child, and get my arm properly underneath him. I began to tug him towards me inch by inch. He was not co-operative. He screamed and wriggled, kicked and waved his arms. I managed to pull a blanket with him and rolled him in it. He hated this too, but better for him to have his face in the blanket than be in danger of being choked and blinded by falling plaster.

Inch by inch I edged myself and the baby to safety, praying that the roof would not collapse on us. At last I gained the side of the room near the door where there was space to straighten up. I got to my knees, lifted Juan Bautista in my arms, and brushed the pieces of plaster from his face.

My aunt was behind me. "Give him to me."

I passed him over, struggled to my feet and followed her out of the door. Gimeno, our *mestizo* butler, appeared behind her.

"Take the child to India," she said, and passed him the howling bundle.

"The señora—?"

"I'll see to her."

My aunt put her arm around me. "Can you walk, *querida?*"

"Yes, I'm all right, thank you. There's nothing wrong with me."

"Dios, no!" she said grimly. "Only five months pregnant, under cannon-fire and risking your child crawling around a shattered room."

It was not until that moment I thought of the danger to my own baby, and began to shake. But she said no more, and helped me down to the cellar.

Having herded the servants out of sight she sponged and bandaged my cut and bruised knees and hands and told me, as she did so, that it seemed the great explosion was caused by an unlucky cannon ball falling into one of the gunpowder stores of the fort. One of our menservants had looked out and said the place was on fire, the soldiers divided between trying to put out the flames and return the fire of the English ship.

And Miguel? Now I had time to think a dozen different fears caught at me, making my heart thump sickeningly and the sweat start to my forehead. Miguel had almost certainly been dining with Colonel Guzmán —and in that case would have been with him when the attack started. He would have stayed at the fort; if he had been near the explosive store. . . . You can do no good by thinking about it, I told myself. My baby—was it safe? I felt in a wretched condition, but the child might not be affected. I must carry my baby,

I must have something of Miguel . . . I must not think about it.

I ordered some bottles of wine to be opened and each of the servants to be given a drink, enough to hearten them, but a strict ration so that none of them had the chance to get drunk. I was glad of a glass myself.

I wanted to send a servant to the fort for news of Miguel, but I had no right to risk another life. Besides, I should hear bad news soon enough; with no news I still had hope. The firing seemed to have stopped. Gimeno went upstairs and reconnoitered through a ground-floor window. When he told us the attack seemed to be over we all trooped up. The ground floor was very little damaged; most of the shutters had been closed and had blown in, and broken glass was much in evidence; otherwise the rooms were habitable. After all the firing it seemed very quiet outside.

I was wondering whether it was safe to go to bed when I heard a new sound. Distant at first, it grew slowly louder, and seemed composed of shouts and cries, crashes and a kind of general confusion. I looked at my aunt. She too was listening. Gimeno appeared, his lined brown face and dark eyes anxious.

"Señora," he began, "can you hear—"

"Yes, what is it, Gimeno?"

"I think, señora, it is a riot. There are always people who will take advantage of such a situation."

What a fool I was, not to have guessed.

"I see. Then will you make sure that both the outside doors are bolted and barred, and all the shutters on this floor wedged back into place? Nail wood across them if necessary. Is there anything else we should do?"

"That is all we can do, señora. It should be enough. But—the señor Don Miguel . . . ?"

"Without news of him we must believe he is helping Colonel Guzmán at the fort. I dare say he will stay there until morning. Please hurry and see to the doors."

He bowed and left us. I was thankful to have an old

manservant I could trust. I had learned enough of the Viceroyalty to guess that the *mestizos* more than the Indians might cause trouble at times when they thought we had our hands full. Some *mestizos* bore a grudge— to some extent justified, I thought—and they were more sophisticated, more knowledgeable, and more active than the Indians.

The night seemed never-ending. At intervals we could hear the mob which seemed to be ranging up and down the streets, breaking windows, battering at shutters, entering houses where they could, possibly plundering—and worse. That was something else I tried to avoid thinking about.

As far as possible I turned the house into a fort. I kept myself busy by touring every room on the ground floor and having all vulnerable windows barricaded. All those accessible from the street had iron *rejas* as well as shutters; one hoped to keep marauders out of the patio. My precautions were necessary; there were three separate attempts to break in, but our barriers held. I checked the windows on the next floor, made sure that the most agile climbers could not enter or even throw anything into the rooms. When there was nothing more that I could do I let Tía Amalia persuade me to lie down on a sofa in the *sala,* and pretended to sleep. I may have dozed a little, but I seemed all the time to be aware of the fluctuation of noise and quiet, of smells of burning, and of Gimeno moving to and fro on self-appointed sentry-go.

The lamps died down, the candles guttered, and at last it was gray dawn. As it became light I ordered the cook to make coffee and give a simple breakfast to everyone. I felt exhausted and appallingly low in spirit, but I was determined not to show it. I did my best to eat and drink, spreading the yesterday's bread liberally with conserve to help it down. The coffee was good.

I set about getting some order into the house. We heard more trouble in the streets, noises and firing, but it turned out to be a party of soldiers dispersing the last of the rioters, and after that everything was quiet. I was just deciding it might be safe to open up the house when I heard knocking at the door. I waited, knowing that Gimeno would first open the grilled hatchway and see who was outside. Then I heard the bolts being drawn, and my heart leapt with hope. But perhaps it was only a messenger. . . . I clutched the back of a chair and held my breath. Miguel came into the room.

I stood there, too relieved to move or speak. I had never seen him in such a state, though he had made some attempt to improve his appearance. His clothes were filthy, torn and bloodstained, and his face and hands must have been quite blackened with smoke and dirt for they were gray and streaked where he had tried to wipe them clean. There was a cut on his jaw and others on his hands, but otherwise he seemed unharmed.

He came forward and caught me by the hands, and I could smell smoke and gunpowder on him.

"Marta! Praise God—I thought you might have come to harm—if only I could have left before."

"What happened, Miguel? Are you all right?"

Then he saw my bandaged hand.

"*Ay, querida!* What—"

"It's nothing. What happened to you?"

"A number of soldiers were killed, and others injured when the store blew up—poor devils—but since Gaspar has too much sense to allow all the explosives to be in one place we were able to keep on firing at that damned English ship." He looked at me anxiously. "You are sure you are well? No harm to the child?"

"I am well. Go on—"

"It's only by the grace of God!" Tía Amalia interposed. "She should be in bed, resting, after all that—"

"Don't fuss, Tía! Go on, Miguel, what happened?"

"We don't know what the English were after—to reduce the fort, certainly, perhaps make a landing—they had no hope of coming in unnoticed—but though they got their blow in first they took too long to get our range, and our guns had a couple of lucky hits. It was too dark to aim well at the ship—and we disabled her. She had to pick up her skirts and run for it."

He looked at me closely. "I agree with Doña Amalia. You are very pale. You must go to bed."

All at once I was dropping with exhaustion; I let myself be persuaded; I went to bed and slept.

With all the sensational affairs of that night you would have thought my pulling India's baby out of the rubble would have been passed over, but no, to my embarrassment people remembered and made far too much of it. Miguel felt obliged to thank me, and was even more embarrassed than I, though he covered this with the cool formality I now realized was his mask for all unadmitted emotions.

"India has asked me to thank you for what you did. To risk yourself in that way was noble, even though it was foolish, and I thank you too."

Foolish to risk your unborn child to save your first-born, I thought. Perhaps, if one had stopped to think.

"There was nothing else to be done. It was a child's life—one doesn't stop to consider anything else. India was not fit to get him out, so I did."

"She is truly grateful. You saved her too, and I thank you. Her safety—their safety—is important to me."

"I know."

If that remark of mine was unnecessary, so was his, I thought bitterly. I saw him bite his lip.

"It is not the way you think. She is a chief's daughter—ah, Marta, I should have explained it to you long ago—I suppose it was foolish pride that prevented me, but it is not the way you think."

"No?"

"She has been my mistress, I admit that—but even so, I do not feel I was entirely culpable—"

"I am sure you do not."

How clever men were at making excuses for themselves, I thought. I was suffering from reaction against the events of the previous night. I still felt sick and exhausted, and I could not bear to discuss a subject which was so painful to me.

"Please do not say more," I said to him. "I know why you married me. It was a bargain, a business-like marriage, you called it—and I shall try to keep my side of it. Beyond that, as long as you allow me to keep my dignity I will not interfere with your personal affairs. They are no concern of mine."

He looked at me, and once again his eyes seemed more hurt than ashamed. How unfair men could be!

"If that is how you feel there is no point in explanations. I had hoped that by now you would have felt it mattered enough to ask me or Doña Sara—but if you do not care, then I suppose it is unimportant."

Unimportant! As he left me, half of me wanted to call him back, to ask him what else there was for me to know; but the other half said: I can't bear it; she has had everything that matters—his interest, his comradeship, his love, his son—everything I may never have. I must put up the barriers, stop myself from being hurt any more, and concentrate on making the best of my part of the bargain.

11

The house had suffered considerable damage, and the combined effects of the bombardment and the explosion followed by the rioting had reduced a number of other buildings to a similar or worse state; over a much larger area most of the houses had lost windows and roof tiles. Doña Sara had been lucky; although quite near the fort her house had been protected from the blast by intervening buildings, and had only suffered superficially with the loss of a few windows, tiles, and some plaster. The services of builders were at once in demand, and it would be some time before our house could be repaired; meanwhile living there would be at best an uncomfortable business. As soon as she heard of our state Doña Sara insisted that we all moved in with her.

I did not view the prospect of a prolonged stay under Doña Sara's roof with unmixed pleasure, but I accepted gratefully. Bearing with her autocratic ways and busybody habits would be a small price to pay; to offer us hospitality was a most kind action, and for all

I knew she might find my disposition as irritating as I found hers.

As it turned out, living with Doña Sara was not as difficult as I had expected. Perhaps it was my pregnancy that made her mellow towards me; she even went so far as to compliment me on my reactions to the attack, saying that for someone with no experience I had got the house into a defensive state with satisfactory speed and efficiency. Someone had been telling her a fine tale, I thought.

"You didn't lose your head, and you took the right action," she said. "You'll make a good wife for Miguel yet, if you work at it."

From her that was praise indeed.

One benefit of living with Doña Sara was that I shared in all her callers. In this way I got to know Varena society better, and was kept in touch with all the gossip. There was one meeting I would have given much to be able to avoid; sooner or later I was bound to be confronted by Doña Isabel, Alfonso Sánchez's wife, who was a regular visitor to Doña Sara's. They had much in common, notably a keen intelligence and a fearless tongue, such qualities which might have made them cross swords but which in fact made allies of them. In addition, Don Gaspar, when he was at home, found Doña Isabel good company, appreciating her wit and brilliance. He himself was a charming man, though quite ugly, being broad-faced, short-nosed, with one side of his face badly scarred. He possessed a pair of eyes as black and shrewd as his mother's, which in his face looked like shiny boot-buttons, while his hair was short, stiff and as wiry as a yard broom.

I have noticed that it is one of life's inequalities that while men never consider a woman charming unless she is pretty, a lack of looks is no hindrance to male attractiveness, and ugly men frequently seek, and succeed in getting, the attentions of the best-looking women. Don Gaspar was the exception in that he did not seem to need to compensate for his own lack of looks by acquiring a beautiful companion. In fact he treated the pretty, flighty types with indifferent politeness, and soon ran out of small talk; with Doña Isabel he would have a discussion when the occasion presented itself, to the satisfaction, it seemed, of both parties. Sometimes I wondered why Don Gaspar had never married: he was a dedicated soldier, but no misogynist.

A very few days after our move to Doña Sara's, I heard Doña Isabel announced, and braced myself for the meeting. In view of what had passed between our husbands I expected her to cut me, and was prepared to accept the situation with what dignity I could muster. To my surprise she greeted me very pleasantly, inquired after my health and hoped I had not come to any physical harm through the bombardment. I assured her I had not.

"And did your house suffer much damage?" I asked.

"Mercifully, no," she answered. "Some of the windows blew in, but even so we escaped with a cut or two between us. My old father was wonderful. He is very frail, you know. It would not have been surprising if he had succumbed with shock, but it only made him angry and he spent his time shaking his fist and cursing the English!"

I was quite astonished when, a little later, she said to me in a confidential tone, "I hear that your husband has taught mine a much-needed lesson. I am glad their enmity does not mean that we must be bad friends."

"I am so happy that you do not hold it against me," I answered quickly. "I do not see why their differences should concern us."

"No. And I admit the bad blood has all been of Alfonso's making. The man has a genius for alienating decent people. Your husband did a public service in thrashing him, though he will certainly have made more trouble for himself by so doing."

I did not know how to answer her, and she threw me a quizzical look and continued.

"There is no need to look so surprised! One may as
well be honest. Everyone knows that although I
thought I loved him when I married, I soon saw him in
his true colors. Now I heartily detest him. Because I
was a gullible fool I am permanently saddled with
him, and must put up with it. But I do not have to
participate in his feuds."

"That is good of you, Doña Isabel."

"Not at all. I have few enough friends, why should
I reduce their number because of Alfonso's quarrels?
And now I will give you a warning, although I expect
it is unnecessary. Alfonso never forgets a slight, much
less forgives it, and the humiliation he suffered at your
husband's hands is something he will be determined to
repay. His new position will give him great power to
strike at your husband financially, but apart from that,
I would remind you to be on your guard, for no action
would be too mean or cruel for him."

I had hardly stammered out my thanks before we
were interrupted, but I did not forget what she had
said.

At that time Sánchez was still in Buenos Aires, but
he returned shortly afterwards, and it was my ill-luck
to meet him in the street a few days later.

I was walking with Tía Amalia in the Plaza Mayor,
where we had some trivial business. It was a busy
morning, and the arcades around the square were
thronged with people. My aunt and I were talking together and I did not notice Don Alfonso until we were
nearly upon him. I would have preferred to avoid a
meeting, but it was too late, and in view of the insin-
uations he had made to his friends in Buenos Aires I
did not intend to show him any signs of friendship—or
of fear. So I looked him full in the eye, and gave him
no smile or acknowledgement.

He flushed—whether in shame or anger I could not
tell—then as we were almost level with him he spoke
my name.

I paused and looked back at him, and he went on
speaking, his voice low, his manner intense.

"The insult your husband gave me has not made you less desirable. But it has rid me of any feelings of mercy. I warn you that I intend to strip your husband of everything he has, starting with his money. When he is a poor man he will have to ask me favors. He can send you, and perhaps we will come to terms."

Now I could see the blood had risen to his face with anger, and not only anger; resentment, greed, jealousy and lust—they were all there.

There was a hot fury inside me at his insolence, and I retorted, just managing to keep my self-control, "My husband will never ask you for a favor. And if you make him poor in money, you will never make him poor in spirit. As for sending me, he would sooner die!"

I saw another flash of fury in his eyes, and then he smiled. It was the smile of a man gloating over his thoughts.

"It may come to that, Doña Marta."

He bowed, and walked away.

I felt profoundly disturbed, and could see that Tía Amalia was pale with anger and fear. I told her we could have expected nothing less from Sánchez in the circumstances. The best thing we could do was to forget it. Sánchez had always been one to boast of what he might do; but his performance rarely reached the level of his prophecy.

And yet I could not forget it. Nevertheless I kept my own counsel, for to tell Miguel would serve no useful purpose and would only increase the chance of more trouble between him and Sánchez. Then, in a little while, I had another more immediate problem with which to concern myself.

I was alone in my bedroom one morning when India came in with an armful of Miguel's shirts, freshly ironed. She made a great business of putting them away in the press, and then instead of leaving the room she stood looking at me. I turned to her in some surprise.

"Your baby—it comes in three—four months?" she said.

"Yes," I agreed, thinking: What business is it of yours?

"It is a long time. A long time for Don Miguel to stay here. He will want to go to Valdoro."

"That is for Don Miguel to decide," I answered, determined to keep my temper.

"You will see, he will go. And he will take me. When I had my son it was in his house, with him there. You wait. You will have your child not in his house, he will not be near you. He will be with me!"

"I cannot stop you imagining that," I said coldly. "But Don Miguel will decide."

"Yes, he will decide—to be with me! Always he wants me, and while you have your baby, he will be with me! Perhaps it is then we shall make another baby, he and I!"

She smiled triumphantly at me and left.

I sat down feeling physically sick. She was so sure she had Miguel's love—would she never be satisfied until she had ousted me? One thing was plain, I was having no success with her. She was more firmly entrenched than ever. I could not get rid of her, and if I was not careful, she would soon be lording it over me in my own house. I had thought to keep my position by holding myself aloof, but I had failed or was in danger of failing. It was time I took action. But whatever I did it would have to be most carefully considered, or I would antagonize Miguel as well and ruin everything.

How much did India really know? I wondered. Was she guessing that Miguel would not want to be so long away from Valdoro, or had he already said something like that to her? I burned at the thought that he might be staying with me out of duty, and that she was receiving confidences I did not share.

It was not long before that suspicion was apparently confirmed. A soldier brought Miguel a letter from Valdoro, one which he read quickly with every sign of dissatisfaction. Then he tossed it on to the table and said, "That Ruíz! He is too tight-lipped by half! He writes me a letter and tells me nothing."

"Is anything wrong at Valdoro?" I asked.

"I believe not. The building progresses slowly—he says; the fields are being worked—he says; the *vaqueros* are caring for the cattle—he says. But not a word more."

"What more should he have said?"

"Something about the movements of the Indians—whether there is any hostility between tribes; if the *mestizos* have been stealing cattle or horses—anything that gives the feeling of the place."

"I see."

Then, more to himself he went on, "It is four months before the baby is due . . . ?"

"Nearly that."

"Four months. More than four months before . . . "

"Before you return to Valdoro?" I supplied the words.

"Yes."

"If you are not happy about it there is a way you could keep in better touch."

"I should be glad to know of one," he replied grimly.

"I have been thinking, Miguel," I said. "We are still constantly having rumors of English ships in our waters, and another bombardment is not impossible. It it not as safe here as we thought." That was true, up to a point. "In addition, it will be months before the house is repaired, and four months is a long time to trespass on Doña Sara's hospitality."

"What has that to do with Valdoro?" he asked, a frown creasing his brows. "You are surely not suggesting that we return there? That is impossible for you until—"

"Until after the birth, yes. But there is no reason why we should not move inland. If we took a house in Platinas you would be nearer to Valdoro, and much more in touch with affairs in the area."

"Platinas . . . "

He was actually considering it.

It was true that Platinas had been no more than a

mining settlement, but with the development of the
mines a town had grown up, and there were now many
good houses and a fairly large Spanish population,
quite enough for it to be a comfortable little town with
such facilities as we would need. The fact that
Sánchez's mines were there was not likely to affect us.
They were managed for him and he had little to do
with them and now he had a crown appointment his
visits would be even more scarce. He would be busy
giving himself airs in Varena.

"Platinas . . . " Miguel murmured again.

"You would be only about two days' journey from
Valdoro." (As if he didn't know that!) "Besides, it
might be better for me to make the longer journey now
and the shorter one to Valdoro after the birth."

If I make it look as if he is doing me a favor it might
work, I thought. If he must go to Valdoro then I prefer
not to be so far from him. Platinas would be much
better.

"That is a good idea," Miguel said. "I'll think about
it."

He did more than think about it. He set inquiries
going at once. The result was that he himself went to
Platinas—without India—and in a very few weeks we
were ready to leave Varena for a house he had rented
there.

The night before we left I had a private talk with
Doña Sara. Miguel's words to me, that he had thought
that I would have asked him or Doña Sara about India had stuck in my mind, and I decided that if
there was anything more for me to know this might
be my last chance of finding out, for I could not bring
myself to talk to Miguel about her.

I waited all evening for a private moment, but none
came, so in the end I let her go to bed and then
stopped the maid who was taking her her posset and
carried it in myself.

I remembered the night before my marriage. The
room, full of shadows, looked exactly the same, with

the old lady perched in her bed like a night-capped hawk in the circle of candlelight.

"Oh! So it's you! What do you want, Marta?" she asked sharply.

"A little talk, that's all, Doña Sara," I said, placing her posset cup beside her.

She shot me a suspicious look, lifted the lid, stirred the contents and took a spoonful. Silence. Another spoonful.

"Well, what is it, girl? What do you want to talk about? Miguel, I suppose."

"In a way, yes," I said, as calmly as I could. I was determined not to let her intimidate me. "I want to know what you can tell me about India."

"India? What's there to know about her? It's all pretty plain."

"How did she come to—to join Miguel?" I asked. "I was only told that Miguel saved the life of a *cacique's* son, and the chief gave her to Miguel as a servant in gratitude."

She gave a short dry laugh. "A *servant!* Only an innocent who knew nothing of the Indians would believe that! Yes, the chief gave her to him, a life for a life—but not as a servant! The *cacique's* daughter! As an Indian wife, of course."

"I see," I said slowly. "And Miguel accepted her—as that?"

"Accepted? What else would he do?" She laughed again. "What else would he want to do? She's beautiful in her own way, she's got a fine body, and the Indian girls, so I'm told, are passionate and clever at pleasing a man. He's not a monk, why shouldn't he enjoy a woman?"

I sat there, choking down my disgust. He was married to *me*, I thought—to *me*. The deep cracked voice went inexorably on.

"Besides, he knew what would happen if he didn't. If he'd refused her, or if he'd taken her with him and kept apart from her, it would have been a deadly insult. The Indians are used to the idea of Spanish men

having Indian women when their white wives are not
with them. Such an insult—and he would have had
them at his throat in no time. They'd have been everywhere, stealing his cattle, killing off his *vaqueros*, burning his fields—burning Valdoro if they could. There
would have been no peace, no *estancia*." She sipped
her posset and smacked her lips. "No, he did well. He
got the peace he wanted, and a lovely Indian mistress
into the bargain. And you must learn to live with the
situation. He's not going to insult the *cacique* by sending her back now. And why should he want to? He
has no reason."

"I suppose not," I said stonily.

"Oh, no," she said, and I could hear her gloating
over me. "He has everything to gain by keeping her.
Peace—a lively bed-mate—and her help when he
needs her."

I clenched my fists. You horrible old woman, I
thought, you are deliberately tormenting me. I must
keep calm, let her talk, and without knowing it she
may say something that matters.

"What help?" I asked.

"Don't be a ninny! Miguel speaks one or two of the
dialects quite well, but he needs her as an interpreter."

"Why? He can talk to the tribes near Valdoro."

"There are others—farther afield—the army has to
know."

The army! At last something dawned in my mind.
I remembered how he had gone to and fro with the
patrols, with India; how on his return he had gone
straight to the fort, perhaps not just to wine and dine
and to enjoy himself—perhaps to give information.
Somehow he and the military had always been hand
in glove, even before I came. Wasn't the scar on his
face the relic of some campaign?

I gripped my hands together to stop them from
trembling, and looked Doña Sara full in the eyes.

"Perhaps you will tell me," I said, "how long Miguel
has been working with the army as a spy?"

"Not as a spy!" she burst out hotly. "He is—"

Then she realized that I had trapped her into an admission, and rattled her spoon in her saucer with irritation.

"There is no need for dramatics, miss!" she went on. "Very well, you've guessed it. They rely on him for a lot of information, but he isn't a spy. He's fought with them too, unofficially, but that was against the Portuguese, when they were trying to push out their borders at our expense. That's why he needs her as an interpreter." She looked sideways at me, and her eyes glinted maliciously. "But that makes no difference. He's lucky to have a mistress who is also an interpreter, that's all. That way she can always be with him—no doubt it makes his expeditions more enjoyable."

Why couldn't she leave that alone? Why was she always trying to make me feel as if I weren't good enough for Miguel, as if I failed him in one way or another?

"It's time you were used to running in double harness with her," Doña Sara croaked. My gorge rose at the revolting expression. "You ought to be like her —give him what he wants, and don't ask questions. There's no woman fit to claim him exclusively. He's a fine man. There aren't many of them, men like Miguel and Gaspar."

I stared at her as if I was seeing her for the first time. And so, in a way, I was. In one flash of insight I was seeing her, not as the terrifying old autocrat who kept me in awe, but as an old woman of whom I was no longer afraid. It was as quick as that. I no longer feared her, for she was just a possessive, jealous old woman, as I was a possessive, jealous young one. I found my voice.

"Miguel's like a second son to you, isn't he? He's Peninsular-born, which your own son isn't, but he helps Don Gaspar, giving him news, so that makes it all right. Whoever she was, a wife of his, a wife who might win some of the affection that you want for yourself—would be a rival. Oh, you were right. He married me for Valdoro, and to have an heir; he is ambitious, but not so ambitious that I couldn't have aroused a little fondness in him if I had really tried. But there was India. She was always a thorn in my flesh, and that suited you, didn't it? You wouldn't let me forget. You intended that she should always come between us. Perhaps she will. But, thank God, I've seen your game at last."

For once she did not answer back, but stared at me in silence, her stricken look telling me that I was right.

"Good night, Doña Sara." I said. "I will say goodbye to you in the morning."

12

There were times during the journey when I almost regretted having instigated the move to Platinas. Previously when we had travelled it had been in good weather, and we only had to contend with dust and heat. But this time there was rain; every day, it seemed, we had a downpour, and though they were of varying duration, each time the riders were soaked and the road turned into a rubble-strewn morass. Going was slow and difficult; the ground had rarely dried out by the time we made camp, and although everyone endured the situation stolidly and without complaint it was not conducive to comfort or lightheartedness.

On the third day I thought of something which could be done to help, and during our mid-day break, there having been as yet no rain, I gathered up such twigs and dead branches as I could find and put them in the back of one of our wagons. During the afternoon the heavens opened, and I thought that, thanks to my foresight, we would be able to start a fire more easily than before.

We broke for camp in the evening; I slipped on the wooden-soled clogs I had bought in Varena to keep me above the rubbish of the streets should I need to walk; and I went to the wagon to get my little store of dry wood. To my amazement it was not there. But of course someone—India probably—had already taken it. I looked around. A man was striking flints over a little pile of tinder, but the twigs beside it were all new gathered, wet. Then I saw India watching me.

I felt the old anger at her rising in my throat. I went up to her.

"What did you do with the dry wood, India?" I asked.

She did not even bother to pretend ignorance.

"I threw it away. I am the one who looks after my lord."

I clenched my fists to stop myself from shaking her.

"Then I suggest you do so. In future you may collect dry wood each day ready to make the fire when we camp."

She drew herself up proudly, resentment showing in her face.

"I am a *cacique's* daughter. I do not collect wood."

I was sure her position in her tribe would not have precluded that action, but I was not going to argue with her.

"Do not behave like a child, India. I do not mind who collects the wood, I simply want a fire made quickly. You make a fuss about caring for Don Miguel's comfort; then either collect the wood yourself or leave it alone when I do so. Now, which of us will collect wood tomorrow?"

She looked at me long and sullenly. "I will. I care for my lord."

The next evening she produced a large armful of dry twigs, and a fire was soon started. Miguel came up and stretched his hands to the little blaze.

"That's good," he said.

India smiled at him. "It is because I collected wood

when it was dry, and put in the wagon," she told him.

"That was clever of you, India."

"I shall do it each day."

"Splendid. Then we shall have a quick fire each day."

I cannot pretend that I was noble and forbearing.

"You would have had one yesterday if she had not thrown out the wood I collected," I said tartly.

Miguel shook his head despairingly and did not reply.

I had been surprised when Señora Enríquez had asked whether I would like her to go to Platinas with me. Since she was more than willing to do so I was glad to have her. My aunt and I found her congenial and hardworking, and I greatly wished there had been hope of her replacing Señora Ruíz at Valdoro, but that seemed impossible. She would certainly ease our life in the rented house at Platinas.

I was sorry that her first experience outside Varena was of such an uncomfortable journey, but she did not let it bother her.

"I can imagine what it would be like in good weather, and even now, when the sun shines it is quite splendid to see the open country," she said cheerfully. "I have nothing to grumble about. In the carriage we are dry—unlike the poor men on horseback."

And so, between rain and sun, soaking or steaming, we reached the few cabins at Puenterojo. I explained to Señora Enríquez the lie of the land.

"You see, this is where the river bends," I said. "It flows in from the west, and that way lies Valdoro. The house is on the edge of the great pampa. We shall follow the tributary and travel north-east—Platinas is roughly as far in that direction as Valdoro is in the other."

"Do you know Platinas, Doña Marta?"

"No, I have never been there. I am told it is very small, but pleasant enough. I dare say we shall manage to put up with it for two months or so."

I was very glad to get there. I had developed a heavy cold, and was quite feverish when we arrived, so I made only a quick inspection of the house and allowed Tía Amalia to put me to bed. And there I stayed for several days. Miguel seemed concerned at my illness, and would come two or three times a day to see me; but in order not to disturb me he slept in another room. I thought I was more likely to disturb him, but agreed it was a wise proceeding.

While I suffered from the fever I had strange dreams, and sometimes was so confused that I hardly knew what I had dreamt and what was reality. One evening Miguel had visited me; I lay tossing in bed and could not talk to him properly, so he said he would not tire me with conversation, wished me recovered in the morning, and left me to try to sleep. He drew the curtains around my bed so that the firelight should not disturb me. I sank into a kind of sleep. Then I seemed to be dreaming; I did not know where I was but I could hear voices.

"You should not be here."

That was Miguel's voice. I tried to answer, but could not speak, and another voice replied to him.

"Why should I not? I wish to be with you."

"Not here—not now."

"Then come to me. It is so long—always you have some reason not to come. But it is time—time for me to please you with my body—time for us to make another son. . . ."

Always those nightmare words in India's voice . . . and rustling sounds . . . and . . .

"You see, am I not more beautiful than before? Why will you not come? Come tonight. . . ."

"No, not tonight. She is ill. It is not right."

"Not right! And when she is better, it will be something else. . . ."

"India, you must go."

I struggled to release myself from the dream, to move my heavy limbs, to call out, and after an age I heard a gasping cry and knew it came from my throat.

Then with a rattle of rings the bedcurtains parted and Miguel was bending over me. I stared at him, panting, incapable of speech, hardly able to move as his arm went out, came under me and lifted me to him.

"Miguel, I dreamed—" I moaned.

"Hush, *querida,* hush. You had a nightmare. It's all right, you'll be better soon."

"Is she here?"

"Who? Tía Amalia? No."

"No. India. Send her away—send her away—"

"India is not here. Come, have something to drink. You must not get excited. It was only a nightmare."

I let him put the glass to my lips and then settle me back on the pillows. I did not know how much had been dream, how much reality, but his presence reassured me and eventually I slept. The next morning I was a little improved, and thought that it must have been a nightmare. But I could not be sure.

A week later I felt recovered. But I was fairly far advanced in pregnancy, and it was not easy to be comfortable in bed. Miguel thought it best for me to continue to sleep alone, so he no longer shared my room. I knew it was sensible for us not to disturb each other, yet I could not help feeling lonely and unwanted, solitary in the large room, enclosed, isolated in the great bed. And Miguel—was he alone? I could not ask. But I did not trust India.

The first Sunday after my recovery I went to Mass in the great church of Platinas. No one had prepared me for the sight of Nuestra Señora de las Minas. It had been built and furnished by the mine-owners out of their profits, and I came to look on it as one of the great ironies of our Spanish civilization in the Americas—a viewpoint, I must admit, which few people in our society shared.

As we approached it across the square it looked fairly typical—a huge baroque building, large for so small a town, more extravagantly decorated than some churches of the same period, but not so different that it gave me any warning of what lay within. We passed through the great door and stepped inside. I was expecting the customary gloom relieved only by candles faintly illuminating areas of gray stonework and dark wood, touched here and there with painted color and gleam of gold. I could not stifle a gasp of surprise as I entered and looked about me.

Instead of soft darkness and points of candlelight, everywhere there was a pale gleam like moonshine, for everywhere one turned, instead of wood—and often instead of stone—was silver. The candles shone pale gold against shrines and figures totally fashioned in silver, chapels silver-vaulted, and I moved in a daze down the church towards a silver altar, a *retablo* of silver, a Christ and Our Lady sculptured in silver against walls of silver which rose in a mass of Churrigueresque decoration from floor to ceiling, saints, angels, cherubs, everything mounting up in a shining, gleaming, glowing fantasy. My first reactions were—how incredible, how beautiful, and how splendid that so much should be given to the glory of God.

We had arrived in good time; we found places, and gradually the church began to fill. Just before the service started there was a sound of many bare feet shuffling their way into places at the back, and I thought that the ordinary people here were poor but devout.

When the service was over and we turned to leave I had another shock. The back of the church was filled with Indians who seemed to be in the last stages of poverty; ill-clad in the extreme, sunken-cheeked, hollow-eyed, their skins unhealthily pale, their expressions showing suffering, apathy, and despair. Then I saw several *mestizos*—big, strong, healthy men, roughly but adequately dressed, with good boots, who carried heavy staves and were obviously in charge of the Indians. Realization struck me like a blow—these were Indians from the mines. These were the poor wretches whose slavery had built this church. It cost the mine-owners nothing to erect this silver temple: with their vast profits they would not miss whatever they gave, but slaves had given everything: freedom, happiness, health, and eventually life itself. I felt ashamed to walk past them in my decent clothes to go to my carriage and drive home to a good meal.

I could not get the contrast out of my mind, but apart from Tía Amalia I found few people who were in the least troubled by it. The Spaniards of Platinas considered the Indians as no better than animals, and were unmoved by the knowledge that they spent so long in the mines that they hardly saw the light of day except when once a week they were given the inestimable treat of being taken to church to offer prayers and thanks for the life they were leading.

I had to speak to Miguel about it, and tried to moderate my language, for I knew he would be more affected by reasonable argument than expressions of outrage. But he could see I felt very strongly about it.

"I know, Marta," he agreed. "It is dreadful. But no good can be done by trying to rouse people with wild accusing speeches. The people who could change conditions are the ones whose only interest lies in maintaining things as they are. The only way to alter things is first to get the present laws enforced—and that means having right-thinking men in power—and then getting laws passed which are progressively more humane."

"You mean, the mine-owners are breaking the law? And nothing is done?"

"The mine-owners, or their friends, are in power. Legally, Indians cannot be made slaves; legally, any of the mine-workers can leave at any time; legally, they must be paid wages and should not in the first place have been moved from their own areas of land—but in practice, as you have seen, matters are very different. It is only because the Indians are fatalistic and accept so much that there has not been real trouble before."

"And will there be real trouble?"

"It is always possible."

"If so, what would you do?"

He frowned and thought for some moments before replying.

"I could not encourage a revolt. I should have to try to mediate, to get better conditions for the workers, better pay and a basic freedom. But I doubt if I should achieve anything. The owners want their profits, enormous profits, and want them undiminished. In a revolt they would use force on the workers, and, naturally, they would crush them. I hope it does not happen."

"Is there nothing you can do, Miguel?"

"Without a crown appointment, nothing."

"Then, please—oh, there is no need to ask it."

"To ask what?"

"I know you have no mines and would never touch profits made like that. I like to feel that anyone we employ is considered a human being, given fair treatment, allowed to live as a person. You would always do that."

He took my hand. "Marta, I give to every man his human dignity—and every woman too. I am building my *estancia* on that principle, and, God willing, it will flourish long after the mines and their misery are finished."

I leaned over and kissed his cheek, the first kiss I had ever given him spontaneously, for I had always been enough in awe of him to wait for him to show affection; and as I spoke he gave me one of his rare smiles, swift and brilliant.

"Of course it will, Miguel. Valdoro will be a great name—and a respected name. In days to come everyone will know what the Mourales of Valdoro stand for."

"Then the credit will be as much yours as mine, *querida,*" he said, and I felt a glow of pride within me.

As I had expected, as soon as we were well settled in Platinas Miguel went off to Valdoro. But it would be as short a visit as possible, he told me, and he did not take India with him. So I was reasonably content.

I found Platinas very different from Varena. There the society formed itself into different coteries: the upper-class families, the military, the professional class of doctors, lawyers and the like, who were mostly *criollos*. There was a little overlapping and interchange, but on the whole society kept in its groups. Here in Platinas, there were no groups, only the upper class in general, which was small in numbers and mainly consisted of mine-owning families and the merest sprinkling of professionals and military. So while in Varena there were many undercurrents, the pull and tug of varying interests, the stimulation of controversy and at times downright antagonism, in Platinas there was no variety. There were no divisions or diversions; everything came back to the mines: to yield, to the profits, and what was being done with the money that the silver produced. I was horrified and disgusted by the ridiculous extravagance of some of the women who vied with each other in demonstrations of opulence, without a thought of how the money came to them.

The same women would treat their house servants with less regard than they would a dog. The Indians in the mines had every reason to hate the owners, but I could see that the *mestizo* managers and servants had reason to bear a grudge as well. I was glad that in my condition I was not expected to go visiting to any extent. When I did so I could not escape a certain impression—that this was Sánchez's town. He was not there, he was in Varena, and yet he seemed to dominate affairs even at such a distance. I saw now that he was not just a dissolute pleasure-seeking young man; he was greedy and ruthless, and in a town where greed and ruthlessness were rampant he had set the standard.

It seemed to me that if I appeared when the conversation was turning on taxes the subject was quickly changed, and I soon saw why. The mine-owners, Sánchez's friends, were expecting to get off lightly; and they knew that Miguel was going to be made to pay for Sánchez's enmity.

I went to church during Miguel's absence, hoping

that the Indians would not be there, for their presence made me feel a hypocrite. Of course, their absence would not have made any difference, save that I would not have had to feel their sad despairing eyes on me. But they were there, and as before, they waited while we filed out first. As I walked down the church I noticed one man, a little taller and bigger than most of the other Indians. It was not this which made me single him out, but the fact that while every other Indian had a vacant, downcast look, this man had raised his head and was gazing about him, some alertness and spirit remaining in his manner. With a sudden shock I thought: I knew that man. But it was impossible. And then I remembered . . . surely he was the husband of the woman I had bought from the slave-runners?

I touched India's arm and whispered to her. "India, you see the man who is looking about him—the big one."

"Yes?"

"He is the man whose woman I took from the slave-drivers. Try to get his attention as we pass, and tell him his wife and child are safe and well at Valdoro."

She shrugged. "I'll try."

He was the third man in from the aisle, and peeping covertly from behind my mantilla I saw India trying to catch his eye. She had to be careful: if we made our interest obvious enough for it to be noticed by the foreman the Indian might well suffer for it.

We went past, and India murmured in her own tongue. The man's eyes flashed in an otherwise impassive face; I guessed that he had heard and understood.

When Miguel came back I could tell that something had displeased him. It was late and we were almost ready for bed; I ordered food for Miguel and when he was settled at the table Tía Amalia excused herself and left us alone. I poured his wine and let him eat, pretending to sew until he was ready to talk.

Finally he left the table, stretched himself into a chair by the fire with his refilled glass, and lit a cigarillo.

"Was everything in order, Miguel?" I asked.

"More or less," he said, and then after a pause: "The Ruízes have left."

"Left!" I echoed in amusement. "Before you came?"

"No. They were perfectly proper about it. When I arrived they said they wished to resign, and to leave as soon as possible. You can imagine I did not ask them to work out their notice."

"But why did they—?"

"Oh, some excuse that it is too remote—after all this time! I would like to know their real reason."

"I am not sorry they are gone," I said. "I always felt they were disloyal—or could be."

"Disloyal! *Querida*—"

It was no time for burdening him with my reasons.

"Well, I didn't like them. So what is happening?"

"I have left Father Marcos in charge—an odd situation for a priest, but he does not seem to mind."

"You will replace them, but not, I hope, from Platinas."

"Why not?"

I spoke my mind. At that time, although where our affections were concerned I felt as if I stood near quicksand, in matters of business I sensed that Miguel would now take my opinions and consider them with almost as much weight as he would have accorded a man of his acquaintance.

"Because Platinas is full of Sánchez's men."

He looked at me darkly. "Is he here? Has he been . . . offending you? Or trying to ingratiate himself again?"

"No, no! There's no need for you to assume—"

He laughed shortly. "No need, but I do."

I could not bear these doubts of his. "Miguel, do you still not trust me?"

"Trust you?" He looked surprised. "I always trust you. But don't you realize how confoundedly jealous I am? It tortures me."

Looking back it sounds ridiculous, but I had truly not realized that jealousy was strong within him.

"Jealous? You? Of me?" I asked in surprise.

"What else? You should know by now. *Caray*—I shall still be jealous of you if you live to be a hundred."

A little spurt of excitement warmed my heart. What a sweet, odd thing to say.

"I should think by then there would be very little point," I said.

His frown disappeared, he leaned back and laughed unrestrainedly.

"*Ay,* what a practical thing to say! You are indeed a practical-minded woman!" Then he became serious again. "So Platinas is full of Sánchez's men? It's as bad as that, is it? Then tell me what you know."

It was little enough, but it gave him something to think about. As for me, I was altogether too practical for my own good; it might have been much more interesting if I had pursued the subject of jealousy; but the mood and the moment were gone.

Señora Enríquez was a surprising woman. I was resigned to the thought of finding Valdoro mismanaged and deep in dust when we should eventually return there, with no one but Father Marcos to keep the servants up to scratch, but she had other ideas. She was quite willing, she told me, to go there ahead of me and put everything in order; in fact, she would be honored if I would allow her to do so. I talked it over with Tía Amalia and Miguel, for before I accepted, as I was selfishly tempted to do, I must be sure there would be adequate safeguards for her. In the end it seemed quite practicable. One of the serving women was prepared to go with her; we had a very reliable driver and a good spare wagon and if we chose our time they could travel from Puenterojo with the military. Miguel himself, with two of his men, would escort them as far as Puenterojo, where he would collect any mail from the army train and exchange information with the commanding officer. Since Miguel was satisfied that the tribes were happy and the country absolutely quiet it sounded a good arrangement.

Before my household was thus depleted I became involved in—or rather, I involved myself in—a crazy scheme.

It started the very next Sunday we went to church. The Indian mine-workers were there, and as we began to walk out at the end of the service I saw "our Indian," as I came to call him, among them. This time he was standing next to the aisle, so that we should pass close by him. As we drew nearer I could see him staring at India, and when she was level with him I heard him murmur a few words.

When we were outside India exclaimed, "That man! He is a bold one!"

"Why? What did he say?" I asked.

She glanced around her and lowered her voice. "He said to me, 'Help me to escape!' As if I could!"

I said nothing to India, but my mind worked on the man and his wretched situation. No doubt all the slaves wanted desperately to return to their people, yet had no hope; but he had a link, a frail, a most tenuous link with his family, and we were it. What right had I to send him a message about his wife and child, to give him a grain of comfort and hope, and then refuse to help him? It would be compounding the cruelty of his fate.

I thought long and hard about it, and eventually told the poor result to Tía Amalia and India.

"It may seem foolish to help one man out of hundreds," I finally said, "but I feel a responsibility towards this man. Do you think we could get him away, and if so, are you prepared to do so?"

"It's crazy, *querida*," said Tía Amalia. "And is it right? If it were discovered Don Miguel would be accused of harboring a slave."

"But legally they are not slaves," I insisted. "The man has a perfect right to return to his people—if he can manage it."

"And if he's caught?" said Tía Amalia. "From what

I've heard, the foremen would either beat him to death as an example to the rest—or, since he's strong and has some work left in him, they might settle for a flogging and make him work in chains, keeping him underground for months on end, perhaps for the rest of his life."

I shuddered, but went on. "He must know that. He must be prepared for the risk. We must try to ensure that he isn't caught. Will you help me? I can't do anything without you."

I looked at India. Her face was impassive.

"Why do you do this?" she asked.

"Because I would like to help them all. That of course is impossible—but isn't it better to help one person than none at all?"

"What will Don Miguel say?"

"I don't know. I would rather not tell him until we have the man safe. Once he is here I am sure Don Miguel will help to send him to Valdoro."

"I will help," India said after a few minutes.

Tía Amalia nodded.

"But how can we do it?" she asked.

"I've been thinking about that. The foremen seem to herd the workers to and from the church, and I don't see how one of the men could leave the group and not be noticed. It just doesn't seem possible for the man to separate himself then—and inside the mine compound they are kept as close as birds in a cage. Besides, we can't go there; and if we're going to help him at all we must not make ourselves conspicuous."

"So there's no way?" My aunt said.

"There's one chance," I told her. "We must do it inside the church."

"Inside—!" She was aghast.

"How?" said India.

"The man would have to manage the first part— the worst part—himself. The church is dark, which is our one advantage, but it will still be difficult. I was thinking that it might be just possible, if he could position himself not by the aisle but on the farther side. . . ."

"Yes?" My aunt's eyes were sparked with interest.

"There is a confession box against the wall, level with the front group of slaves. If only he could, at some point in the service, get across the gap and hide in the confession box—"

"The guards are always on the watch," said Tía Amalia.

"It is possible," said India. "Even the guards pay some attention to the service. But what good would that do?"

"The rest would depend on you, India. You're the only one who can talk to him, and the only one who could manage the rest."

"What would I have to do?"

"You'd have to go to the service, but not with us. You'd have to go dressed as a servant, and wearing a poncho. You must get as near to the confessional as you can. After the service you'd have to join him in the confessional."

She wrinkled up her nose.

"Oh, I know it will be a tight fit, and he will smell, but it's the only way," I told her. "Inside the box you would give him the poncho to cover his clothes. Then you would come out and wait for him, praying. After a few minutes he could come out and join you. Then you could walk together out of the church, and you could bring him here."

With any luck they would give the impression of being two Indian servants going back to their employer's house.

We talked it over, and we were unable to improve on it. It was risky, and it would depend absolutely on whether the man was able to make the initial move from the ranks of the slaves into the confessional, but it seemed worth trying.

On the following Sunday, India passed the message: "Can you get into the confessional during the service?"

He would have a week to consider his reply.

The next Sunday we could not see him anywhere, and I spent the following week wondering what had happened to him. Had he suffered an accident in the mines—they were not uncommon? Was he terribly injured, perhaps dead, just as he had some hope of release? The following Sunday as we left the church I saw with a lightening of spirit that he was in his usual place.

India passed next to him; he said one word, "Yes." And she responded, "We will tell you when."

India had been in favor of telling him to hide himself the next week, but I thought it better to give him more time to decide when, and how, to do it. A few days later we discovered it was a good thing we had not fixed a day for the escape, for India became unwell, and by the Sunday was confined to bed with a fever.

By this time Señora Enríquez had left for Valdoro; Miguel had gone with the escort as far as Puenterojo, and had returned with mail brought out by the Varena detachment. Sánchez was beginning to exert his power; new taxes were being levied, and they were heavy. On Miguel they would press very hard; but it was not only the wealthy landowners who were being penalized; tradesmen, merchants and small traders were coming under the screw.

"We are all expected to bribe our way to lighter assessments," said Miguel grimly. "It will bear heaviest on the small tradesmen: they cannot afford to bribe, nor can they afford to pay."

"What will you do?" I asked.

I received the reply I expected.

"I shall pay. I do not approve of bribery—and if I did, to bribe Sánchez would only be giving him another weapon to use against me. I shall appeal, but I shall pay, much as I begrudge it since I know full well most of it will go into his pockets."

We both knew an appeal would be a useless formality, since Sánchez was at present in high favor with the Viceroy. About that, "We shall have to wait for the wind to change," was all Miguel would say.

It was now more difficult to run the house smoothly. My staff was depleted by the loss of Señora Enríquez and the one really capable woman we had brought with us. The servants we had engaged with the house seemed a dull lot and inclined to laziness. Tía Amalia had her hands full trying to keep them up to scratch, and often went out to do the marketing herself since the cook was an unreliable shopper. She would return home, followed by the Indian boy who carried her purchases, full of grim satisfaction at holding her own with the rascally Platinas traders, and with tidbits of news gleaned from overheard gossip or her own observation.

"It's a pity India is a-bed," she said to me one day. "If she came out with me she might be able to find out more than I can."

"About what?" I asked.

"Oh—things in general." She answered a trifle evasively, I thought. "There's a funny sort of feeling in the town, to my mind."

I urged her to tell me more, but got nothing more definite from her.

I was not happy about India's condition, and even less happy about that of her child. They had both developed the same sort of fever, and were not responding well to my aunt's capable nursing. They each had a distressing rash on face and body, and little Juan Bautista was a pitiful sight, so feverish and wretched was his state.

"What is wrong with them?" I asked my aunt.

"It's one of the fevers our people get in childhood," she told me. "With us it's usually of no great concern. But I am beginning to think that the Indians are not used to it, and so it is much worse when they catch it. We shall have to wait and see what happens. If they do not improve we will send for the doctor."

I was disturbed by this, for my aunt was a good nurse. What was more, she had very little faith in doctors, and would not call one in unless she felt she was out of her depth and unable to cope with the patient. With her it would be a last resort.

When Miguel had suggested that I should see a doctor during pregnancy and arrange for his attendance at the confinement Tía Amalia had given a short laugh and remarked, "A doctor! She'll be better off without one, from most of them I've seen. All they can do is give purges and saw off legs—and that's not much use to a woman with child. Now a good midwife—a good one—is another matter. That's what she should have. I'm not experienced enough, and if the birth should be difficult I wouldn't be sure what to do for the best. If you'll take my advice you'll settle for a good midwife."

And settle we did. So you can see her mention of a doctor was more than a little disturbing.

Then quite suddenly everything came to a head. Miguel was away, having gone to Puenterojo to meet the returning detachment, and we were alone in the house with the minimum of servants. The condition of India and her baby suddenly worsened—and Platinas erupted in revolt. All at once we were virtually in a state of siege.

13

The first warning we had of trouble was hearing gunshots in the distance. A few moments later one of the servants appeared, white with fright, and when we could calm her enough to make sense of what she said we discovered that a riot had been started by *mestizo* traders who had been joined by disaffected servants and that not only property but people were being attacked. With the Varena troubles fresh in my mind I ordered the outer doors to be secured and all outside windows shuttered and barred. I was glad I had kept the house well provisioned. Order should soon be restored, and in the meantime we would not starve if we could not go to market for a day or two.

In the distance we could hear the sounds of disorder, shouting, crashing, odd noises, but not many shots. It was unlikely the rioters would have much in the way of firearms. A detachment of soldiers would soon disperse them, I thought, but Platinas had only one unit in residence and that was on training maneuvers some distance from the town; the rioters naturally knew this. We should just have to sit it out and by the time Miguel returned the chances were everything would be quiet again, for I was not expecting him for another day, perhaps two.

"I thought something like this was brewing up," said my aunt grimly. "There was a feeling, an atmosphere, I didn't like when I went to market. It's been there for days, threatening, like a thunderstorm."

"Do you think the new taxes have brought it to a head?" I asked.

"Certainly. It's the rich property that is being attacked, it seems."

"Then let us hope this is not considered unreasonably rich," I answered, and my aunt went back to see how India was faring.

Tía Amalia would not let me help with the nursing duties, for besides the fact that my presence always excited India when she was ill, I was near my time and my aunt feared infection for me and the baby, although I had almost certainly had the illness in childhood.

"If you caught it again now I would never forgive myself," she said. "You must keep out of the sickroom."

But even from the door I could see that India was seriously ill.

Outside the house the tumult ebbed and flowed, and later in the morning the rioters came rushing down the street. A hail of stones crashed against the shutters, and it was frightening to hear all the noise and shouting, realizing we could do nothing. I pretended to be calm and kept myself busy, but my heart was in my mouth until the crashes outside became fewer and fainter, the shouting drew away and the mob moved into the distance.

The servants were useless fools and cowards. Our own people at Varena or at Valdoro would have put a good face on it; the weakest might have shown fear but they would not have panicked and collapsed in terror as these silly wretches did. Try as I did to encourage them by telling them they were in no danger as long as they stayed indoors they would not heed, but sat crouched in corners moaning, crossing themselves and showing the whites of their eyes like frightened cows. There was nothing we could do for them. They would not even help themselves by getting on with their work; they were so contemptible that I eventually left them to their own devices and began preparing a meal for everyone and some broth for India.

I was worried about India. Her child was not weaned, and with the sickness in her body and the fact that the child was too ill to suck I did not know what the effect on her might be: it must be worse than if she had not been nursing the boy. I forgot all the sorrows and irritations she had caused me, and ached with pity for her condition.

India took no more than a sip or two of broth. My aunt shook her head gravely and hurried through the light meal I had prepared for her, and went back to the bedside. I went with her as far as the door and waited while she looked at the girl again. She came back to me, her eyes full of concern.

"They are both very ill," she said. "As soon as the rioting is over one of the servants must go for the doctor."

"It's quiet outside now," I said. "I think it would be possible for one of them to go."

But when I went to their quarters there was not one of them who would set foot outside.

"Very well," I said. "I shall send the coachman."

That would be better, I thought; he could take the small carriage and bring the doctor back in it.

I went into the courtyard to find the driver. Our good driver-coachman had gone to Valdoro with Señora Enríquez; the boy could not manage the horses. There was only one man left who could drive, and when I went across the court to the stable my heart sank. The man and the boy were sitting on a pile of straw, and the boy was terrified and tipsy; the man, with empty bottles at his feet and another in his hand, was blind drunk.

There was no point even in being angry with them; that would come later. I went back into the house.

At any other time I would have harnessed a horse to the *calesa* and driven myself, but I realized that would be folly. If anything frightened the horse I might not be able to hold it, and I could not risk being overturned in my condition. There was, too, the point that a solitary woman driving a carriage through the empty streets might attract unwelcome attention should she meet rioters round a corner.

I went back to Tía Amalia. One look at her and I did not need to ask her how urgent it was.

"There's no one who will go, and the driver is dead drunk," I told her. "I'll go myself."

"Ay, querida, you cannot!" she cried.

"I must," I said. "You must stay with India—you know how frantic she becomes if she so much as sees me when she is ill. There is no one else. Luckily it is no distance. I know exactly where he lives, in the street beyond the Plaza Mayor. I will wear something dark and simple and look like a servant. I'll get there quite unobtrusively—and I shall have the doctor with me on the way back."

"No, Marta, you must not go! It would be madness in any case—but as you are—Don Miguel will be fit to kill me if I let you go."

"You know she must have extra attention. We cannot take the responsibility of her life. There will be no danger to me as long as I avoid the rioters. Let us not waste time arguing."

But she followed me to my room and pleaded with me as I changed my dress. I told her to go back to the sickroom and not to worry about me.

I put on a plain dark dress, the simplest I had, and covered myself from head to knees with a large black shawl. I could easily pass for a respectable upper-class servant, I thought.

"You had better come and let me out," I told my aunt. "And listen for my knock when I return—none of those idiots would open up for St. Peter if he banged with his keys on the door."

My aunt opened the door, I crossed the threshold and heard her shut and bolt the door behind me.

The street was quiet and deserted. I pulled my shawl about me, and with a thumping heart I set off. All went well. I could still hear sounds of disturbance, but they were at a considerable distance, and here one could only see where the trail had passed by damaged windows, broken shutters, and the debris in the street. I had to walk the length of the road, turn left and go on down into the Plaza Mayor. Crossing the square past the church I must take a street on the far side; a little way down was the doctor's house. Normally I would have made nothing of it, but in my state I could not walk well. I was clumsy and heavy: in fact, happy as I was at the thought of the baby, I was ready for it to be born. I was tired of carrying the weight of it, tired of the physical enslavement and of the way whenever I wanted to rest, the child decided to move and kick and keep me awake. Trying to hurry along I was more conscious than ever of the burden I bore.

It was strange to find the streets, normally full of people, bustling with activity and humming with cheerful noise, now silent and empty. I do not think I saw more than three people on my journey, and they were men scuttling along, quick and furtive as a fox with a stolen fowl. I dare say I looked the same. I reached the square; the great mass of the church loomed up above me, impressive at the top of its steps, its stone golden in the sunshine. I'm glad it's not raining, I thought, and then wondered whether a good downpour would dampen the rioters' enthusiasm.

I turned the corner of the church and gasped as a figure rose up in front of me and grabbed me by the wrist. It was a ragged man, dirty, unshaven, and drunk. As I struggled my shawl fell from my head.

"Ah, my pretty, where are you off to?" he asked, grinning in my face. I could smell the raw spirit on his breath.

"Let me go. I'm going to get the doctor," I cried.

His eyes swept up and down me.

"Oh, it's like that, is it? Well, you can spare a minute for a kiss—"

He leered at me and put out his other hand, but with a sudden burst of strength I twisted myself free and pushed him away. He was so unsteady that he fell headlong, and I stumbled off as fast as I could down the road. I heard him swearing but he was too drunk to follow me, and I reached the doctor's house, my heart hammering, my breath panting, and banged and banged with my fists on the door.

It seemed an age before anyone came fear and desperation were rising in me; then I heard shuffling steps and the door opened a crack.

"The doctor!" I gasped.

The door opened a little wider; an old woman in a black dress and loose slippers looked at me with beady black eyes.

"Wait," she said.

The doctor came; I knew him by sight, a middle-aged, pompous, inflexible-looking man, whose mien I did not much care for.

"Please, will you come at once?" I asked. "I have a mother and baby in my house, very ill with fever."

He looked at me closely. "Isn't it—Doña Marta Moural? What on earth brought you out?"

"My servants were too frightened to come. Please come back with me now," I urged.

"Surely you have someone who can nurse a fever?"

"Yes, but there's no more we can do. We need your help."

"I'm just on my way out to another case. I'm sorry."

"Can't you go there afterwards?" I laid a hand on his arm. "If you will only come for a moment, and tell me what we should do—they are so ill."

"Who is the patient?" he asked, a glimmer of curiosity, but very little feeling, lighting his eyes.

"My—my husband's servant—and her baby," I stammered.

He looked at me, his eyebrows lifted. *"Por dios,* señora, you amaze me! You risk your life, in your condition, to get a doctor·for your husband's Indian mistress! I never heard such folly! No, I cannot come; I have a gentleman with a gunshot wound who needs me at once."

"Then come afterwards," I begged.

"I can promise nothing. With these riots I expect I shall have too much to do to bother about Indians with fever. What are you doing for her?"

In desperation I gabbled out the treatment my aunt was following.

"You cannot do better. Either she'll live or she'll die, with or without me. These Indians have no physique. I'll bid you good day."

"But, doctor—"

"No, señora, I have more urgent calls. You had best go home. I am sorry I cannot escort you, but I must go in the other direction. I'll tell a servant to walk back with you."

As he spoke a lad drove out the doctor's little carriage. He spoke to the boy, who got down and gave him the reins. With no more ado the doctor got into the carriage, called to the lad, "See the señora home, Juan," flicked the horse and rattled down the road.

The boy eyed me doubtfully. I pulled my shawl about me, numb with frustration and hopelessness.

"This way," I said to him, and set off, the lad following unwillingly a couple of paces behind.

I had become accustomed to the steady background of noise in the distance, but as we approached the square I had the impression that the sounds were growing·nearer. I listened. The rioters—or a group of them —were certainly moving in our direction. In the square the position of the buildings and the narrowness of the streets would make it impossible for me to see from whence they were coming. I could only hope that they were not in the street I wished to take and that I would be able to cross the square and gain it before the leaders of the mob appeared.

I reached the square and began skirting it. I was still on the first side when two or three men came into it. Behind them was a crescendo of sound, not as yet frenzied and out of control, more a steady roar like a puma on the prowl, as if the mob was considering a new victim. The doctor's lad took to his heels and fled back the way he had come and I could not blame him; he was young and I was nothing to him. Fear gripped my heart. There was only one thing I could do. On the next side of the square was the church. Hugging my shawl about me, my heart beating sickeningly in my throat I forced myself in a stumbling run up the long flight of steps to the great door.

I reached it and caught the handle—claiming sanctuary, I thought—and turned it, but the door would not yield. It was bolted—bolted—secured against the mob, but also against me, at the moment when my need was so great. I lifted my hands and beat them against the wood, knowing in my heart that no one would hear me inside.

I turned, despairing, to see the first men moving towards me up the steps, and every moment more figures were pouring into the square. Then I thought, the side door, that might be open. But it was too late. The men barred my way. I stood and faced them.

They halted at the top of the steps, a few paces away from me, and we eyed each other. They were *mestizos,* and in the gathering crowd I could see all shades of color from Spanish skins where only a trace of Indian in the features betrayed the admixture of blood, to faces almost copper-dark. Most of them had been decently dressed, but their recent activities had made them look dishevelled, unkempt; their faces and clothes were dirty and some streaked with blood.

A man at the front challenged me. "What are you doing, señora?"

I must be calm, I thought. Answer him rationally, show no fear and they will let me go.

"I was trying to get the doctor," I said aloud.

"In the church?"

"I was going to wait inside until you had passed."

"What mistress sends you out like that when you may meet trouble?"

I hesitated, my brain would not work fast enough for my needs. The men were pressing nearer, and another shouted, "She's no servant! Listen to her—"

The first man came up to me and pulled my shawl from my head. His fierce eyes glared into mine, his thin lips twisted in a bitter smile.

"You're right! I know her. She's a newcomer—the Moural wife!" He looked at me more closely. "What are you doing out of doors, now, in your state?"

"I have told you. I was trying to get the doctor for my servant."

He threw back his head and laughed, and the others around him joined in. It didn't sound like laughter; it was a taunting, frightening cacophony.

"You expect me to believe that! You—out on foot —to get the doctor for a servant! Señora, we are not fools!" He grabbed my arm. *"What message were you carrying?"*

"Message?" I said helplessly.

"Yes, what message? Your husband's away—so you're carrying on his activities. It must be important to bring you out. *So what is it?"*

I felt completely trapped. If they would not believe me, what could I do? And what would they do? The noise in the square was mounting all the time; there was a crowd of *mestizos* in front of me, and what was more, from another street more figures came trickling in.

"There is no message—nothing!" I cried.

"If she won't tell us, it's got to be important—and against us!" someone shouted, and there was a roar of agreement.

"Why won't you believe me?" I cried. "My husband is not against you—and he would never ask me . . . My servant is very ill, please let me go back to her."

Their attention was distracted by someone at the

back of the crowd who shouted, "There they are! The slaves are out!"

Heads turned. They raised a shout and then a cheer at the sight of the newcomers who were now pouring in. One glance was enough to confirm that these were workers from the mines. Now escape was impossible. I was completely surrounded. How could I persuade them to let me go?

I was forestalled, and hideously so, by a shout from the back.

"A mine-owner's wife! Teach her a lesson!"

The cry was taken up. Now I was really frightened. Some slaves were rushing up the steps as the *mestizos'* leader dragged me from the shelter of the doorway's arch. All around me I could see faces full of hate, faces wild-eyed, with flaring nostrils and snarling mouths, men like animals. Then one Indian rushed forward, faced me, and raised a pick-axe over my head.

In that second I thought: This is the end. The end of me, and of Miguel's child. It's all over. . . . Then the man's hand was caught by another, and an Indian pushed himself in front of me facing the crowd. To me it was a miracle—for it was "our Indian," the one whom we had been plotting to help, who had intervened. Now he and the other Indian were talking, arguing, and the *mestizo* leader pulled me aside.

"While they're quarrelling I can decide what to do with you," he said. "Are you going to tell me what I want to know?"

"There is nothing!" I protested.

"Look, I can make you talk very easily, and in your condition you'd be a fool to—"

His head jerked up, he was listening—but for what, in all the confusion around us?

Then I heard it, faint but sharp amid the roaring, the clatter of hooves on stone; and I saw riders come into the square. The man relaxed.

"Only two—we'll soon settle them."

I flung out my free hand in appeal—would they see me? My heart sank as one of them touched spurs to his horse and charged up the next street, but the remaining rider came straight at the crowd, which, intimidated by his sudden appearance and evident determination, parted as he came on. My breath caught in my throat. It was Miguel.

On he came, urging his horse, thrusting aside restraining arms, till the animal reached the steps—and still urged, clattered up them—then he leapt from the saddle and stood beside me. At the look on his face the *mestizo* let go of my wrist and Miguel put his arm around my shoulders. With the other he tried the church door.

Now the crowd was recovering from its surprise, and began to press around us. Miguel drew his pistol, but used it to hammer with the butt on the church door. He turned and faced the crowd again.

"There's little glory in molesting a woman," he shouted. "I advise you all to go home before the army arrives."

"The army! We'll settle with them!" someone shouted.

"They have more guns than you," he retorted, "and will use them. As for you—" he turned to the mineworkers—"you've escaped—if you stay in the town you'll be taken back. Get out into the country now, while the going's good. Then you'll stand a chance of getting back to your own people."

Some of the *mestizos* were wavering, some I could see were too fanatical to be influenced at all. I knew our situation was still desperate, but we were in it together. Then over the shouting came another sound—horses again, but this time more of them, a steady rhythmic trot—and from the direction Miguel's man had taken there appeared a cavalry detachment. They were ready for action, carbines slung across their saddles, and to my amazement I saw, riding with the officer, Alfonso Sánchez and Ruíz.

"Go while you can!" Miguel shouted to the mob, as the noise suddenly stilled.

I could see Sánchez weighing up the situation. There we were, caught between the cavalry and the rioters. He drew a long horse-pistol from his saddle-holster, and pointed its muzzle in our direction.

He turned to the officer, gesturing at us as we stood, the *mestizo* leader on one side, our Indian on the other. In the quiet I could hear what he was shouting.

"There are the ringleaders! Tell your men to fire!"

In the silence the jingle of harness clinked menacingly on the air, the mob was holding its breath, waiting for the next move. The organized troops were outnumbered but fully armed, confronting a rabble whose weapons, apart from a sprinkling of guns, were hatchets, clubs, pick-axes, shovels, knives—and the accumulated hate and fury of the years.

There were sounds behind me of bolts being drawn, and the church door creaked open a little way. Miguel swerved, peered inside, took me by the waist and thrusting at the door he pushed me through.

"Keep her safe," he said, and pulled the door closed behind me.

"Miguel!" I cried, and threw myself at it, but the priest shot the bolts and took my hands in his, restraining me as I clawed at the handle.

"*Calma! Calma, señora!* He has man's work to do outside. In here you are safe."

"I don't want to be safe!" I sobbed. "I want to be with him!" I leaned against the door, straining my ears to hear. Outside it seemed utterly quiet, but the massive walls and the thickness of the great door would cut off all but the loudest sounds. I thought I heard voices—was one of them Miguel's?—and a faint low rumble of sound which came from a hundred throats. Then, even in the close depths of the church, I could hear the sudden outburst—shouts, gunfire, cries, and screams which might be human or animal. Muffled as it was, the noise seemed to enter my very brain, bringing with it the knowledge that Miguel was caught between the two forces, and that lurking to one side, waiting his time, full of malice and hate, was Sánchez, ready to take any opportunity to put a bullet into my husband if fate did not do it for him. If Miguel were killed in the mêlée it would be ascribed to an unlucky chance. One way or another, what hope had he of survival?

All my strength left me and I collapsed against a pillar, clutching the cold stone, laying my cheek against it, my body racked with dry sobs. If Miguel died everything would have been in vain. My life would have been in vain, and his would have been thrown away, wasted in trying to rescue a woman who was too proud or too fearful ever to have told him that she loved him. In those hellish moments I regretted that more than anything. What would I have lost beside a little pride? He did not want my love; he had never asked for it, only for a child—but it might have helped him to understand my jealousy of India; it might have made him more tolerant of my bursts of anger and unreasonableness. He might then have found some affection for me. And I should have accepted his need for India. In keeping my silly pride I had lost him for ever, and there would be nothing left to make my life worth living.

"Courage, my child." The priest laid his hand on my head. He was an old man, white-haired, frail, with a wrinkled face and eyes full of compassion.

"Let us pray together," he said. "God will give you strength."

I was beyond praying, but I knelt in the silver-shining gloom beside him, and amazingly the strength came, I know not how. A resolution hardened in me that everything should not be in vain. I still had Miguel's child within me, and I would find courage for the two of us. I would not do what Sánchez would expect, go back to Spain with my child and leave him to swallow up Valdoro and bloat himself on Miguel's land, taking Miguel's people as slaves to his mines. I

would stay, I would fight him, I would keep Valdoro,
for Miguel's child I would do anything to safeguard
the inheritance.

I found that I was praying.

14

How long I huddled there beside the priest I do not know. I think that for part of the time I was near to insensibility. To me there was no time, just an agony of mind which blacked out everything else. My senses would not function. I was deaf, and blind, and dumb.

Then I felt a touch on my arm. I turned my head and looked into the face of the priest. He pointed down the church. I heard quiet footsteps, and saw a young priest approaching; then came a sharper sound of boots on stone—there was another man behind him. Miguel.

He hurried to me and put his arms around me. He lifted me and had to take all my weight for at first my legs would not hold me. I was helpless, speechless. He sat me down and began to rub my hands.

Then he turned sharply to the young man. "Can you not get her something? Some brandy?"

He shrugged. "I do not think—"

Miguel's jaw set and he turned to the old priest. "You have communion wine! Would God grudge it to a woman in this state?"

The priest looked startled. Then he gestured to the

young one. "The señor is right. Get a glass of wine—quickly."

I felt as cold as death and was shaking from head to foot, so that Miguel had to hold the glass to my lips, and even so it chattered against my teeth and some of the wine spilt down my dress. But after I had drunk it I began to feel better and was able to take a grip on myself.

"Is there somewhere she can rest until I can get her home?" Miguel asked the old man.

My voice returned in a whisper. "No—no—I can walk. Don't leave me. We can go together."

"Marta, you cannot. I will find some way—"

"No," I said more firmly, and dragged myself to my feet. "I can walk."

He looked at me doubtfully, but he put my shawl about me, draping it over my head.

"The side door," he said to the young priest, and they supported me, while the old priest went ahead and led us to a smaller door at one side of the church, presumably the one by which Miguel had entered. I was feeling a little stronger.

"I will manage," I said.

Miguel paused on the threshold. "Now, Marta," he said firmly. "Keep your shawl about your face. Look straight ahead, and keep your eyes to the front all the time."

I thought he intended it so I would not be conspicuous, but as we stepped outside I knew that was not the reason.

It was quiet; strangely, unnaturally quiet. I could hear that in the square to our left not a soul was moving. Everyone had gone. I hoped the Indians had gone quickly enough to escape being rounded up and returned to the mines . . . and the *mestizos?* . . . But everyone had not gone.

Miguel twitched my shawl further forward over my face, and led me across to the narrow street we must take; but the smell of blood was reeking in my nostrils. I saw nothing but a man's leg thrust out at the edge

of the roadway I did not need to see; something told
me that the square behind us and even the steps to the
church were hideously littered with bodies. My stomach
retched and I pressed my fingers to my mouth, fighting
back the bile which rose in my throat.

"Come, Marta. You are a brave girl. Can you walk,
or shall I carry you?"

"Of course I can walk. I'm just a bit unsteady."

He looked sideways at me, his eyes dark with anxiety. "What possessed you to go out?" he asked.

Until that moment I had forgotten India. I told
Miguel how ill she was, and of my vain attempt to
fetch the doctor, as we made our way along the deserted street.

"You are too brave, *querida*. You should have considered yourself first."

"But she is so ill—the baby too. And I know how
—how important they are to you."

I could not bring myself to say: I know how much
you love her. So I used the phrase he had spoken to
me.

"Important to Valdoro—if her father thought that I
had been careless of her life—but not compared with
you—"

I turned to smile at him, but halted suddenly and
involuntarily gripped his arm as a pain shot through
my body.

"What is it?" he asked.

The pain stopped.

"Nothing." I said, and began to walk again.

I was in a near-trance as we made our way along
the street, our steps sounding in the horrifying silence,
meeting no one. Before long another pain racked me,
and I knew.

"Marta, something is wrong. What is it?"

There was no point in pretending.

"I think it's the baby," I told him.

He drew his breath in quickly and looked at me
more anxiously than ever. "What shall we do? I'll carry
you—is there time?"

I managed a smile. "There's plenty of time. And I can walk. Just help me to get home."

At last we reached the house and Miguel hammered on the door. An upstairs window opened and Tía Amalia's face peeped between the shutters. Then they were quickly closed and I knew she was hurrying down to let us in.

"*Ay, dios!* How is she?"

"The baby's coming," said Miguel shortly, then bent to lift me in his arms. I protested, but he carried me upstairs and put me down on the bed.

"I'll leave her to you," he said to my aunt. "Tell me what you need now, then I'll get the midwife."

"How often are the pains?" she asked me.

"How is India?" I asked her.

"The pains?" she insisted.

"Not frequent yet. And India?"

She paused in undoing my dress. "She is no worse. But Juan Bautista—" She looked at Miguel. "The boy is dead."

"Dead?" I whispered.

My aunt continued to undress me. Miguel said nothing.

"Miguel," I said. "You must go to India. She will need your comfort."

He bent over and looked into my eyes.

"No," he said. "She does not know I am here. I am going to fetch the midwife, and if the servants are useless there will be jobs for me to do."

I did not want him to leave the house, but he went for the midwife, and returned in a fine state because she was not at home and all he could do was to leave a message. Then, under my aunt's direction, he cleaned himself up, for he was marked with dirt and gunpowder, and wearing a clean shirt and breeches he fetched and carried for her, getting water and cloths. Never had I imagined my great *hidalgo* doing a servant's work for me, but he did, and it was more than adequately done.

All this time I had been wondering how long it took

a baby to be born, and if it mattered that the child was arriving two weeks before it should. The pains at first were sharp but not severe, and I thought: If this is what childbirth is like it can't be worth the fuss that is made about it—or perhaps I am one of the lucky ones.

Later I revised my opinion. The pains were wrenching at me, tearing at my body so that the thoughts dissolved in the rising agony. I sweated and ground my teeth together, fighting to make no sound. Miguel bent over and gripped my hands.

"Is it very bad?" he asked.

When the pain subsided, I said, "Bad enough. You had better leave me to get on with it."

"You men have no idea," muttered Tía Amalia.

"Then it's time I had," Miguel answered. "It's my child she's having."

I gazed up at him, astonished. Men had nothing to do with childbirth. They waited outside and played cards—or got drunk—or went riding and forgot all about it, to come back and say, "It's a boy, of course?" when it was all over. And he had not been like this with India.

"Hold tight to me when the pain comes again," he said.

I did so, and it seemed to help. I saw Tía Amalia giving him a sharp look, and then she said, "How much can you stand? You'll be no use to me if you faint or get sick—men are so squeamish."

"I won't be squeamish," he answered. "If Marta can stand it, I can."

"Miguel." I whispered, and he leaned closer to me. "When I was waiting in the church . . ."

"Yes, *querida*?"

"I thought you were dead. And I said to myself, what a fool I've been. . . ."

Another pain swept over me.

"Shout if you want to," my aunt said, and wiped my forehead with a damp cloth. "Sometimes it helps."

"You've never been a fool, Marta," Miguel answered.

The flood of agony ebbed. "Yes—yes. I was too proud—or too afraid to tell you—"

More pain. Miguel looked at my aunt and said, "*Sangre de dios!* How much more?"

Through half-closed lids I saw her shrug. Was she looking anxious? My eyes went back to Miguel's face.

"Was it important, *chiquita*?" he asked.

"It is, to me." I had to say it. Some women do not survive childbirth, and if I were to die, he would never know. "I love you," I said.

There was silence. Miguel's hand clasped mine, his face was over me, his eyes wonderfully tender, his lips smiling. He bent and kissed me on the mouth.

"What fools we both were. I was as bad," he said gently. "I thought you wanted it to be a business-like marriage. I was too proud to court a wife who might remind me of the limits of our contract. All the time I was waiting for some encouragement."

"A fine time to tell me," I said between clenched teeth.

When I could smile at him again, he said tenderly, "We have years ahead of us."

Then I could not talk; I could only try to ride each pain as it rose, swelled, and broke over me. Each time I thought: How many more? How much longer do I have to stand this? I was beyond rational coherent thought, living from pain to pain, my body sagging with exhaustion in the brief respite between spasms. My aunt gave me a cloth to put between my teeth, and I found myself grinding and groaning on it at the climax of each agony. I lost all track of time.

A great wave of pain suffused me. I felt light-headed —surely I would float on the tide of it into unconsciousness—I could not bear it. Then everything dissolved in a rushing, sweeping tumult of sensation, and suddenly it was over. I was empty and at peace. There was something warm against my leg, and it was not my aunt's hand—and in the heavenly quiet there came a high, fierce cry. I lay back, utterly relaxed, and closed my eyes.

I heard Miguel's voice, sharp with fear. "Tía! Look at Marta! Is she all right?"

"The baby—"

"Never mind the baby! Marta—*dios,* is she—I cannot lose her now."

"She's all right. She's resting, poor girl. It's been a hard struggle."

I opened my eyes. "The baby?" I whispered. "How is she?"

Miguel leaned over me, his look bright with love. "Marta—*mi amor*—"

Tía Amalia put a warm bundle into my arms.

"There, hold him just for a minute. He's a fine boy."

"A boy!"

Miguel and I gazed at each other, and I began to laugh, weakly, hysterically. Miguel looked puzzled at this.

"A boy! Oh, Miguel, I should have known! You were bound to have your own way!" I looked at the tiny wrinkled face in the crook of my arm. "I suppose I shall get used to the idea of a son in time!"

I stayed in bed for a few days, floating in that blissful state of euphoria that first follows birth, when one's body is free of its burden and one is glowing with the triumph of producing a healthy child. My son seemed wonderful to me. I did all the foolish doting things a mother does: counting his fingers and toes, kissing his chubby body and talking nonsense to his screwed-up face as he protested his hunger.

One day when I was rested and refreshed Miguel came to me and put his arms about me as I lay in bed with the child at my side.

"This is the moment I have waited for," he said. "Now it has come I don't know where to start, what to say."

I was in his arms and his mouth was on mine, taking the kisses I had dreamed of giving him for so long. For the first time there were no reservations, no holding back, and we both knew we were in love and totally committed to each other.

"Marta—my dearest Marta," he murmured. "There must be no more misunderstandings! So many of them were my fault. I was too proud—and a coward, too."

"A coward! How ridiculous!"

"No, it's true. I should have told you about India when you first arrived in Varena. But I thought, if you knew, it might make you change your mind about marrying me. I said to myself: I will tell her when the ceremony is over—but each day it became more difficult."

"Why was that?"

"Because I loved you! How could I expect a girl like you to believe that I could do so and still take an Indian mistress? And knowing you had married me out of duty I wanted to win your love before I humbled my pride and gave you my explanation. And so it went on. Besides, if I had swallowed my pride at the beginning and told you, wouldn't you have thought I was trying to buy your love and forgiveness by pretending to love you?"

"Perhaps. How silly we were! You did not know, but I soon realized I was not marrying you for the sake of my family. Yet I was sure you did not love me, or any one of us. And I was such a second-best; you offered for Serafina."

"I offered for one of your father's daughters. I had to have a wife—but I wanted you. I was gambling that you would be one of them. I didn't even know if you were . . . eligible."

I looked at him incredulously.

"I knew you were a girl of spirit the moment I saw you. It was something in the way you looked at me."

"I thought I kept my eyes very modestly cast down when we were introduced."

"And so you did. But not when I saw you first— standing there barefoot with a hen tucked under your arm."

I gasped.

"For all I knew marriage with you might have been . . . impossible," he added delicately. "But I'd had my fill of languid sophisticates who fainted at the thought of South America, and I had to try. And then, when I met you—to find you were the middle sister and I was expected to take the eldest—*caray!* But what could I do? I shudder to think how nearly I lost you—both before and after marriage!"

I stroked his hair and laughed at him.

"There was little danger of that, although I simply wouldn't admit to myself at first that I could find any charm in a man who looked for a wife in the way you did! You really are like an old-time conquistador! But I think I loved you from the beginning."

"*Querida,* we were meant for each other."

Then his mouth was on mine, conquering me with kisses. It was selfish of me to be so happy. At last I thought of what I should have asked long ago.

"Miguel, how is India?"

"She is improving each day now. She will recover."

"Thank God. But . . . Juan Bautista—?"

"We could not risk telling her at first. I think she is only just beginning to accept it." He paused, then added: "I have promised he shall be buried as my son. I owe that to her."

"Of course, Miguel. Try not to grieve too much."

"I have not grieved enough. I feel ashamed of myself for not feeling more deeply. But he always seemed such an alien little creature. I hoped, as he grew older . . . but then, he might have grown to hate me. I shall never know."

There was nothing I could say except, "India will suffer terribly from her loss."

And indeed she did. Tía Amalia told me that at first she feared for India's reason, but at last her grief subsided into a dull acceptance.

The days spent in my bedroom insulated me from all that was happening in the town, but as my life returned to normal and I began to ask questions I was told, little by little, of the horror that was past.

"What happened while I was in the church?" I
asked Miguel. "I must know, sooner or later. Were
many people killed?"

He nodded gravely. "Many in the square—and
others later."

"I was terrified that in the confusion Sánchez would
take the opportunity to shoot you. I saw it in his eyes."

"Sánchez! Without him there might have been no
killing. I was trying to persuade the *mestizos* to sur-
render to the army, and hoping that the Indians would
take the chance of escaping, to get to the country. At
that stage they had done nothing but break out of the
mines. Sánchez was shouting at the officer to order the
men to fire, and calling me the Indians' friend and
saying I had provoked insurrection. "There is Moural,
the traitor!" he was saying as he levelled his pistol at
me. 'And you are Sánchez the mineowner!' someone
shouted—and then all hell was let loose. The crowd
rushed forward and he was dragged from his horse.
The *mestizos* and the Indians began to attack the
soldiers. It was then the officer gave the order to fire."

"And Sánchez?"

Miguel shook his head.

"Dead?"

"They clubbed him—and cut him to pieces."

I was silent with horror. Miguel took my hand.

"They had good reason to hate him. And a mob out
of control is like a wild beast. He was unconscious
before . . ."

"Ruíz was with him. Did he—?"

"He escaped, only slightly hurt. There were few
casualties among the soldiers; they fired on the mob,
and then charged with sabres. It did not take them
long to clear the square," he added grimly.

I could not bear to think of it.

"I had suspected for some time that Ruíz was Sánchez's man, but how could I say so without proof?"
I told Miguel.

"You were sharper then I. Even when he left Valdoro I did not guess. He showed his hand too soon:

he thought Sánchez couldn't lose. If he had stayed I
would never have known."

"He served two masters, and now he has none. Well,
that's justice," I said, with un-Christian satisfaction. I
did not want him dead, but I could not wish him pros-
perity.

When India was fully recovered she came to see me.
She showed no resentment at the way fate had treated
her; all she would say was: "My son is dead. I have
failed my master."

I tried to tell her that she could not possibly be responsible for the death, that no one blamed her or
thought her a failure, but she was unconvinced.

"I know my lord will not give me another child," she
said. "Now you are his true wife and I have lost his
son it is all over. I have decided. I will serve my lord
back with my own tribe."

"India, what do you mean?"

"I shall return to my father. I can still help Don
Miguel to speak to the tribes when he visits them, and
I can tell my people about Valdoro, how they will get
fair treatment and kindness—that way I can help
keep peace and stop my people thinking that all Spaniards want to make them slaves."

"Did you hear that 'our Indian' saved my life?"

She nodded.

"And I heard that he escaped the shooting. Perhaps
he will reach Valdoro."

I believe he will, I thought. He has the spirit of a
survivor.

I had never liked Platinas; now I hated it, and persuaded Miguel to let us leave it as soon as I was fit.
He did not need much persuading. He was as anxious
as I to quit Platinas and return to Valdoro.

Our son Diego was baptized in the great silver
church, and that happy occasion gave me one good
memory of the building. The baby was a month old
when we brought him to Valdoro.

It was early evening, and we had been travelling all day. Tía Amalia took turns at nursing Diego, for there was no room in the carriage for the carved wooden cradle Miguel had ordered in Varena months before our first-born. We neared Valdoro just before sunset. I called to the driver to stop, for this was a moment I wanted to savor. Miguel turned his horse and came to the carriage window.

"I want to get out and look, just for a minute," I told him.

He dismounted and handed me down, and we stood together, the low sun glowing on our faces, the light wind fanning our cheeks. In the distance Valdoro was a mass of sun-gilt stone, red-roofed and, remembering that I had once thought it like a fortress or a prison, I realized with a glow in my heart that now it looked to me strong and solid, but a refuge and a home. I knew that time would mellow it into a gracious house, and generations to come would live happily there. If God so willed, Miguel and I would see our children grow up within its walls.

Before us, stretching illimitably to the red-streaked horizon was the great pampa, like shot-silk green and gold as the wind rippled it and brought sweet scents of grasses and wild herbs to our nostrils. This was our land, and my son's heritage. I reached inside the carriage for my baby. Tía Amalia handed him to me and I walked a few steps with him in my arms, revelling in the sun and the breeze.

"You must get used to this, Diego," I whispered. "You are going to be a country boy."

Miguel held out his hands. "Let me hold him. I want to show him Valdoro."

Laughing I gave him the child, and watched as Miguel, cradling him so carefully in the crook of his elbow, lifted the baby's face to the great open country.

"Look, Diego. Someday it will all be yours."

I smiled at Miguel—what fond folly it was for us to talk in that way to an uncomprehending infant—and his eyes as they smiled back were full of love.

"It's not too soon for him to learn," he said teasingly. "We'll have a lot of work to do here, he and I."

There was so much I wanted to say, and in good time I would say it. But for now I only whispered, "Miguel, I am so glad you brought me here. I've learned to love Valdoro."

"Then my happiness is complete."

Diego woke, chuckled and waved his little fists, and Miguel bent over him, one lean brown finger playing with the tiny pink hands.

"You are home, my son," he said.

I looked at them both and said to myself: We will succeed. This might not be the end of our difficulties, but we would meet them together, and together we would build Valdoro into the great *estancia* Miguel dreamed of owning in a land at peace. Miguel would always have two loves, but I was one, his only woman; the other was Valdoro, his golden land. And I had reached the end of suspicions, of jealousies and fears. I was capable of being the wife he needed.

I had proved myself. I was the mistress of Valdoro.